Praise for the novels of

Barbara Michaels

Books by Barbara Michaels

The Sea King's Daughter

ELIZABETH PETERS
WRITING AS
BARBARA MICHAELS

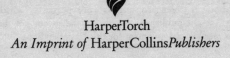

HarperTorch
An Imprint of HarperCollinsPublishers

This is a work of fiction. Names, characters, places, and incidents are products of the author's imagination or are used fictitiously and are not to be construed as real. Any resemblance to actual events, locales, organizations, or persons, living or dead, is entirely coincidental.

HARPERTORCH
An Imprint of HarperCollins*Publishers*
10 East 53rd Street
New York, New York 10022-5299

Copyright © 1975 by Barbara Michaels
ISBN: 0-06-074517-7

First HarperTorch paperback printing: May 2005

HarperCollins®, HarperTorch™, and ❦ ™ are trademarks of HarperCollins Publishers Inc.

Printed in the United States of America

Visit HarperTorch on the World Wide Web at www.harpercollins.com

10 9 8 7 6 5 4 3 2 1

To Jessica
with—if she will excuse the expression—love

The Sea King's Daughter

Chapter

———————— *1* ————————

DON'T CALL ME ARIADNE. THAT'S NOT MY NAME ANY-more.

I changed it legally a few years ago. Not that anyone had ever used it, even Mother. She called me Sandy, like everyone else, even when she was mad at me.

I must have been about ten years old before it really hit me that Sandy wasn't my real name. That was the day the package arrived—a fascinating package, big and battered and plastered all over with bright foreign stamps. The package itself looked foreign, with its thin shiny paper and unusual string. It was addressed to Miss Ariadne Frederick.

I was disappointed. I had hoped it was for me.

I didn't know any Ariadne Frederick. My last name was Bishop.

I knew it wasn't really—at least I knew Jim Bishop was my stepfather. Mother had left my other father when I was a baby, not because he didn't love us, but because he loved something else more. I couldn't get it into my juvenile brain precisely what it was he loved—some strange, hard-to-pronounce word that was my father's job. That was incomprehensible to me. How could a person love his work more than he loved a person? Mother tried to explain; I remember her soft, anxious voice going on and on, while I fidgeted, picking at the scab on my knee and wishing she would stop talking so I could go back to the baseball game down the street.

It may seem strange that I had forgotten my own name. A psychiatrist wouldn't find it strange; he would say I wanted to forget it. Maybe so. But I think the explanation is simpler. Children have a culture of their own; they are no more interested in adult values than an Australian aborigine is interested in the rules of Emily Post. I wasn't interested in the name, or in the forgotten father who had given it to me.

I remember thinking it was a weird name, not one I'd have wanted to claim. People didn't have names like that, except in the boring stories we had to read for English. My friends had sensible names, like Debby and Jan and Penny.

Mother arrived while I was inspecting the package. She always tried to be there when I got home from school, but the lines at the grocery store had been longer than usual that day. I went to help her carry in the bags, and then I saw that she was standing quite still, staring down at the big battered parcel. She had the most peculiar look on her face. I know now that what I saw was a struggle, internal but intense, and when I said casually, "Hey, I guess the mailman made a mistake," the struggle showed in a facial contortion so extreme that I mistook it for physical pain. I asked her what was the matter.

It was several seconds before she answered.

"He didn't make a mistake. It's for you. Have you forgotten?"

If I felt chagrin at being reminded that the weird name was my own, it was quickly forgotten in delight. The package was for me, that was the important thing.

I dismembered it there in the garage, too excited to notice Mother's silence. She stood watching while I tore the wrappings off and removed the lid. The interior of the box was filled with scraps of newspaper. Even in my anxiety to reach the object buried within, I realized that the paper was unusual. The language wasn't English. Even the writing was funny, not like English print.

My groping hands found a hard surface among the shreds of paper. I pulled out the object and held it up. My first thought was that someone had played a mean trick on me. This wasn't a present. It was a joke, a piece of junk.

The object was a statue, about a foot high, made of white stone. The arms were missing and so was the nose. The stone was stained and chipped and worn. At first I couldn't even decide whether it was supposed to be a man or a woman. It wore a long robe, carved in stiff pleats; but I knew that men used to wear long robes, and this object had an air of extreme age. Yet as I continued to stare, disgusted and disappointed, some quality of the small, marred face got through to me, and I felt sure that the subject was female.

Not that I cared. I was about to set the thing down, with a decided thump, when Mother's hand caught mine.

"Be careful. It is probably valuable."

"Valuable! This dirty, beat-up, old—"

"Very old. Over two thousand years old."

I sat back on my heels and looked at the statue again. I felt more respect for it; the difference between ten and two thousand has to command a certain awe. The more I looked, the more the thing got to me. Even the disfigurement of the nose could not destroy the haunting quality of the face. The mouth was curved in an odd, disquieting little smile, and the sunken eye sockets seemed to stare directly into my eyes.

Mother was on her knees, digging with both

hands among the crumpled papers. She leaned back with a short, high-pitched laugh.

"Not even a note," she said, as if to herself. "How typical."

I paid no attention to the comment, which was obviously not addressed to me. I couldn't rid myself of the notion that this was some kind of practical joke. I turned the statue upside down, thinking there might be a note, or a rude remark, on the base. Sure enough, something was written there in black ink. It wasn't a word; the shapes looked more like code than letters of the alphabet.

I showed it to Mother. She gave another of those funny little laughs.

"Ariadne," she said. "Just like him! How could he know? It might be anyone—Aphrodite or Hera, or an anonymous worshiper."

"Ariadne? This is supposed to be me?"

This time Mother's laugh sounded more like her own. She was wearing jeans—she had a nice trim figure in those days—and she sat down on the garage floor with her legs crossed and the statue on her lap.

"The writing is in Greek," she explained. "It's a Greek statue—archaic Greek, about five hundred B.C. Ariadne was a princess who lived on an island near Greece, even earlier than that—a thousand years earlier. She was like a fairytale princess to those ancient Greeks. They told stories about her, and I suppose they did make statues of her. But no one can tell who this statue is supposed to represent. It must be his idea of—no, not a joke, he never jokes—of an appropriate gift for a little girl. I wonder what reminded him of your existence."

I had lost her again. She said "you," but she wasn't talking to me.

I joggled her elbow. "Who?" I asked. "Who sent it?"

"Your father," she said. "Now, Sandy, don't look so blank. Don't pretend you've forgotten about him too; I told you the whole story years ago, you must remember—"

Her voice was getting high and shrill. I couldn't figure out why she was upset—I thought I was the one who should be mad, getting such a dumb present—but I didn't want her to be upset, so I said quickly,

"Oh, sure. I remember. It was silly of me not to think of him right away."

She put her arm around me and pulled me against her. It was an uncomfortable position; my face was squashed against her shoulder, so I couldn't see her face. I could see the statue, though. She was holding it against her breast with the other hand, holding it pressed against her as she was holding me.

"Why should you remember?" she said softly. "I'm sorry. I had no right to snap at you. I was angry for you, not at you."

"You were mad at him," I said intelligently.

"Yes. And that isn't fair either." She let me go. I sat upright, relieved to see that she was smiling faintly. "I should be amused," she went on. "This is just the sort of thing your father would do. All these years ignoring our existence, and then, out of the blue, a completely inappropriate gift. I wonder if he remembers how old you are. He certainly doesn't remember your birth date. But, you see, that's the sort of man he is. He isn't interested in living people, and the only dates he can remember are dates before Christ. He didn't let us go because he disliked us; it was just that he liked—"

"His job more," I interrupted. The discussion was beginning to bore me. "You told me. He's a— a archae——"

"Archaeologist. A classical archaeologist. That means that he studies about ancient Greece."

"And that's where the statue came from. Are those Greek newspapers?"

"Yes. Presumably he's in Athens now. I suppose he found this in an antique shop and decided to send it to you. You should be flattered. It's really a lovely thing. Someday you will be proud to own it."

"I don't think it's lovely. It's all banged up, and I'll bet it never was pretty, even when it was new. I'd rather have a new football." I stood up. "I'm going for a bike ride now, okay?"

"Okay." She looked up at me, smiling and shaking her head. "Atalanta would have been more appropriate," she said obscurely. "Heredity is the most mysterious thing. How did that man and I ever breed a female Olympic star?"

That was my first introduction to Ariadne. I didn't meet her again for years, not until I studied the Greek myths in high school. Nobody knew I was her namesake, and I was careful not to tell them. Privately I thought she was a pretty feeble character. A traitor, in fact. She betrayed her country and her father for her boyfriend, and then he walked off and left her flat. All she could do was sit and cry until some god came along and made her his mistress.

Atalanta wasn't much better. Imagine letting some man con you out of winning a race by throwing goodies along the way! My personal hunch is that Atalanta wanted to lose. She had outrun a lot of prospective husbands, and being an old maid wasn't acceptable in those days.

I understood by then, however, why Mother had referred to me as Atalanta, and made that cryptic remark about heredity. Mother is short and getting a little—plump is the word we use. She has no more muscles than an amoeba. She's bright, though; has her M.A. Now I am not academically inclined, to put it politely. I never had trouble with schoolwork, not after Jim laid down the law: "A B average, or no after-school activities." But I never did more than I had to do to make that average, and maybe a little extra, just to be on the safe side.

The activities? Track. Swim team. Basketball. Hockey. I tried out for the boys' baseball team, and caused the biggest flap in the history of Morningside Junior High; that was a few years before the sexist bias in sports made headlines. Jim backed me up. He thought it was funny, since I was taller and better coordinated than most of the boys on the team. But Mother got upset; so I had to let it drop. I wasn't that crazy about baseball anyway.

In high school I really wanted to try out for the football team. I'm a little light, but I could have played quarterback. Mother burst into tears every time I mentioned the subject, so I gave that up too. I went to practice one afternoon, just to show the coach what he was missing, and completed twenty passes out of twenty-two, with eleven guys doing their best to cripple me and my receivers. They were nice guys; most of them were friends of mine. The center, Randy Sullivan, told me the coach cried after I left. He was probably exaggerating, though.

Jim, my stepfather, is a former All-American.

No, I'm not trying to say that heredity doesn't count. I'm saying that the question of identity is very complex. What makes you the person you are? How much of you is bred in the bone, de-

fined in embryo by a bunch of minuscule cells;
and how much comes from your environment—
friends, parents, physical factors such as diet and
freedom from rat bites? Environmental influences
aren't that simple either. Maybe the most important ones are the implicit, unstated assumptions
you carry with you, like a heavy knapsack—or
like wings. Some of them can drag you down,
and some can lift you up, let you fly.

These are old questions. They've been argued
by biologists and sociologists and psychologists
for years. I don't suppose the answers will ever
be definitely settled. But. . . . What if those
aren't the only things that make a man or
woman? What if there are other influences that
shape one's life? Influences that once lived and
then died and crumbled into dust—and lived
again? Silent inner forces from a past so distant
that even the metal of its artifacts has crumbled
into dust?

II

I heard from my father, off and on, during the
twelve years that followed the arrival of the package. (I thought of him, and spoke of him, when I
had to, as "Father." Jim was always "Dad.") The
communications were just as peculiar as the first
one. One was a reprint of a scholarly article he

had written, filled with Greek quotations and references to stirrup cups and Late Helladic IIIb. I didn't even try to read it. The craziest gift of all was an elaborate embroidered, lace-festooned modern Greek costume, complete with coin-trimmed headdress and red boots—for a child about six years old. I was fifteen at the time. Mother laughed till she cried over that. . . .

By the time I went off to college the communications had petered out. There had been no more scholarly articles.

It was pure accident that I learned why. The dentist was running late that morning, and there was nothing to read in the waiting room except issues of *Healthy Teeth* and an old copy of *Saturday Review,* or *Harper's,* or something of that ilk. I forget which one. I was thumbing through it when the face jumped up out of the page at me.

I didn't exactly recognize it. I couldn't have, because I had never seen a picture of my father. If Mother had any, she had never shown them to me. I didn't know that the man in the photograph was my father until I started reading the article. But even before I saw the name the face was inexplicably familiar.

The article was very amusing if you enjoy the kind of humor that consists of cutting someone else down. The author started out by referring to Professor Frederick's distinguished past career, and then tore him to pieces. Professor Frederick, it seemed, had gone off the deep end. He believed in the Atlantis myth.

I had heard of Atlantis. It was a wonderful island, a kind of earthly paradise, which sank into the depths of the ocean after being wracked by violent earthquakes and floods. The story is in Plato, than whom there could hardly be a more respectable writer, but scholars used to believe that Plato made up the whole thing. I had a friend, though, who was into mysticism and Rosicrucianism and all that; she thought the Atlanteans had inspired the Egyptians and Mayans and the other early civilizations. According to her and her fellow mystics, there really was an island of Atlantis, and the remains of the palaces and temples are still down there, draped with seaweed, at the bottom of the Atlantic. I had seen some science-fiction movies about it, too.

From the article I learned that the Atlantis theory has become more respectable in recent years. The island couldn't have been in the Atlantic Ocean, because deep-sea soundings have proved that the ocean floor has been under water for millions of years. But the island that disappeared in a sudden catastrophe could have been somewhere else, and as far back as the late nineteenth century, scholars began to wonder if the basis of Plato's story might not be found in the Minoan civilization.

We studied the Minoans for a week in World

History, preceded by Prehistoric Man (three days) and the Egyptians (two weeks), and followed by the Greeks (two months). So I knew who the Minoans were. They lived on the island of Crete in the Mediterranean, two thousand years before Christ; they built elaborate palaces, with plumbing and bathtubs. They had a king called Minos, whose daughter was named Ariadne, and a great scientist named Daedalus, who built the Labyrinth. What I didn't know—or if I had known, I had forgotten—was that Minoan civilization had ended around 1500 B.C., when the great palaces were destroyed in a violent catastrophe.

A thousand years passed between King Minos and Plato, plenty long enough for the true facts to be forgotten and legends to grow like coral. The location of the island was lost. The storytellers moved it out into the Atlantic, where there was more room for a civilization whose accomplishments had been magnified by generations of literary liars.

It was a plausible theory, but that is all it was until a few years ago, when archaeologists began digging on the island of Thera, north of Crete. They found the remains of Minoan houses buried under thick layers of volcanic ash. Thera is the largest island of a group of islands named Santorini, which are the remnants of a volcano. Back in 1500 B.C., or thereabouts, the volcano blew itself to pieces. The entire crater collapsed into the sea, forming a deep bay, or caldera, and the remainder of the island was buried under ash and pumice—like Pompeii, only deeper.

The Atlantis story suddenly looked pretty good. Not only was Thera, with its Minoan colony, annihilated, but tidal waves and earthquakes sparked by the vast explosion hit Crete, sixty miles away, with devastating force. The Minoans were merchant sailors, and all their big cities were on the coast. I was familiar with the effects of wave action, so I could imagine what waves fifty feet high would do to the Cretan palaces. And there were other side effects of the eruption—earthquakes, falls of windblown ash that rendered the soil infertile for years, local land collapses that drowned harbors and cities. The daughter colony and the mother island had both died in that unimaginable cataclysm. It was no wonder that the memory of it would linger even after the names had been forgotten.

As I have said, I'm not academically inclined. But the idea of sunken palaces fascinated me. I've always loved the water. Living in Florida, with a sports buff as a stepfather, I grew up practically amphibious, and Jim and I spent our summers looking for sunken Spanish galleons. The article expanded my imagination; I could see myself swimming through the columned porticoes, gathering the golden diadems of drowned queens.

The dentist had two emergencies that morning. I finished the article and then went back and reread parts of it. What I couldn't figure out was why the author was so antagonistic to my father. He had been one of the first to support the Atlantis-Crete identification, long before it was fashionable. Now it appeared that he had been right all along. Yet the author had nothing good to say about him. I decided that maybe the man had met Professor Frederick somewhere and had taken a violent dislike to his face, or his habit of eating peas with a knife, or something. After all, my mother hadn't been able to get along with him, and she was a pretty tolerant woman.

However, the tone of the article set my teeth on edge. Every sentence held a veiled insult or an open sneer. The ultimate effect was exactly the opposite of what the author intended: my sympathies were with the victim, not the attacker.

Don't imagine that the article was a big turning point in my life. I didn't develop a sudden passion for classical archaeology or burn to defend my poor abused father. I didn't think more kindly of him; I rather suspected he had brought the abuse on himself.

Yet that article was the first of two coincidences (if they were coincidences) that were to change my life. The second occurred a year later. Jim and I found our Spanish galleon.

I'm an excellent swimmer. I don't claim any

credit for it; most people would be good if they had spent as much time in the water as I have, with a coach like my dad. I'm not Olympic class, but I'm good, and I took to scuba gear the way the Ugly Duckling took to being a swan.

No, the Ugly Duckling reference is not meant to be a subtle description of myself. Swimming is a good way to develop the body, and my figure is all right. I look healthy. Reddish-blond hair (hence my nickname), green eyes, and the usual number of other features—nothing extraordinary, one way or the other.

Where was I? Oh, yes, the Spanish galleon.

The part of Florida where I live, about a hundred and fifty miles north of Miami, has seen hundreds of shipwrecks. There's a reef out from our beach that has murdered ships for centuries. If Columbus had come this way, the *Santa María* might not have made it back to Spain. We call it Devil's Reef. The Spaniards called it El Diablo, and they knew it well.

After the conquistadores conquered Mexico and Peru, they started looting on a scale that makes other conquerors look like amateurs. Tons of gold and silver and jewels were carried away to Spain. Every year the treasure fleet assembled in Cuba, convoys of six to ten ships. They planned to set sail for Spain in June, before the hurricane season. Some fleets carried as much as thirty million dollars' worth of treasure. They crossed the Florida Straits and followed the coastline north until they hit the Gulf Stream; then they turned eastward for the long, hazardous crossing.

Some of them never made it. Pirates and storms took their toll, but the greatest danger came from the condition of the ships themselves. Clumsy, topheavy, loaded to the gunwales with treasure, they were difficult to maneuver in any weather, and doomed in a hurricane. The coastline they hugged on their way north has some of the worst reefs in the world, and navigational skills were not highly developed. I don't know what percentage of the great galleons were lost during that period, but I know that the coast is thick with the wrecks of ships driven off course and ripped apart by the jagged rocks. Devil's Reef claimed its share.

So why are the wrecks still there? Why isn't everybody bringing up gold bars and pieces of eight?

There are a lot of reasons. Sometimes a vessel sank straight down into deep water. If the depth is great enough, salvage operations become prohibitively expensive. Most of the time it's impossible to pinpoint the exact location of a wreck, even when survivors described it to Spanish authorities. When a ship struck a reef, it was usually traveling at high speed, driven by winds. A projecting spike of coral would rip off the bottom, but the ship itself might be driven on over the reef, scattering cargo from the wound as it went. The remains could be strewn over hundreds of yards of territory, and as time passed, the hand of nature smoothed over the intrusive material. Heavy objects sank into sand or mud. Chemicals in seawater corroded metal. Marine organisms ate wood and clustered on other materials. Within a few years nothing would be recognizable—just lumps and bumps, indistinguishable from natural formations except to a highly trained eye. And it isn't all fun and games down there. Sharks, barracuda, moray eels, and other live hazards have to be handled with care. Sharp edges of coral and rusty beer cans add their kicks. Then there are the so-called "diving diseases"— nitrogen narcosis, oxygen poisoning, air embolism, and caisson disease, popularly known as the bends, to mention only a few. Treasure hunting is a chancy profession. The big discoveries make headlines, but most people spend their whole lives looking in vain. The successful strikes are usually the result of back-breaking work, long months of research in dusty colonial archives, and luck.

Our find was one of the rare exceptions. In our case, it was pure luck.

Jim always said there was a wreck somewhere offshore. We had been picking up stray coins for years—blackened, irregular scraps of metal that bore no resemblance to the gold doubloons of historical fiction. Once I found half a dozen pieces of eight on the sandy bottom, thirty feet out. That discovery moved Jim to some halfhearted research, but he didn't get far; like me, he is not academically inclined, and the records are all in archaic Spanish. So we weren't expecting anything that day in June when we went for our morning swim. We hadn't been to the beach for several days. The weather had been bad, and the night before we had had a humdinger of an early tropical storm, with high winds and heavy rain.

It was a gorgeous day. The beach was covered with debris, but the air sparkled. I went down seventy-five feet offshore, and I spotted the cannon immediately, by its shape. It was too regular to be a natural formation. But I couldn't believe it. I had been in that area a dozen times before. Apparently the storm had swept the sea bottom like a big broom, removing a deep layer of sand.

There were three other cannon behind the first. Then I saw *it*. It looked like a jagged greenish-brown rock, but the minute my eyes lit on it I felt a funny prickle run down my back. I swam over to it. There were coins all over the bottom around it, silver coins, some lying singly, some stuck together in clumps. I had read about finds like this, and I knew that the big lump also consisted of coins—hundreds of them, welded together by chemical action.

I don't know how I got it out. We found out later the darned thing weighed over thirty pounds. All I remember is doing a war dance with Jim. We were both whooping and jumping up and down and smacking each other's hands.

Jim called the museum right away and the state archaeological service took over, but they let us work along with the pros. The historians figured that the ship was one of the galleons from the plate fleet of 1735. It had carried a couple of million dollars' worth of gold and silver coins. Of course we didn't find nearly that much; the cargo had been scattered and washed away over two hundred years.

But it was a fabulous summer. Mother couldn't hassle me about getting a job, not with an opportunity like that available, so I spent most of the summer in the water, which is just the way I wanted to spend it.

I also enjoyed the publicity we got. Most of it was from local papers, but some of the national magazines sent photographers, and there was one smashing picture of me in the *National Geographic* article. I was back in school for my senior year when the issue came out, and I had to take a certain amount of ribbing. "Pretty young Sandy Bishop, the discoverer of the wreck. . . ." They posed me lying languorously on the beach, half buried in silver coins.

I managed to live that one down, and by Feb-

ruary everybody had forgotten about the article—
everybody except me. I caught myself daydream-
ing when I should have been studying,
remembering the glory of it all, and wondering if
that was the last exciting thing that would ever
happen to me. The weather was bad—it is bad in
February, even in Florida—and I was not looking
forward to graduation, assuming I would graduate, which was not at all certain, thanks to a particularly boring Soc course and a professor who
was giving me a hard time. I knew I had to make
it, though. Jim and Mother were worried about
money.

Worried about money, after finding millions of
dollars worth of treasure? Most people would
read that sentence with an incredulous smile. If a
professional treasure hunter read it he would
smile, too—a wry, pained smile of sympathy. I
know of one pro who dumped his coins back into
the ocean after getting his tax bill. There are complicated laws governing the way the find is di-
vided—it isn't a case of "finders keepers." The
value of the treasure depends on what you can
get for it on the open market, but you pay taxes
on the basis of a standard determined by the mysterious gentlemen from internal revenue. The
problem got so complicated I never did understand all the ramifications, but poor Jim used to
sit for hours, brooding over the masses of accu-
mulated legal forms, holding his head in his

hands and groaning softly. Eventually we might make money out of the discovery, but it would take years to settle the accounts, and there were times when Jim thought it would be easier to donate the coins to a museum. The point is that at that moment we were hard-up; and I knew I had to get out and stop sponging off my parents. Work, in other words. It was a depressing thought.

I was considering my prospects one evening in February. I had a single room that year, so there was nobody there but me and an unfinished, overdue Soc paper, which lay on the desk staring accusingly at me. I had just had a talk with my adviser about job prospects. They were as grim as the weather. I was preparing to be a Phys. Ed. teacher, not because the prospect of coaching fat little girls appealed to me, but because there isn't much else you could do with my skills, or lack thereof. Assuming I could latch on to a job for the following year, it wouldn't start until September; and that meant a summer of clerking in the drugstore or waiting on tables. The idea was less than alluring, especially after all the fun I had had the previous summer.

So, when I heard the knock on the door, I was glad to have something interrupt my gloomy thoughts. I was a little surprised, because I had stuck up a big sign—"Term Paper. Do not interrupt on pain of death"—and usually my friends were pretty good about that sort of thing. At that point, though, I'd have even welcomed an enemy.

Maybe that's who it was—an enemy. I knew him right away, although he had changed a lot since the picture in the magazine was taken. I knew him in my blood and bones. It was my father.

Chapter

2

I COULD HAVE RESPONDED TO THE APPARITION IN ONE of two ways. I might have said coolly, "Yes?" as if I didn't know him. Or I might have come up with something coolly ironic—"Well, well, long time no see," or some other equally witty remark. The key word is cool. I was not cool. I was thunderstruck; and my expression showed it.

I would have found him easier to deal with if he had been shabby and stooped and defeated. He was shabby, all right; his suit coat didn't match his pants, and it was worn and spotted, but the impression was one of disinterest, not of poverty. And physically he looked impressive. He was taller than Jim and he didn't have Jim's little pot tummy. I couldn't help making the comparison; it was disloyal, but I couldn't help it. If you had seen the two of them side by side, you'd have picked this man as the athlete. He had hardly any gray in his thick brown hair. Even his face was young looking. His eyes were a funny, frosty gray; they studied me with detached interest from under heavy dark brows. He didn't smile. His chin was square. It was *my* chin. I had never particularly liked the shape of my chin.

He looked me up and down, with that irritating, impersonal stare. I felt like a horse being appraised by a prospective buyer. Then he said,

"Ariadne. Yes, I would have recognized you, even without the photograph in *National Geographic.* Aren't you going to invite me in?"

Still speechless, I stepped back. He came in and closed the door. Then he sat down in the sole armchair the room boasted. Casually, quite at ease, he glanced around. The room was a mess. Papers, books, clothes, sports gear all over. The bed wasn't made. He didn't seem to notice. His eyes lit on the photo on the dresser. It was my favorite picture of Mother and Dad, enlarged from a snapshot I had taken. They were in the front yard. It was a breezy day, and Mother's hair was blowing. She was laughing, and she looked about twenty. Jim had his arm around her. He was laughing too, and he looked like the wonderful guy he is, bald head, pot, and all.

Something in my father's expression made me angry. The warmth loosened my tongue.

"Mother is fine," I said.

"I assumed she would be."

"Oh, did you?" I sat down on the bed and glared at him. "You certainly never bothered to find out."

"Why should I?"

If he had sounded angry or defensive, I would have had an answer. But he didn't. He just sounded surprised. Before I could find sufficiently cutting words, he went on, in the same calm voice.

"It was obvious, even when you were an infant, that you would not be interested in pursuing a scholarly career. Perhaps if you had been a boy I might have communicated with you more regularly."

"Male chauvinist," I said.

"I beg your pardon?" His broad forehead wrinkled. Then it cleared. "No," he said, in the same dispassionate voice. "It was not your sex, but your lack of intellectual capacity that guided my decision."

A funny thing happened then. I looked at him sitting there, perfectly at home, with a daughter he hadn't seen for almost twenty years—a daughter whom he had rejected because at the age of two she had failed to display sufficient intellectual capacity. He looked—no, not smug, that word is too strong—he looked self-satisfied. He had explained himself, and he expected me to understand, and to agree with his assessment. The notion that he might be wrong—that he might be irritating or cruel or unreasonable—had never entered his head.

Oddly enough, this didn't anger me. You can't feel anger with a blind man because he can't see. For the first time in the insane interview I relaxed.

"How could you tell?" I asked curiously. "What tests do you administer to an infant to find out whether she has an aptitude for classical archaeology?"

He waved the question away with an impatient flick of his hand.

"That is beside the point, Ariadne. What does matter is that I was mistaken as to your usefulness. Not because my assessment was incorrect, but because circumstances have changed. The field of underwater archaeology has developed since then. Not that I had any reason to suppose that you would develop a talent for that sort of thing—"

"You should have tried throwing me into a pond," I suggested.

Mother had once said my father was the only man she had ever known who had absolutely no sense of humor. My remark wasn't all that funny, but it should have won a small social smile. The corners of my father's long, thin lips remained straight.

"That would not have answered," he replied, with complete seriousness. "And, as I have said, the field of underwater archaeology has developed since—"

"Okay, okay," I interrupted. "I get the point. See here—uh—"

"You had better call me Frederick. A more intimate appellation would not only be out of place, considering our relationship, but it would prove an embarrassment in the situation I propose to outline."

"Frederick," I said experimentally. "Fred?"

"I dislike nicknames."

"Well, I don't. Nobody ever calls me Ariadne. I hate the name. If I call you Frederick, you'll have to call me Sandy."

He considered the suggestion thoughtfully. Then he nodded.

"Although," I added, "I don't know why we should call each other anything. Is this supposed to be the beginning of a new and beautiful relationship? Because I don't think—"

"You don't think," he interrupted. "If you did, you would understand what I am leading up to. I assure you, I should be more direct if you would stop distracting me with side issues."

"Oh, I'm not that stupid. You saw the article in *Geographic*—what were you doing reading a pop mag like that? Anyhow, you decided that your stupid daughter might have a few talents you had not expected. Have you got a specific job in mind, or are you propositioning me generally?"

"I have a specific job in mind."

It was the weirdest conversation. The most peculiar thing about it was that it didn't seem weird, like the events of a bizarre dream that seem entirely reasonable in the context of the dream. The man's self-confidence was so complete that it made his behavior seem right, somehow. I had never met anyone like him. Few people have, because most human beings suffer from self-doubt and insecurity, whether they express it openly or try to hide it under blankets of arrogance. Not this guy. Frederick. My father.

". . . I could have obtained all the personnel I needed if those fools in the antiquities service hadn't refused me permission to dive," he was saying, as I came out of my reverie.

"Wait a minute," I said dizzily. "You mean. . . . Start at the beginning. Where is this dig of yours?"

"On Thera," he said impatiently. "One of the islands in the Santorini group. They have assigned me an area where they do not expect me to find anything of importance. Fortunately Mistropolous has just been appointed head of the service and he has some respect for my ideas. But even he—"

He went on berating the Greek archaeological department, while I tried to sort things out. I suspected I would have to do a lot of sorting with him. He took so much for granted. I pitied his poor students, if he ever taught a class.

Thanks to the magazine article in the dentist's office, I knew that Santorini was the volcanic island that had blown itself to pieces in the fifteenth century B.C. Several archaeological expeditions had worked on the main island of Thera; I gathered that Frederick's concession was not near any of the places that had produced juicy finds, but off in a corner where, it was fondly hoped, he wouldn't cause any trouble. I already knew him well enough to suspect that was a vain hope.

Then another point hit me and I interrupted the tirade.

"What do you mean, you don't have permission to dive?"

"The words seem plain enough to me."

"Yeah," I said. "They seem plain to me, too. In other words—correct me if I'm wrong—you have permission to dig, but not to dive. You can't hire divers—no pro would be fool enough to risk his career and his reputation by breaking the law—so you are suggesting that I do so. Thanks a lot."

"You have no career and no reputation to lose," said Frederick.

"How tactfully you put it," I said. "What makes you so determined to risk *your* reputation? Why can't you just dig, like a good little archaeologist is supposed to do? It just so happens that I know about Thera, about the Minoan houses that were dug up—out of the dirt that is, not out of the ocean floor. And if you're thinking about my diving down into the caldera, where the middle of the island was, forget it. A diver couldn't work down there with ordinary scuba gear, it's hundreds of feet deep."

"Three to four hundred meters, to be exact," Frederick said. "Obviously I wouldn't propose any such absurd idea. Water pressure would have destroyed any remains in that area. If you knew as much as you claim to know, you would realize that the outer portions of the island were also subjected to seismic action. Parts of the coastline have subsided since ancient times. Local divers have reported seeing ruins underwater. I want you to investigate a—a particular area. The situation is ideal. Even our names are different. No one will suspect you of being motivated to—"

"Break the law," I said. "Won't they get just a teeny bit suspicious when they see me diving?"

"The village is remote. We will take all possible precautions."

"But it's impossible! I'll need gear. Tanks. Air. How do I get my tanks filled without some smart character suspecting that I just possibly might be diving? It's crazy!"

The madman—my father, for God's sake—looked vaguely around the room.

"I'd like some coffee," he said. "We'll discuss the details. They can be worked out."

I made him some instant on my hot plate. I

didn't want to go out to the coffee shop with him. I didn't want to be seen with him. But I knew what was going to happen. I even knew why it was going to happen.

Breaking the law didn't bother me, although I had made a big point of it to Frederick. As he said, I had no reputation to lose, and I didn't consider that I was planning to commit a crime, merely bend a minor regulation. I doubted that they would put me in a Greek jail even if they caught me. I could always claim my revered parent had ordered me to do wrong.

That danger I could dismiss, but the other dangers were more serious. Diving is the greatest fun on earth, but it is not a game. You have to know what you're doing, and you have to know the terrain. Thanks to Jim's super coaching, I felt competent to take care of myself in home waters, but I didn't know anything about the Mediterranean. For all I knew, they had man-eating plants down there. And my father didn't strike me as the greatest person to have around if you got into trouble. I had a feeling I could drown ten feet away from Frederick if he happened to be thinking about something else.

Money was no problem, apparently. Somehow or other Frederick had conned some nutty foundation into sponsoring the dig. There are more of them—nutty foundations—than you might suppose, supported by millionaires with more money than sense, or by groups of earnest fanatics. They want to find the Fountain of Youth, or the secret of the Great Pyramid, or—in this case—Atlantis. The Atlantis bit suited Frederick's plans; that's what he was really looking for, although he put the problem in more pompous terms. So I could get my fare and expenses out of Frederick. I might not be earning any money, but at least I wouldn't be a drag on Mother and Dad.

Which brought me to the main problem.

I had no intention of telling my parents—my real parents—about Frederick. Mother would flip, and I wouldn't blame her. It had taken me only half an hour to realize that my begetter was ruthless, unreliable, and incapable of feeling responsibility toward another human being. Mother had better reasons than anyone in the world to know these things. For the first time in my life I allowed myself to contemplate that marriage. It had lasted for three years. . . . I shivered. Cold. Cold—it must have been like embracing a block of ice.

So what I had to do was think up a convincing story. I considered lying about my whereabouts, writing a dozen letters and arranging to have incoming letters forwarded by a confederate in some safe neutral town, or one of the state parks, where I might reasonably be expected to find a summer job. The idea didn't appeal to me. If I got caught, it would destroy a relationship that had taken me twenty years to build up. I hated to risk it. And yet it was because of that relationship of trust that I could get away with what I planned to do that summer. Mother and Jim would believe me when I told them . . . anything. They trusted me that much.

I was already starting to talk away the difficulties. The decision wasn't hard to make. It was a choice between Joe's Pizza Parlor, with a lot of beer-drinking high-school big shots making grabs at me, and . . . Thera. Brilliant sunlight and cobalt-blue waters, olive groves and white beaches and bronzed Greek sponge divers with dazzling smiles. . . . My ideas of Greece were pretty vague. But underlying the hazy tourists' picture, motivating the decision that altered my life was the prospect of what might be waiting for me in the blue waters off Thera. Sunken treasure, cities under the sea. The columned halls of the sea kings. Gold ingots, piled in stacks. Crowns and diadems, jewels spilling out of rotted chests bound with silver. Pretty Sandy Bishop, the discoverer of the treasure . . .

I'm not ashamed to admit I was a fool. Even now, after all that happened, I'd rather be foolish than too dull to respond to a lure like that.

After Frederick had left I tried to get back to my term paper, but it was a lost cause. His aggressive presence still pervaded the room. After a while I put on my raincoat and went to the library. Instead of looking up references for my paper, I took out three books about ancient Greece.

Things worked out about the way I had expected. Lying to Mother and Jim left me with a nasty feeling. I hated to do it. But there was no other way.

So I set up a deal with Betsy, a friend of mine who was planning to spend the summer backpacking around Europe with a couple of other guys. She agreed to forward mail, read telegrams or anything that looked urgent, and telephone me right away if something came up. (That was before I found out about telephone service in remote parts of eastern Europe.) She was also supposed to scribble an unintelligible postcard from time to time.

Mother and Dad accepted my plans with a readiness that made me squirm inside. I had about two hundred dollars in the bank. I told them it was more. They believed me. And I felt like the A-1 heel of the universe on graduation day when Jim handed me a check. He had to borrow the money, I was sure of it. I almost told them the truth then, they were so teary-eyed and proud and gullible. But I didn't. I promised myself I would pay Jim back at the end of the summer, with interest. I could get the money from Frederick, and believe me, I had no qualms about doing just that.

I had seen him a couple of times since his first

visit. Finally I told him not to come to the campus. He made me nervous. It was okay with him. We communicated by letter after that, and I must admit he was relaxing to deal with. He wasn't like a parent at all. I mean, with parents—parents you love—you have to go through all kinds of contortions to keep from worrying them or hurting their feelings. I didn't have to pretend with Frederick. He treated me like an equal—no, not like an equal, he didn't think he had any; he treated me like a functioning adult, no more incompetent than the other adults he knew. Like, in making the arrangements for the trip. He just sent me a check. No reservations, no "I'll meet you at three thirty-four at the customs desk, and for heaven's sake, don't miss the plane." Love is fine. But it is also confining, it ties you down. My parents were the greatest, but even with them there were times when I felt like Gulliver, pinioned by a million tiny strings, and I wanted to leap up and yell and throw my arms wide and break loose.

I wanted to be free. And if that sounds corny, adolescent, immature—it's the truth, and I've made up my mind to be as honest as I can. I know. Freedom's just another name for nothing left to lose. I had plenty to lose and no intention of losing it. I didn't want to be free of Mother and Dad, not permanently. But for a while. . . . With Frederick I was free. I didn't give a damn about him and he didn't give a damn about me. If I ever came into conflict with his precious work, then heaven help me. He would sacrifice me as quickly—and with less regret—than Agamemnon had sacrificed his daughter to get favorable winds. (You see, I had been doing my homework on ancient Greece.)

I knew from the start I couldn't live long in that arctic cold that was Frederick's emotional environment. But after twenty years of cozy warmth, it felt bracing. He was an interesting man. I was curious to find out more about him. And there were the sunken halls of the sea kings, waiting. . . .

They weren't such bad reasons. There was no way I could have anticipated what was going to happen.

III

I took my time about getting to Thera. Frederick was probably pacing up and down the volcano, looking at his watch and cursing me in several languages; but after all, it was my first trip abroad. Besides, I felt I had to establish my relationship with Frederick right from the start. If I wasn't firm with him, he would walk all over me.

So I spent a couple of days in London and a couple of days in Paris, seeing the sights and sending lots of postcards home. I was always with a crowd; there were a lot of people my age traveling, and it's easy to spot a fellow student, whatever his or her nationality. I said good-bye to Mike and Sally and Joe in Paris, and met another group in Athens. We visited the Plaka together, and I learned how to do that Greek dance, the kind where the dancers have their arms around each other's shoulders.

Oh, yes, we went up to the Acropolis one afternoon. If they would only fix the place up, it would be rather impressive. There's no reason why they can't patch the holes and put up some new columns.

I mention this not to show what a boor I am, but because my lack of response to the great antiquities of Greece proves that I am not susceptible to that sort of thing. I had no emotional reaction to the place, and it's a place that brings out the hidden romanticism in many people. "The birthplace of democracy.... The stones trodden by the sandals of Socrates. . . ." That sort of thing.

Which makes my experience in Crete all the more peculiar.

I hated to leave Athens. I had met this guy named Aristotle—really—who was a student at the university, and he was showing me parts of Athens most tourists don't see. He wanted to show me some other things, too; and although I was having fun, I decided maybe it was time to move on. I wanted to spend a couple of days in Crete, to keep up my tourist pose, before I went to Thera. I suppose I was overdoing the camouflage, but I rather enjoyed it; it made me feel like Mata Hari.

I took a boat. There were quite a few other students on board, and we stayed up most of the night singing and talking. The cabins were stuffy little cubicles with four or five people in each of them. I guess every safety regulation was violated on that boat, especially the one that limited the number of passengers. I figured if we hit a rock or something, I'd have a better chance on deck, so instead of going to bed with my four roommates, I just lay down on the deck when I got sleepy.

When I woke up, with the sun shining down on my face, I felt awful—sick and stiff and depressed, the way I'd felt when I had Asian flu. It wasn't the hard deck or the fact that I'd had only three hours sleep. I had done that plenty of times. I wondered if I was catching some kind of bug, and I lay there for a while with the smell of bilge and sour wine strong around me, regretting my boasts about never getting seasick. Then I remembered the dream.

When I was young I used to have nightmares— not often, but when I did, they were bad. It would take me a long time to fight free of the dream, even after I woke up; I can remember lying in bed in a cold sweat of terror, shaking and sick, before I came fully awake. It hadn't happened for a long time. Until now.

I felt a little better when I realized that the main thing wrong with me was a bad dream. I tried to recall the details of this one; but the harder I concentrated, the more the memories slipped away, like small wet fish between my fingers. At first all I could remember was that it had something to do with Crete and the old legend—with which I was now very familiar—of Theseus and the Minotaur.

The Minotaur was a good theme for nightmares. Half man, half bull, he was the result of a temporary liaison between the queen of Crete and—right. The queen couldn't help herself, actually. Poseidon, the god of the sea, had made her fall in love with the bull because her husband had kept the animal for himself, instead of sacrificing it. The Greek gods were always doing things like that. They were a mean, vindictive group of divinities, not nearly so well behaved as the poor humans they harassed.

Anyway, King Minos couldn't destroy the Minotaur because it was sacred. So he had his brilliant architect, Daedalus, design the Labyrinth as a sort of kennel for the monster, and every nine years he fed it with hostages from the conquered city of Athens—seven young men and seven maidens. One year, when the sacrifice was due, the prince of Athens, Theseus, volunteered for the draft, hoping to kill the monster and save his fellow Athenians.

He wouldn't have succeeded if the Princess Ariadne, Minos' daughter, hadn't fallen in love with him. She gave him a clew, a ball of string, to unwind as he went into the Labyrinth. Without it, he couldn't have found his way out again, even if he succeeded in killing the monster, which of course he did, being a hero. He took Ariadne with him when he escaped from Crete, but he deserted her before he got home—sailed away, leaving her on an island where they had stopped for provisions. At least that's what one version of the legend says, and it's the one I'm inclined to believe. Another version claims Theseus' ship was blown away by a storm while Ariadne was on shore.

The part I had dreamed about was the part where Theseus meets the Minotaur.

I had seen a picture of that scene in some mythology book. It was a line drawing in black and white—nothing like my dream picture, which had been in living color, complete with all the sensory impressions. As I lay there, the dream came back to me, my memory nudged by the Greek sun beating down on my upturned face, the boat rocking gently under me, the smell of fish and seawater and close-packed bodies. . . .

The walls were rough, rock cut; they dripped with moisture and shone with a rotten greenish luminescence. There was a horrible smell—not the smell of manure and hay, which is wholesome and clean by contrast, but the stench of organic things decaying. The air was thick with it. No wind from outside had entered that place, to sweep it clean, since it was built. This was the heart of the Labyrinth, the lair of the monster. Maybe the outer walls and corridors were man-built and straight; I hadn't seen that part in my dream—but here, at the very core, the rocky maze seemed to be cut out of the body of the earth itself. The earth mother was the oldest of all the gods, and the slimy, curving corridors were horribly suggestive of the entrails of some gigantic animal. The light pulsated feebly, as if something breathed.

In the center there was darkness, utter and absolute. But I knew something was there. I could sense it, waiting. The man knew it, too. He was afraid. The sweat ran down his face in streams, and yet his half-naked body shook convulsively, as if he were cold. He was wearing a queer short skirt, with a wide belt that shone like metal. It pulled his waist in and made his chest and shoulders look even broader than they were. There was a chain around his neck, with an amulet or locket hanging from it. He had dropped the clew. There was something on the ground at his feet. How could I tell it was a box, the box that held the ball of twine? I don't know. But I was sure.

Yes, I was there. That was the worst part of the

dream. I was there, invisible, impalpable; watching in an agony of fear and hope.

Something stirred in the central darkness. There was a rustling sound, not the rustle of dried grass or hay, but a clicking rattle, like dead bones rubbing together. Then It came out into the light.

Half man, half bull. It's all right when you see something like that in a drawing. You can accept the grotesque because it is unreal. But this was real—alive and breathing. The mingling of animal and human wasn't as neat as it is in the illustrations—a well-shaped man's body with a bovine head, like a mask. This creature was indescribably blended. But the face was human, and that was horrible, because it was aware. It knew what it was, and it felt the same loathing its victims felt—for its own body. Imagine being trapped, not just for a single lifetime, but for eternity, inside something you loathe and despise with a sick hatred. . . . Hate was its only emotion. Hatred for itself and for humanity and for the immortal gods. I caught one glimpse of that ghastly face and blacked out.

When I could see again, the two, man and monster, were wrapped in a struggle to the death. They rolled over and over, in and out of the light, arms and legs entwined as if they were being molded together into a single, even more monstrous, being. And I knew that one of the two must die; and I knew that whichever one it was, I would suffer a loss in that dying, for the monstrous thing was part of me, bone of my bone. As the two rolled and tore at each other, among the brittle, breaking bones of earlier victims, I woke up.

I remembered the whole thing now, and it was almost as bad as dreaming it. Then somebody's arm went around me and rolled me across the deck. Two sleepy brown eyes stared into mine and a fur-fringed mouth opened in a wide grin.

"Guten Morgen," said—I had forgotten his name. He was Austrian.

"Hi," I said, and freed myself. I stood up, holding the rail for support.

The view almost made me forget my queasy stomach. The air is so clear in that part of the world that everything seems to sparkle. The water was aquamarine, sprinkled with lines of foamy white bubbles. The sky was a big inverted bowl of blue, with fat white clouds in it. We were gliding along the coast of Crete, and I could see the harbor of Herakleion, with a rash of houses and buildings enclosing it. The island was a bright, cheerful green, but behind the coast rose brown, bare mountains, and in that marvelous brilliant light it seemed as if I could make out the separate boulders on the slopes.

"We come into harbor," said Hans, or Fritz, or whatever his name was. Joining me at the rail, he threw an enormous arm around me and squeezed my shoulders till the joints cracked. He was a great believer in touching. That arm had been around somebody, usually me, the whole evening. He was a big, blond, sleepy-looking guy who looked like a linebacker. There were 220 or 230 pounds of him, and most of it showed; he was traveling in a pair of shorts, sandals, a knapsack, and a beard. I put my arm around him and squeezed him back. The solid warm feel of him was wiping away the memory of my nightmare. But what a dream that had been!

"So," said Fritz, or Hans. "Where we go? First we drink a beer, eh? Then to museum, then to Knossos, then to Haggia Triada, then—"

"First some coffee," I said.

There was no dining room on the boat, but the crew cook ran a little concession on the side. I got coffee for me and Hans, at an exorbitant price. I figured Frederick was paying for it, so why should I be cheap?

Fritz continued to hang around. I didn't know whether it was the coffee or my girlish charm that kept him, but I didn't care. He knew a few words of Greek and found a guy, one of the ones who were lounging around the dock, who had a sister who rented rooms. He—the brother—agreed to take my luggage to the house. He told Hans where it was—the house—and I gave him my luggage check and some money, and we went looking for a café. I might add that when I describe such transactions to adults they almost die; but I never lost a piece of gear or a drachma.

After I had stocked Hans up with food—he ate an incredible amount—we headed for the museum.

The minute I walked in the front door I began to feel funny. I've tried to think of how to express it; the only thing I can say is that I *recognized* the objects in those cases. Not all of them. But some things. . . . It was like the time I found a beat-up, half-disintegrated object under a bush in the backyard and recognized it as the remains of a doll I had lost a few years earlier.

I remember what brought on the first stab of recognition—it felt like that, like a sharp, physical pain. The object was described as a gaming board. I could see that it had been absolutely gorgeous, all inlaid with lapis and crystal and gold and ivory. There was a border of daisies around the edge, and reliefs of shells and things, in miniature. The board was cracked and battered, but it didn't take much imagination to see it the way it had looked when some proud artisan presented it to the king. It had to have been a king's plaything, that glitter of crystal and gleam of gold could not have been designed for any but a royal household.

Okay. So an imaginative person could picture that without much strain. Only I knew that board. I knew how to play the game. The pieces started on the right side, in the central one of the four circular spaces, and followed a path I knew, ending in the ladderlike section at the left—"home." The men moved according to the throw of dice—ivory dice, larger than the ones we use today. I could almost feel them between my palms; one was a little jagged because I had flung it against the wall one time, when I made a losing throw. . . .

The room came back into focus, and I realized that Hans-Fritz was holding my arm in a grip that hurt.

"Do not fall on the case," he said calmly. "It is always so in museums, do not fall on the case."

I realized that he had not seen anything peculiar in my behavior. That was a relief. *He* was a relief, with his big, lazy, good-natured grin. Not a nerve in him.

"You mean, don't lean on the cases," I said. "Uh—Hans, I think we ought to go. Let's go to Knossos or someplace."

"No, no, we must see museum. All in order."

I don't think I could have gotten through the museum except for Hans. Although he looked like a football player, he had a brain like a Rhodes scholar—the two are not necessarily incompatible, in fact. He knew a lot about the Minoan culture, and he communicated it to me in his cheerfully ungrammatical English. I just nodded and made noises. I was feeling queerer and queerer, Hans's hand, to which I clung like a kid afraid of losing his mother, was a lifeline anchoring me in the present.

Some of the other objects hit me almost as hard as the gaming board—a gold necklace, a mirror—but the one that shook me most was the clew box.

It's a small, squarish box made of clay, with holes in it. It could be used to hold a ball of string; I've seen similar gadgets in modern kitchens, containers with a hole for the string to come through so you can pull out the length you need without having the ball unwind all around the room. Such a device would have been equally practical for Ariadne and Theseus; the clew, or ball of twine she gave him, so he could find his way back out of the Labyrinth, might well have been enclosed in such a box. But there's no way of proving that theory. The name of the mysterious object in the Herakleion museum is pure fancy, the suggestion of some imaginative scholar. Ariadne is a mythological character, and nobody knows what the function of the clay box was. Nobody but me.

I don't remember what else we saw in the museum. I must have walked and talked and looked normal, like a well-constructed mechanical doll, because when I got my wits back, Hans didn't appear to have noticed anything unusual about me. We were in a grocery store at the time. It was almost noon. I gathered that we had decided it would be romantic to eat lunch among the ruins of Knossos. So we bought goat's cheese and a loaf of bread and a bottle of local wine and went to the plaza to catch the bus.

The bus ride was so normal and crowded and human, I forgot what had happened in the museum. We were jammed in like sardines. Hans took up a lot of room, and he kept apologizing to people, who nodded and grinned back at him. Everybody seemed to be in a good mood. I couldn't help thinking of the buses in Miami at rush hour during the tourist season—the scowling, worried faces and hard voices.

Knossos was the end of the line, so we all piled out. It seemed funny to ride a bumpy little local bus to an ancient Minoan palace; twenty kilometers and three thousand years out, so to speak. There was a grape arbor outside the entrance to the city. The grapes were little green balls, but the leaves were thick and shady, so we sat on the ground in the shade and ate lunch, with Hans quoting inaccurately from Omar Khayyám. Then we paid our entrance fees and went in.

Most archaeological sites are pretty boring, just low foundation walls, drab brown brick and gray stone, with dusty weeds growing up over the thresholds. Knossos has been restored by the excavator, Sir Arthur Evans; and although the purists criticize his restorations, claiming that he used more imagination than research, the result is so handsome you can't condemn him. The palace is truly labyrinthine in size and complexity. The rooms, roofed and columned, are complete; the grand staircase really is grand, the queen's bathtub is in place in her bathroom. And the colors! The queer Cretan columns, larger at the top than at the base, painted black and red; the faded terra-cotta of the giant storage jars; the soft blues and yellows of the painted walls. The frescoes are clean modern copies of the originals, which are now in the museum. Like most of Knossos, they have been restored—over-restored, according to some critics. But they give some idea of how gay and bright the place looked in its heyday. There are flying blue dolphins and golden griffins; processions of young men with long black curls falling over their shoulders and their waists pulled in by broad, tight belts; frivolous Cretan ladies in costumes that look like the latest Paris fashions, the skirts long and full and flounced, the bodices baring their breasts.

Perhaps the most famous fresco is the one of the bull leapers.

Hans liked that one.

"*Achtung,*" he exclaimed, or some vigorous German exclamation. "How could they do such dangerous thing? I would not jump over bull!"

"You might if the alternative was being killed," I said. "Maybe the bull dancers were prisoners who were trained for the job."

"Yes, yes, I have read the books that say so. But I doubt that it happened. Even, I doubt the picture when I see it! It is a fantasy."

"No," I said. "No, it could be done. It doesn't

require any more skill or coordination than modern-day gymnastics. The only difference is that it's more dangerous. The mortality rate must have been high. But that didn't seem to bother the Greeks. I wouldn't choose you, though, Fritz. You're too heavy. A bull dancer had to be light and lean—pure muscle."

Like the man in my dream.

"Like you." Fritz looked me over approvingly. "You would dance well with the bull, *nicht?*"

The big brown bull was in full charge, his head lowered. The three athletes were naked except for queer little calf-length boots and close-fitting loincloths, fastened at the waist by the broad, stiff belts that seemed to have been fashionable in Crete. One of them was standing behind the bull with her arms raised, as if she were about to catch the man who was doing a handstand on the bull's back. His legs were flung back, and it was clear that he was about to somersault over the tail and land on his feet, behind the bull. The third of the three vaulters was just starting her leap. She had hold of the bull's horns, and she was right in between them, you could see the points on both sides of her body. The technique couldn't have been more clearly expressed in a games manual. The athlete grabbed the bull's horns when he charged, and when he tossed his head back she vaulted up over his head, landed on his back, and jumped to the ground. That is, she did it unless she got caught on the horns.

Yes, I said "she." Two of the athletes were girls. No mistake; not only were they shaped like girls, but they were painted a pale yellowish white, in contrast to the third athlete, who was reddish brown. Hans explained that coloring the men darker than the women was a convention in Minoan art. The Egyptians did the same thing, perhaps because the women usually stayed inside and protected their complexions from the hot Mediterranean sun.

I wondered if I could get a postcard of the scene. If so, I would send it to Mr. Barnes, the gym teacher who had refused to let me play baseball because girls were too fragile for such a violent sport.

This was one sport I wouldn't have tried out for. Oh, it could be done; as I had said to Hans, it didn't require any more coordination than a lot of the tricks gymnasts learn. Only here, if you slipped, you didn't get up, rubbing a sore fanny, and try again. But the danger wouldn't deter the bull vaulters, any more than it stops bullfighters and mountain climbers and Evel Knievel. Maybe the vaulters weren't prisoners. Maybe they were kids who saw themselves as superstars, strutting down the stone-paved streets with everybody pointing and whispering and asking them for their autographs. And, as Hans said, there might have been a religious meaning to the game. That would strengthen an athlete's nerve too. The bull was the sacred animal of Poseidon, the sea god, and the games might have been rituals in his honor. Remember the Minotaur, half man, half bull. . . .

You see, I was thinking quite reasonably and coherently. All the while, however, another process was going on inside me. What had happened in the museum was only the overture before the main event, which began as soon as I set my sandaled foot on the soil of the city. The feeling was so strong that it overpowered my sense of congruity. It no longer seemed strange that I should find so many things familiar. It was as if I were two people in the same body. The real me— Sandy—was in control. She walked around and talked to Hans and admired the sights. But down underneath, in the dark places of my mind, someone else was waking up from a long, long sleep. That someone didn't have a name. I didn't dare give her one. But she knew this place, as she had known the gaming board and the clewbox.

"We" stood in the big central courtyard, and one of us remembered the games.

It was midafternoon by then, and hot. The sun beat down on the dusty gray surface, where a few hardy weeds survived the trampling of tourists' feet. Along the four sides of the court were the walls and columns of the enclosing palace. There were quite a few sightseers. The ones who had come on the big gaudy tour buses were mostly over sixty and overweight. They had gray hair or white hair or no hair, except for a few of the women, whose bright-gold heads had come off a shelf in some shop. They huddled together like sheep, listening to the guide's lecture. The younger tourists seemed to be students, for the most part. Some of them, with their long hair and short shorts, their legs and torsos bared, might have stepped out of the old frescoes—slim-waisted, brown young men.

"I" saw the tourists and the sunbaked earthen flooring. The other person in my mind saw great stone paving blocks, ominously stained; rows of spectators watching in breathless silence; the great brown bulk of the bull, and the man who stood waiting for its charge, hands raised and ready for the horns. His body was lean and brown, and his face was the face of the man in my dream.

Chapter
3
_____

WHEN I WOKE UP THE NEXT MORNING I DIDN'T KNOW where I was. The events of the previous day were hazy and dreamlike, as if they had happened to some character in a book I had been reading. The hallucination in the great court, when I had seemed to see a color replay of the bull games, was my last coherent memory. The rest of the day was a series of isolated fragments.

Hans and I had explored the palace, met a couple of students from Denmark, and had supper with them. I remembered their faces; the names were gone. Afterward I must have found the house where I had rented a room. . . . Yes, one of the memory fragments concerned the house, and the smiling, motherly Greek lady who owned it.

She had shown me the room and brought me water so I could wash. After that—blank.

Calling the experience a hallucination reduced it to terms I could accept. Mentally I added another acceptable word. Sunstroke. Too much sun, unfamiliar food, illness—hallucinations. Reassured, I looked around the room.

The window was wide open. Sunlight made the whitewashed walls so bright they hurt my eyes, and there were so many flies they sounded like a vacuum cleaner. I had a couple of little red bites I hadn't had when I arrived in Crete, but otherwise I felt fine.

I went downtown and had breakfast. The coffee was the kind you have to strain through your teeth. We call it Turkish coffee at home, but I had been cautioned against using that term. The long Turkish occupation of Greece still rankles; the beverage is Greek coffee, if you please. Anyhow, the bread was good and the jam was a little bit like glue, and after I got my tongue unstuck, thanks to the water that is served with the smallest order in Greece, I went down to the dock and found that I could hitch a ride on a local boat that was going to Santorini that afternoon. On the way back to my boarding-house I met Hans. He suggested I stick around for a few days and go on to Rhodes with him. I said "No, thanks." He kissed me good-bye; and then he decided he would go with me, wherever I was going; and I had some trouble getting rid of him.

My hostess and I parted on excellent terms. I practiced my Greek on her. I already knew how to say "Thank you" and "Please" and "Where is the toilet/café/hotel/boat/dog of the innkeeper?" Then I shouldered my stuff and started out for the dock. I only had one suitcase, in addition to my backpack, but it was a big suitcase. It held my diving gear. Frederick had assured me I could rent gear on Thera, but I don't like using second-hand stuff. I only hoped Frederick was right about getting tanks and air for them.

I had to hang around the dock for a couple of hours before the captain of the boat got back from his afternoon nap. Jim would have had fits at the sight of the boat. It was a filthy tub that looked as if it would founder in a slight breeze. The deck still showed the traces of its last dozen cargoes—animal droppings, oil, fish scales, and so on. I scraped out a spot and sat down. It's about a hundred and twenty kilometers from Crete to Thera, and from the looks of the scow I figured she'd be lucky to make twenty kilometers an hour. I overestimated the speed. It was late the next morning before we got in.

Santorini is in the guidebooks. I had read about it, but a verbal description can't possibly prepare a visitor for the real thing. It's fantastic.

In an aerial view the group of islands looks like a half-eaten sugar cookie from which a giant child has taken a big bite and let the fragments fall onto his shining sea-blue plate. The main island, Thera, is the largest, crescent-shaped piece. Smaller islands lie like fallen crumbs, outlining the perimeter of the former crater of the volcano. In the center of the bay are two other islands, black intrusions on the surface of the clean sea. They are not parts of the cookie, but new volcanic cores, risen phoenix-like out of the chasm. One of them, Nea Kaimeni, is still active.

Chugging through the channel between Thera and the next-largest island, Therasia, we entered the caldera. The water was a rich teal blue, thirteen hundred feet deep. It seemed funny to think we were sailing over what had been the populated central peak of a circular island. We passed by the ominous black cone of Nea Kaimeni, a desolate heap of cinders and slag, with a trail of pale-green vapor rising from its fumarole. Ahead was a stunning view—the red, white, and black cliffs of Thera, rising sheer a thousand feet out of the blue water, as sharply perpendicular as if they had been cut by the snap of gigantic teeth. The geological strata were defined like the layers of a cake—the black of congealed lava, the pinky-red of pumice, and the awesomely thick layer of white ash that fell during the eruption of 1450 B.C., before the final paroxysm blew the guts out of the island. The cliff glistened in the sunlight, and I remembered Plato's description of the Royal City of Atlantis, built of red and black and white stone.

On top of the cliff, like a starched crocheted edging, were the sugar-white buildings of the island's largest town, Phira. I was reminded of a model of the Taj Mahal I'd once made out of sugar cubes for a school project. The town had an Oriental look, with cupolas and domes and arched porticoes.

Other buildings, docks and warehouses and shops, clustered at the foot of the cliff. Connecting the lower and upper towns was a zigzag path that went up the sheer face of the cliff in a series of acute switchbacks.

As soon as we had docked I made arrangements to have my stuff carried up to the hotel, and then I considered my own procedure. People usually ride donkeys up the path; it's too steep for a wheeled vehicle, and the black lava cobblestones are slippery. The donkeys looked as if they were in worse shape than I was, so I decided to walk. I had been sitting for hours and needed to loosen up.

It wasn't a walk, it was a climb, and by the time I got to the top I was regretting not having taken a donkey. Blinded with sweat and heaving like a spavined horse, I collapsed in the shade of a fig tree, mopped my wet face, and got my eyes focused. And what do you suppose I saw first? Right. My father. He was sitting at a table at a sidewalk café, staring straight at me with an expression of icy disapproval. I paid no attention, being much more interested in the tall glass on the table in front of him. My throat was as dry as death.

I started walking toward him. Then it occurred to me that maybe I shouldn't speak till I was spoken to, so I changed course, heading for one of the other tables. Two of them were taken, but the third had only one occupant. He saw me coming and pulled out a chair. I fell into it. The man grinned and shoved his glass of water toward me. I drained it, pushed the damp hair out of my eyes, and looked at him.

He was worth looking at. As tanned as the Minoan athletes in the frescoes, with brown hair sun-bleached in streaks, he had a thin face and a friendly smile. Handsome? I don't know. After I've known someone for a while I can't judge his appearance. All my friends look beautiful to me. All I remember of that first impression was that he was *brown*. Brown hair, tanned skin, khaki clothes. High, arched eyebrows, which peaked thickly in the center, gave him a permanently surprised look. His frayed work shirt was open down the front to show a chest as tanned as his face. The sleeves were rolled up above the elbows, and his arms were covered with the marks of heavy labor, scratches and scrapes and bruises. So were his hands.

"Health nut?" he inquired. "Animal lover? Skinflint?"

His voice was deep; the accent was western United States. I considered the questions.

"Health nut, I guess," I said finally. "The climb didn't look that bad from down below."

"Live and learn." He gestured; when the waiter came, he ordered, without consulting me. I had no objection to the result, however; it was lemonade, fresh and surprisingly cold, considering that it had no ice in it.

"You speak Greek," I said intelligently.

"Not very well. Not the modern version, anyhow."

"You mean you speak classical Greek?" A qualm ran through me. "What are you, an archaeologist or something?"

"Something. If you ask my boss, he'll tell you I'm a long way from calling myself an archaeologist."

I drank lemonade and tried to think. Frederick had mentioned that there was another expedition working on Thera. It was just my luck to run into one of the staff members before I had a chance to talk to Frederick and find out what role I was supposed to be playing.

My companion was studying me as candidly as I had studied him. He didn't seem to dislike what he saw.

"My name's Jim Sanchez," he said.

"Really? My dad's name is Jim."

I was not trying to be sly. I spoke without thinking. Jim was my father, in every sense but the least important. I had momentarily forgotten about the man who was sitting at a nearby table, as I basked in the warmth of Jim Sanchez's smile.

"What a coincidence."

"Yes, I don't suppose there are more than half a million men in the world named Jim," I agreed solemnly; and then we both laughed immoderately, as if the silly comment had been an epigram.

Why does it happen that way sometimes, with a total stranger? Within five minutes we were talking as if we had shared years of common experiences. We laughed a lot, over things that weren't really very funny. We caught each other's meanings before the sentences were completed. There didn't seem to be any reason why I shouldn't tell him my name, so I did. Then he told me where he went to school—he was working for a doctorate at the University of California—and I told him where I was from and what I had majored in at school. Casual conversation, nothing profound or clever; but I felt as if I had known him all my life.

That's what people usually say when they describe such an experience. It's a figure of speech.

Or is it? I wonder.

The conversation was a little embarrassing because I had to hedge about so many things—why I had come to Thera, for instance, and how long I was planning to stay. I had just about decided it was time for me to make a tactful exit—mentioning that I hoped to be staying at the Hotel Atlantis—when something came between me and the sun. The long shadow fell across the table like a bar of darkness that separated me and Jim. It was very symbolic.

I looked up at the stony face of my father and waited for him to speak first. It didn't really matter what he said. He had ended my little tête-à-tête. The look on Jim's face was as revealing as an essay.

"So you are here at last," said Frederick. "Where is your luggage?"

"At the hotel," I said. "At least I hope it is."

"Come along, then." He moved his head in a brusque commanding gesture and started to turn away. He hadn't even looked at Jim.

"So," said the latter. "That's who you are."

"Who?" I asked warily.

"One of *his* protégées. No wonder you didn't—" Frederick turned back.

"Miss Bishop is the daughter of an old friend, who has offered to give me a hand for a few weeks—typing and recording, that sort of thing. I am extremely shorthanded. But you should know that better than anyone. Sir Christopher hired all the able-bodied men in the village before I arrived. No doubt he had been told I would be here."

Even considering the paranoidal tone of the

last sentences, this was an extraordinary speech for Frederick. As a rule he didn't condescend to explain himself. Jim's quirked eyebrows rose.

"Really, Dr. Frederick, he didn't know. I'm sorry if you feel that way—"

"Your regret or lack of it is irrelevant," Frederick interrupted. "Even if your sentiments are genuine, which I am inclined to doubt, they would be of no practical use, since it is your employer who determines your actions. Come, Sandy, I want to get back to the site this afternoon."

Naturally enough, this piece of rudeness wiped the conciliatory expression off Jim's face and restored his original look of suspicion and hostility. I didn't blame him. I could have slapped my father. However, it wasn't fair of Jim to blame me for somebody else's bad manners. He didn't give me a chance to apologize or explain or smile, or anything. He threw down a handful of change, pushed his chair back and walked off, fairly radiating anger with every muscle in his body. It was a nice body, too, lean-hipped and broad-shouldered, like those of the bull dancers.

Frederick was several yards away, walking fast. I trotted till I caught up with him. He didn't slow down.

"Why the hell did you have to be so rude?" I demanded.

"I cautioned you, I believe, against speaking to anyone you met here on Thera."

"No, you did not!"

"Then you ought to have had the elementary good sense to know it without being cautioned. It is imperative that your identity remain a secret—"

"Then why did you speak to me? I figured—"

"You did not figure, if by that you mean 'think sensibly.' It will be evident, as soon as you appear on the dig, that you are working with me. The important thing is to keep people from suspecting that you are planning to dive professionally. There can be no objection to your swimming or diving for pleasure, and if you are thought to be a casual acquaintance, with no training in archaeology, suspicion will not arise. That is why I explained your presence as I did."

"Well, you might have told me that before," I grumbled. "And I still don't see why you had to be so nasty to—to him."

"His name is Sanchez," said my father obtusely. "He is the assistant to Sir Christopher Penrose, who is conducting a dig on the other side of the village. There is a Minoan town there; house remains were found almost fifty years ago. Sir Christopher is probably preening himself because he believes he has taken the area I wanted. He hopes to find a palace. He is mistaken. The palace is not east of the village, it is west, part of it is submerged, that is why it is necessary for you to dive. Must I explain in laborious detail why I don't want that inquisitive young man hanging around you? His superior is one of my chief antagonists. He would like nothing better than to find me violating some idiotic regulation, so he can have me expelled from the island."

I was tempted to write this speech off as incipient paranoia, but I couldn't. The article I had read in the dentist's office all those months ago had told me what the rest of the world thought of my father and his work. Some of the reading I had done since proved to me that scholars can be as petty-minded and vindictive as mean little kids. Sir Christopher might be like that. And if this incident was a sample of how my father behaved with his colleagues, I didn't blame them for hating his guts.

He had been arrogant enough when I first met him. Here, on his native turf, he was overpowering. He had my stuff collected and put into his rented Land Rover before I had time to draw a deep breath, and my feeble suggestions about lunch didn't even win a glance of acknowledgment. His Greek sounded as fluent as his English. I wondered if the content was as rude. I couldn't judge from the faces of the islanders he was dealing with, they were studiedly blank or studiously polite. Certainly he got results, and we were out of town before I realized that not only had I missed lunch, but I hadn't even gotten a good look at Phira.

To complain would have been to waste my

breath, so I settled back and tried to enjoy the scenery—not an easy job, since the roads were bad and the Land Rover had long ago lost any springs it possessed. Frederick drove the way I would have expected, with competence and with complete disregard for the comfort of himself or his passenger. However, the scenery wasn't awfully scenic. The country was rough, cut by ravines and rising to mountains of considerable height. The soil was a dismal dusty gray, with big lumps of lava and pumice. Volcanic soil is richer than it looks, though; Thera produces good wine and vegetable crops such as tomatoes. The fields, outlined by low stone walls, were terraced to make the most of the uneven terrain. Rows of young vines curved around the flanks of the hills like green contour lines.

We passed a quarry that looked like a lunar ruin, ragged and silvery. I remembered reading that the hardened ash is used in making cement. And I remembered that Thera had once been called Kalliste, "the Beautiful." The name wasn't very appropriate now, and yet there was a kind of stark grandeur about the place.

The village was only about six miles from Phira, but it took a long time to get there because of the roads. They wound all over, skirting ravines and mountain slopes. A mile or so out of town the road I had considered rotten petered out to a goat track, deeply rutted and barely wide enough for the car to scrape between the stone walls. Finally we climbed a steep slope, bumped precariously along the top of a ridge—and down below was the village, Zoa. The white houses, with their distinctive arched roofs, were huddled together as if they needed mutual support to keep from falling down the hillside into the sea.

As we plunged downward, on no road that I could see, I asked, "Where are we staying? Is there a hotel?"

I should have known better. A hotel, even a primitive hotel, would have had some labor-saving devices, such as maids. A hotel would have had people. Frederick didn't like people and he wasn't particularly interested in saving me any labor. No, we had a house, a ramshackle four-room structure some distance from the village. One look at it brought out housewifely instincts I never knew I had. I even forgot about my empty stomach. I couldn't have eaten in that house, and the courtyard was worse.

I spent the rest of the day shoveling out the debris and burying the smellier parts of it. Frederick disappeared while I was working, presumably back to his dig. It was obvious that he wasn't going to help with the housework. I assumed that the cooking was supposed to be my province too. The kitchen was distinguished from the other rooms by the fact that it contained cases of canned goods and a camp-type Coleman stove.

There was plenty of food and enough bottled water to last for weeks. I wasn't so sure that was good news. It implied that Frederick wasn't planning on many outside contacts. Surely, I thought, we could get fresh provisions from the villagers—tomatoes and wine, at least. It was too late to go shopping by the time I had made the house semi-habitable, so I got into my bathing suit. There was a tiny beach below the house, separated from the village harbor by a spur of rock. The path going down to it must have been made by goats, but I managed it without too much trouble.

The water felt like a benediction. It washed away the grime of the house and most of my tiredness. When I came up, a spectacular sunset was streaking the sky, and rosy reflections shimmered across the darkening water. I could have stayed there for hours. The place was utterly silent, except for the swish of the waves. But I decided I had better get back up the cliff before it got dark. I was hungry.

When I reached the top of the cliff, I saw a light in the house. I followed it to the kitchen. Frederick was sitting there eating soup and reading, by the light of a single lamp. He glanced up at me and went back to his book.

I looked from his hunched back to the shadowy, grimy little room, and I thought pessimistically: This is going to be a long, lonesome summer.

* * *

Frederick didn't give me time to be lonely. I was too busy. The routine began early next morning, with Frederick dragging me out of my sleeping bag. (There had been a mattress in my room, but I buried it.) We spent the morning—and it was a long one—at the dig. The area was about a block from the house, at the bottom of a ravine. There were a dozen or so bored-looking men scratching away at the ground. When we appeared they scratched a little faster. I couldn't see that they were finding anything much.

"You'll direct this group," Frederick said, leading me to where three men were poking around in a cleared space about three feet square. He spoke to the men in Greek. One of them grinned at me. I grinned back. It was the first smile I had seen that day, and it looked good. Still grinning, I said out of the corner of my mouth,

"You're crazy, Frederick. I can't direct anything. I don't know what they're doing, and even if I did, I can't talk to them."

"You'll learn," said Frederick.

I learned. I had to revise my impression that he would make a rotten teacher. He wasn't entertaining, but he was effective. For the next few days my head felt swollen with all the information he was jamming into it. But there's nothing like experience on the job; he could explain things as they came up, and in a surprisingly short time the things made sense. Oh, I couldn't have handled it without him right there, ready to jump in when I hit something I didn't know about. But I got by. It's amazing what you can communicate with gestures and goodwill. The men went home for lunch and a siesta break, but I didn't; I stayed on the job, munching crackers while Frederick lectured and demonstrated. In the evening he lectured some more and showed me how to record and classify pottery fragments.

We found more pottery than anything else. Pottery is practically indestructible. I mean, it breaks, but the pieces don't decay the way wood or cloth do, and it's so cheap it isn't worth stealing. Another reason why archaeologists find so much pottery is that it was the universal storage container in ancient times. People then didn't have tin cans or bottles or brown paper bags. Pots were used not only to store food but all kinds of things, from clay tablets to dead bodies. The area we were working in had been a storeroom back in Minoan times. We found one jar with a few desiccated grains of cereal still in it.

The side of the ravine was a colored diagram of the geological history of the island. At the bottom was a level of brownish-black soil—ground level in 1500 B.C., before the big eruptions began. It was at this level, or just above it, that the Minoan remains were found. Above that was a pinky-red layer of pumice ten to fifteen feet thick—debris thrown out by the first stage of the eruption. The volcano had been quiescent for some years after that; a narrow sandy layer above the pumice showed signs of normal weathering. Then came a layer of white ash, thirty feet of it; thick enough to bury houses, kill crops, choke springs and fountains. It had been hot, too; earlier diggers had found burned human teeth. The ash fall was enough in itself to make the island uninhabitable, but it had only been the prelude to the final explosion. Having emptied itself, the volcanic chamber collapsed, and the sea rushed into the chasm.

Seeing the actual remains of the catastrophe made it seem very real. The work was fascinating, actually, but I was too inexperienced to see that it was also rather peculiar. There was an amateurishness about the whole business that was out of keeping with Frederick's reputation and temperament. The very fact that he would allow a novice like me to handle his precious antiquities, even broken pieces of pottery, should have alerted me to the truth: that the digging wasn't his main concern. It was a blind, hiding his real interest.

I was up to my eyeballs in pots and new experiences, and I didn't draw the obvious conclusion. Oh, I knew Frederick wanted me to dive, but I assumed the underwater work would be an extension of what we were doing on land. I was soon to learn that I had been way off base on that assumption.

One thing happened during that period of time. It was an insignificant thing in itself, but it made an odd impression on me.

I was sitting in the courtyard one evening washing potsherds. This occupation is not quite so boring as it sounds. The Minoans made some pretty painted pottery, and every now and then a scrap with a flower or shell or spiral pattern would turn up. It was like magic, seeing the vivid colors and vigorous shapes appear as the masking crust of dirt washed away.

Even painted pots can pall, however; that particular evening I was squatting there with my hands trailing in the water, staring absently at the view and thinking about how bored I was. The wall of the courtyard was in bad shape; parts of it had collapsed completely, and there was a wide gap where a wooden gate had once stood. The sun had just gone down behind the crest of the mountain, and the sky looked like one of Mother's modern embroidery pieces, silky, shiny crimsons and oranges, with sparkles of reflected light like patches of gold thread. There were a few stunted trees on the ridge nearest the house; they made grotesque silhouettes against the garish sky.

Then I realized that there was another shape

silhouetted against the sunset, that of a man on horseback. In contrast to the dwarf-sized trees, he and the animal looked larger than life. They were utterly still, so still that they resembled a monumental equestrian statue instead of creatures of flesh and blood. As I watched, they disappeared, almost as if they had melted into the darkening stones below and beyond them.

I had the impression that the man had been staring straight down into the courtyard. Straight at me.

There was no reason why this should have disturbed me even if it had been true. Nor was there any reason why the sight of him should bring back memories of those unnerving hours in Crete. I hadn't exactly forgotten that experience, but I had rationalized it as the result of sunstroke or illness. I had not felt a single twinge of discomfort since I arrived on Thera, and if my problem in Crete had been an upsurge of ancestral memory, I ought to have experienced it again here, when my fingers actually touched the baked clay those long-dead hands had fashioned.

But the man on horseback was an archaic figure, out of the old legends with which I was now familiar. I couldn't remember whether the Homeric heroes had ridden horseback or not; but they had used horses to pull their chariots. Poseidon was also Hippios, the horse god. The old gods seemed to linger on, here in the regions where

they had once been supreme. It was fitting that
Poseidon should haunt Thera, for he was both a
sea god and a maker of earthquakes.

Frederick came out just then, grousing because
I wasn't washing pots fast enough, and I forgot
my fantasies. I forgot about the horseman, too—
for a while.

Toward the end of the week I had learned more
about ancient Crete than I wanted to know. My
brain was reeling and my body was cramped
with squatting among broken pots. I might have
rebelled anyway, but something happened that
gave me a good excuse for changing my routine.

We went up to the dig as usual that morning.
As a rule the men were there waiting for us, but
that morning the place was deserted. I expressed
surprise, and Frederick explained that they
weren't coming. It was a holy day, a saint's day or
something. He added a few comprehensive
curses on the Greek Christian pantheon.

It was cool down there in the ravine, and
deeply shadowed; but when I looked up I could
see a slash of blue sky and a bird soaring high and
free. I stood up, brushing dirt off my knees.

"I'm taking the day off, too," I said, breaking
into his anathemas. "God knows I deserve it, the
hours I've been working. See you later."

I left without waiting for an answer. We'd just
have gotten into an argument, and arguing with
Frederick was the most useless activity known to

man. He never listened to a word anybody said. I went straight back to the house and changed into my bathing suit.

I know I shouldn't have gone swimming alone. But I was young and confident, and I really had very little choice; either I swam alone, or I didn't swim. I could imagine what Frederick would say if I suggested he join me, especially after I'd walked out on a day's work. He had already turned down several invitations to come for a swim, saying he wanted me to gain some experience with archaeological techniques before I started working underwater. When I pointed out that people did occasionally swim for pleasure, he gave me a blank look.

As I climbed down the cliff, carrying my fins and mask, I promised myself I would be careful. I wouldn't go out far or stay in long, and I would keep an eye out for monsters. But I couldn't wait any longer. It was warm and bright and the blue water drew me like a magnet. It slid over my body like a silken robe as I went in.

In a way, it was like coming home after a long absence. Water is not our natural element. We die if we stay in it too long. But we came from the water, if the theory of evolution is right. Millions and millions of years ago, our remote ancestors were spawned in the seas, and they lived there for more millions of years before some foolish fish wriggled up onto dry land and turned into an amphibian. Maybe that's why some of us keep trying to go back. I don't know. All I know is, I love it. There's a whole world down there, and if some of its denizens are killers, they are less vicious than their two-legged descendants.

Actually, I wasn't too sure what kinds of killers I might run into in these waters. Sharks were a possibility; they inhabit most of the seas. Some jellyfish are unpleasant customers, and they too are common all over the world. I had read about a fish called a weever, which is "capable of inflicting a painful sting." But I figured the chance of encountering anything like that was pretty slim. I was dying to meet a dolphin. I had read about them, how intelligent they are, and how friendly. I also wanted to see an octopus, not a little squid, but a big Kraken-type monster eight feet across. Not that I intended to get familiar with an enraged octopus, but I know most predators are unlikely to attack if you don't bother them.

I didn't see anything particularly interesting that day. I'd never been in water so clear, though; I suppose anything around the United States is bound to be contaminated. The water shimmered with refracted sunlight, and magnified details. I could see the separate, delicate strands of seaweed on the bottom twenty feet below. There wasn't a lot of weed, but it was a rough bottom, covered with rocks and lava fragments. The terrain lacked the spectacular colors of coral and vegetation that I was used to, but it looked fine to me.

When I finally came out of the water I saw that I was not alone. The straight, lean body of the man on the beach gave me a momentary thrill, but almost immediately I realized it couldn't be Jim. His back was turned to me, and it was bleached white in color, not tanned, as Jim's back surely must be. The man turned. I recognized my father.

Half amused and half annoyed I walked toward him. Like his face, his body was younger looking than it ought to have been. I suppose an ascetic, physically active life accounted for that. So far as I could tell, he didn't suffer from any of the temptations of the flesh.

I expected him to be annoyed at my defection, but he greeted me without anger—without emotion of any kind.

"Thanks for coming down to keep an eye on me," I said.

He looked surprised.

"Why should I do that? You are supposed to be an excellent swimmer."

"Even an excellent swimmer can get a cramp," I said, angered at his indifference—and pleased that I could tell him something he didn't know. "I do swim alone sometimes, but I know it's stupid. When I start diving for real, you'll have to stick around."

"I will certainly be on hand, to direct your actions."

"I didn't see anything interesting out there. No pots, no walls—"

"I doubt that you would recognize them if you found them," he said dryly. "In any case, this is not the area in which I am interested. We'll swim around the headland and I'll show you the spot. It's not far."

I followed him into the water, and then north along the coast. He swam with the same economical power all his other actions displayed, but he was a little awkward; I could tell that his technique was the result of concentration, not of training. I turned over onto my side and took a look around. We had rounded the headland and were a long way from shore.

Ahead and to the left, another miniature bay had opened up. Perched on the cliff top was a house. It wasn't a small cottage, like the houses in the village, but an honest-to-God villa, almost a mansion. The walls gleamed white in the sunlight, and the red-tiled roof stood out against the blue sky.

Frederick was slowing down. I moved in closer, blaming myself for not checking him out before we started. He might be well preserved, but he was certainly no chicken, he had to be in his fifties, and for all I knew he might have a heart condition or something. By this time I could see bottom down below, although we were still some distance from the inner wall of the bay. Though the water wasn't deep, there was no beach, only rough rock all around.

Frederick caught hold of a rock, one of several that poked its head up out of the water. He clung there, breathing hard, and I joined him, hanging on with one hand.

"You're out of condition," I said.

"I have one bad lung," Frederick replied, as calmly as I would have announced, I have a pimple on my nose. "I punctured it some years ago."

"You fool, why didn't you tell me? I wouldn't have let you—"

"Let me? I can't imagine how you would have prevented me."

We were both bobbing gently up and down with the motion of the waves, and in spite of myself I started to laugh.

"Look," I said, after a moment. "I take all the orders you hand out, don't I, when it comes to digging? On this subject I'm the expert. I'm familiar with all the life-saving techniques, but I'd prefer not to use any of them on you. Let me do the swimming from now on, okay?"

Frederick's reaction was meek, for him.

"Why do you suppose I'm not doing the underwater work myself? The techniques do not seem difficult; I could have mastered them in a few months if I had been physically able to do so.

I shall certainly leave the diving to you as soon as I have instructed you as to what you are looking for.

"As we know, the Minoans were the greatest navigators and sailors of their age. Cretan experts were responsible for the massive harbor installations near Alexandria, in the Egyptian Delta, discovered by divers in 1910, and a few Minoan harbors have been explored. Five years ago, following certain clues which I need not enumerate to you, I did some diving near here. I found . . ."

He stopped. The rest had restored his color and slowed his breathing, but I didn't like the way he was looking at me.

"If you can't trust me, whom can you trust?" I asked. "You found traces of the harbor installations, I suppose. What's so unbelievable about that? I don't see why you couldn't tell the antiquities people; they might have given you permission to dive, or even supplied money and equipment. You shouldn't be so damn suspicious of—"

I stopped speaking, because he was shaking his head violently.

"You little fool, what do you know about life? Especially my life! This is a cutthroat world, and I have been persecuted more cruelly than most men. Five years ago my career was over. My enemies controlled Greece; not only was I unable to dig, but my very life was in danger. It was a miracle, nothing less, that Mistropolous should have become head of the antiquities department; he is probably the only man in my field who still has some regard for me and my ideas. But he is only one man, and his own position is precarious. If it were known that I had made this discovery, a discovery so astounding, so unprecedented—"

"Okay, okay," I said, in some alarm. "I get your point. But I don't see why a breakwater or a couple of warehouses should be such a—"

He laughed. I think it was the first time I had ever heard him laugh, and if this was a representative sample I knew I wasn't looking forward to hearing it again.

"Don't be so stupid," he said. "Think. You know what happened here in the fifteenth century B.C. on a spring day, when the wind was blowing from the northwest."

It was an unexpectedly poetic phrase for him to use. His voice softened and his face became calm, brooding. There was a far-off look in his eyes. I felt as if I were hearing an eyewitness account of the event.

"There had been signs of the displeasure of the gods. The cloud of fiery gas by night, the pillar of smoke by day, and the rumbling roar of the bull god, Poseidon, the Earthshaker. But these things had happened before. Some fled; most remained, making their ineffectual sacrifices, and hoping. . . . When the cataclysm occurred, it caught them all—women tending their children, the men in the fields, priests in the shrines. . . ."

His voice rose. "And what else? What else, in a harbor town, a mercantile shipping center?"

His eyes bored into me. They were perfectly sane. He was excited, but he wasn't crazy. I knew what he was driving at. But—

"It's impossible," I said.

"Ships!" He slammed his fist against the rock. "Minoan ships, the trading fleet of the sea king himself. They are there, in the water, where they sank over three thousand years ago."

Chapter

4

UP AND DOWN, UP AND DOWN, THE WAVES ROCKED ME.
I was hypnotized by the motion, the warm caress
of the water, and the mesmerizing gaze of this
maniac who happened to be my father.

"Now just one minute," I said, getting a grip on
myself; for a moment the picture had dazzled me.
"Your reasoning is excellent. Sure, there were
ships. Some of them must have sunk. But no ship
could survive underwater all that time. Oh, I
know about the wrecks of Greek and Roman
ships; quite a few of them have been located. But
they date from a hundred A.D. or a hundred B.C.
You're talking about fifteen hundred B.C. Almost
thirty-five hundred years ago."

"A ship could survive that long. It has. At Cape
Gelidonya, in Turkey. That wreck was investi-

gated in 1960. It has been dated to approximately the fifteenth century before Christ. Not only was the cargo found, but even the planks of the ship's hull."

"You're kidding," I said. But I knew he wasn't. He wouldn't joke about anything as important as this. In fact, I had never heard him joke about anything.

"No."

"Okay, it could happen. But how do you know it happened here? I mean, what exactly did you find?" And then, as he hesitated, I said impatiently, "Look, I know what a couple of hundred years can do to the wreckage of a ship. Nothing survives unchanged—except gold. Timber rots and is eaten by worms, metal corrodes. Even pottery would be changed by marine accretions, or by electrolysis from the elements in the clay. And it's easy to be deceived. Rocks look like ballast, and natural formations can imitate straight-line, man-made shapes."

For the first time since I had known him he looked at me with something like respect.

"Essentially you are correct," he said. "Although pottery is not altered as much as you suggest. There are pots here. They are amphorae, vessels containing material meant for export. A heap of such jars almost always indicates an ancient wreck. But that is not all. The ships themselves are there."

I was silent. If anyone but Frederick had told me such a yarn I wouldn't have believed him. I don't know why I believed Frederick. Maybe it was because I just didn't expect his insanity to take this particular form. Paranoia was his problem, not fantasy. If I ever lost my mind, this was the kind of beautiful madness I would create.

"An entire fleet must have been in the harbor," he went on. "Ash had been falling for hours, perhaps for days; the sky was black as night, poisonous fumes made breathing difficult. The rulers of Thera reached a decision—to flee, while flight was still possible. Save the royal treasures, the ritual vessels of the shrines. Seek the safety of the sea, retreat to the motherland. They could not have dreamed of the magnitude of the disaster; they could not know that Crete was also in peril.

"They crowded on board the ships, men, women, and children, with their private treasures and the most precious possessions of the state. But before they could cast off, the volcano caught them. Earthquakes, great tidal waves, showers of molten rock turned the harbor into a scene out of Dante. Some ships caught fire. The flames were quickly quenched when the vessels sank, but I tell you, there are charred ships' timbers down below, in this very bay.

"The sunken ships were covered almost immediately by sand and ash. That is what preserved them. Throughout the succeeding millennia they remained sealed in their natural tombs. And then, by pure accident, a storm, accompanied by earth tremors, shifted those strata. The hardened ash cracked and the sands were washed away. The skeletons of the ships lay exposed as they had fallen. Only for a short time; another storm followed and again the wrecks were buried. It may be that they are gone forever. But I doubt it. I think they are still there. Of all that wreckage something must remain. It will be a long project to search the area thoroughly. I am no longer fit for such exertion. So—"

"So," I said. "Me. It's funny, isn't it, that your long-lost daughter should turn out to be a diver?"

"Funny?" The cold gray eyes grew cloudy, as if they were focusing on some inner vision. "In the cosmic sense, yes; the kind of jest one might expect from a deity who excels in irony. The Olympians would enjoy such a joke. It would have suited their primitive, revengeful sense of humor. I felt at times as if they were taking a hand in my affairs. And why not? I have been so long concerned with theirs. The accident that put an end to my diving was such a jest, and its author is not hard to identify—who else but the Earthshaker, the lord of the sea, who was also the god of ancient Crete? Resenting the interloper, punishing him for intruding. And then . . . you. How is that to be taken, I wonder? Has the god relented, or is this the first part of another of those elaborate, childish practical jokes?"

I shivered. The water was warm, but if you stayed in too long without moving, gradually the chill got to you. It had to be the chill of the water—not my response to that eerie speech, which struck an echoing chord somewhere deep inside me.

Suddenly, for no good reason, I knew there was something wrong with Frederick's story. He had omitted something, something important.

However, this was no time for questions. He looked odd, and I was worried about the return trip.

"Okay," I said. "I'll look for your ships. In fact I'm going to have a look right now. Climb up on that ledge and soak in the sun for a few minutes before we start back."

He gave me a funny look, but did as I suggested. I filled my lungs and went down.

I wasn't expecting to find anything. If the wreck had been located near a landmark as conspicuous as this rock, he'd have remembered. All I wanted to do was get some idea of the depth and the general character of the bottom.

It didn't look encouraging. There was a lot of debris down there, rocks and pumice and old, hardened lava flows. I could see the search was going to take a long time. Every blessed rock would have to be examined to make sure it wasn't an encrusted pot or piece of sculpture.

When we got back to our cove, Frederick was

gray in the face and I had to help him up the cliff.
I pumped him full of hot soup and coffee and
tried to put him to bed, but the food restored all
his normal meanness, and he went back to the
dig. He wanted me to go with him, but I refused.
I hadn't had my holiday yet. Even my swim had
turned out to be an invitation to work.

I put on some white sandals and a long shift I
had bought in Athens, slit up the side and embroidered around the neck. I told myself that I
was paying honor to Saint Irene, or whoever it
was. But of course that wasn't the real reason for
the finery. If our workers were taking a holiday,
so were the men on the other dig.

I was absurdly excited as I walked along the
weed-grown path toward the road that would
take me to the village. Imagine being thrilled at
the prospect of a visit to a metropolis of a few
hundred! But I hadn't seen that many people for
almost a week. I hadn't seen a shop or a café or a
magazine or a radio—or even a tomato. After a
week of canned food, the thought of a tomato
made my mouth water. If I accomplished nothing
else, I could buy some fresh food for supper.

As I marched on toward the center of the village, I began to meet people. They all nodded and
smiled at me. The main plaza was paved with
black lava stone. There was a fig tree in the center.
On one side a flight of steps led up to the church,
a small, squat building with a blue dome. The

shops were closed for the afternoon rest period, but of course the hotel was open; it had a terrace out in front, with a grape arbor and a few tables and chairs. I could read a little Greek by now, and I spelled out the lettering on the faded sign: Hotel Poseidon.

I walked around the village for a while. The whole place was only a few blocks square—but it wasn't square, the streets went up and down the hill and sometimes ended in culs-de-sac, so that I had to retrace my steps. Most of the houses were shuttered and quiet, but some people were out, mostly children, who giggled and ran when I spoke to them. Two old grandmas, wrapped up in dusty black dresses and shawls, were sitting outside the doors of their houses. One had a spindle and a ball of thread, and she was weaving or spinning; the process was unfamiliar to me, but the result looked like coarse lace. Her withered old hands moved with amazing dexterity. I stopped to admire her work and we had a nice talk. Neither of us could understand a word the other said, but we smiled a lot.

The harbor area was the busiest-looking part of Zoa. I gathered most of the traffic came by sea, instead of over the rough roads of the interior. It was also the ugliest part of the village, with the usual man-made mess—oil stains and spills, rusty chunks of metal, garish posters advertising various products.

When I got back to the plaza, people were beginning to come out of their houses. Pretty soon the church bells started to ring, and the crowd eddied toward the church. I followed. I was a little shy about going in, but nobody seemed to mind, in fact some of the worshipers beckoned to me as I paused on the threshold.

The inside of the church was dark. At first I couldn't see anything, after the sunlit plaza, except candles twinkling like far-off stars. Somebody was chanting in a high, inflected sing-song voice. There was a strong smell of sweetish incense and a fainter, underlying odor of goat, or maybe unwashed human.

Gradually my eyes adjusted, but I still couldn't see much. The place was windowless and low-ceilinged, and the candlelight was obscured by the press of bodies. It was rather like being in a cave. The walls seemed to be painted, or maybe hung with pictures, but this wasn't one of the fancy mainland churches, like the famous old ones I had seen in Athens. There were no mosaics, no glimmer of gilded arches; the paintings, what I could see of them, were modern and rather crude. I had chosen a modest place at the very back, so I couldn't see the altar or the priest. I could hear his voice, though, rising and falling in that semi-Oriental chant. People kept wandering in and out and nobody seemed to be paying much attention to the service, except for some older women to my right, who were swaying back and forth and muttering.

Gradually more people began to sway and mutter. Gray clouds of incense billowed out, hanging like fog under the low ceiling. The smell was so strong I felt a little dizzy. A few of the women were keening and wringing their hands, like old Irish ladies at a wake. One woman, near me, was crying; I could see the shiny streaks on her cheeks. More and more people crowded into the small room. I was pressed back against the wall, enclosed by human bodies. Nobody was paying any attention to me, but I began to feel uneasy. I don't like crowds, or mass emotion. People in a mob lose their identity and become part of a great mindless animal. I wanted to leave, but I couldn't see how to manage it. I didn't want to offend anyone, and besides, the space between me and the door was packed full. The incense began to get to me. I could feel myself beginning to sway in rhythm with the bodies all around. In another minute I would have started keening.

Somebody touched my shoulder. I recognized the hand before I looked up into Jim's face. He was smiling.

"Let's get out of this," he said. I think he was speaking in a normal conversational voice, but I could hardly hear him.

"How?" I asked helplessly.

He took my arm and turned. I don't know how

he did it, but people sort of scrunched back and made a path. I followed. Even the steps were crowded; apparently everybody in town had come to the service. The air outside made me feel drunk, it was so clean and fresh. I was surprised to see that the sun was far down in the west.

Not everybody had gone to church after all. The shops were open now, and clusters of tables and chairs had sprouted around the perimeter of the plaza. The occupants were all men, except for a few obvious tourist types.

Jim found us a table.

"Wine or ouzo?" he asked.

We had wine. It was heavily resinated, but I didn't mind the taste; it had a healthy medicinal flavor. At first we talked rather stiltedly about the saint's day and the church.

"Religion in this area is a funny mixture," Jim said. "You find the same thing in all the Mediterranean countries, in small peasant communities—a superficial coating of Christianity over the old pagan beliefs. Local saints are the old gods thinly disguised. The festivals of the church celebrate dates that have been sacred for millennia—the spring equinox, harvest, the winter solstice. And maybe one reason why the Virgin Mary is so popular is because a mother goddess was once the most important deity in these parts."

I decided maybe he liked the intellectual type.

"Ah, yes," I said. "The earth goddess, mistress

of animals, whose sacred creature, the serpent, betokened her role as a goddess of the Underworld. One is struck by her seemingly contradictory nature—the maiden and the mother, ruler of the dead and of rebirth. . . ."

Jim's jaw dropped. Then he started to laugh. After a few seconds I joined him. I hadn't intended to do a conscious imitation, but my voice had sounded just like that of my high school history teacher, Miss Pomeroy.

"You must have had a professor who was the twin sister of mine," he said. "There is an underlying logic beneath the seeming contradiction, of course. The mother was once a virgin, and death must precede resurrection. It startled me, at first, to see how readily the tenets of Christianity could be adapted. But then Christianity was an Oriental religion originally, and the concept of divine sacrifice comes from Egypt and Syria. The god must die in order to ensure the rebirth of vegetation in spring, and the resurrection of the body—"

He stopped abruptly. His funny peaky eyebrows rose even higher.

"Why are we talking like this?" he asked.

"I was trying to impress you," I said candidly.

"You did. But. . . . I guess the trouble is I'm trying to work up to an apology."

"What for?"

In a casual, absentminded way he took my hand.

"The other day. I was rude."

"So was Frederick."

"Sure, but that didn't justify my being rude to you. Quite the contrary." He was still holding my hand. His fingers were long and hard.

"Forget it," I said. "I gather that Frederick isn't too popular with his colleagues. Or do you have a more personal reason for disliking him?"

"Oh, no. My boss knows him pretty well; I guess he's prejudiced me. Look, why do we have to talk about that old—sorry, I keep forgetting he's your boss. Is there any reason why we can't be friends? Just because our employers don't see eye to eye—"

"No reason at all," I said cheerfully. "I'm a great believer in friendly relations."

"Then start out by having dinner with me."

"I don't know. . . . I'm cook and bottle washer at the dig. And Frederick wasn't feeling so hot when I left today. We went for a swim this morning, and he overdid it."

I threw this comment out to see whether Jim would say anything about a ban on diving. His response was more than satisfactory—no suspicion, and considerable interest.

"I'm glad you aren't swimming alone. Don't do it, will you?"

I laughed lightly. "Listen, chum, I live in Florida. I grew up in the water."

"Then you know how stupid it is to take chances. If he can't go with you, how about me?"

"You?" I repeated, in innocent surprise.

"Sure. I don't work twenty-four hours a day. We could set up a time—every day, if you want to."

I considered this handsome offer. And, I mean, it was handsome. It was also impractical. Obviously I couldn't carry out my explorations in the little bay of the villa with Jim hovering around. But it might not be a bad idea to meet him now and then for some casual swimming in another place.

"I couldn't do it every day," I said. "I could let you know. Where are you staying?"

"The hotel."

"Geez," I said. Everything I had seen about the hotel, from the greasy tabletop to the waiter's apron, made me thankful I wasn't staying there. At least I could keep the house clean.

"That expresses it pretty well," Jim agreed. "Fortunately I have a cast-iron stomach and all my shots are up to date. Those qualities, plus a bottle of disinfectant, have kept me healthy so far."

"Are you all staying there?" I asked.

There was a pause. It didn't last very long, but with the intuitive sympathy I felt for this man, I sensed that it was meaningful. Finally Jim said,

"There are just the two of us. Me and Sir Christopher. A couple of the islanders are semi-trained; they worked with Marinatos at Akrotiri, where the first Minoan houses were found."

Another pause followed.

"That's a coincidence," I said. "There's just the two of us, too. Me and Frederick. That's why I ought to go back. I mean, if he is sick—"

"No, don't leave. The food here isn't that bad, if you like olive oil. And you ought to see the procession. It will interest you, in light of what we said about the survival of old religious practices."

"Procession?"

"They carry the saint's image around town and up the hill. It blesses the houses and the fields, and visits a little cave-shrine farther up, which may have been a sacred spot since the Bronze Age."

"Oh, well," I said, abandoning the call of duty. "If it's an educational experience, I owe it to myself to stay."

We sat for a while in a comfortable silence, watching the people moving around the plaza. Some of the women were wearing gorgeous peasant costumes—only these weren't costumes, they were the finery that was saved for special occasions, handed down from mother to daughter. Yards of handmade lace trimmed the aprons and tall white caps. The bodices were embroidered in bright colors, and there were lots of gold coins in evidence, made into necklaces and earrings and heavy collars, hanging in festoons across the women's foreheads.

The sun was down behind the mountains to the

west, and a queer hazy light suffused the plaza. It was still light enough to see clearly, though. I saw the woman as soon as she appeared. She was striking enough to attract anyone's attention; her clothing alone would have made her stand out in that crowd, where the women were wearing either rusty black or the local peasant finery. This woman's dress had never come from Thera, or even from Athens. It looked like Paris—a long, mauvey pinky-blue chiffon, heavily trimmed in gold, with little glitters like rhinestones—only the sparks were rainbow fire, brilliant as no imitation diamond can be. Out of the floating folds of chiffon her throat and head rose superbly. The heavy dark hair was wound into an intricate coiffure, held by gold bands. I could see that she was rather stoutly built, from the way the breeze molded the soft fabric against her heavy breasts and thighs. She moved slowly, and as she moved, so did the crowd. It fell back before her, opening a path down which she advanced straight toward the straggly tree in the center of the plaza. There she stopped. She was half turned away from us, and I could see a fine profile, classic in its straight brow-nose line. The funny thing was that she paid no attention to anyone, neither speaking nor nodding; and although they made room for her, none of the crowd appeared to see her.

"Who's that?" I asked. "Wow, what a gorgeous dress!"

"Too flamboyant for my taste. But she's a flamboyant creature, isn't she? She lives in that villa
on the other side of town—the big white one on
the cliff."

"I saw it this morning. You mean she owns that
place?"

"Not exactly." Jim was silent for a second or
two; then he abandoned himself to the joys of
gossip. Men are worse gossips than women, actually. I noticed that years ago.

"She doesn't live there alone," Jim went on.
"She's either the wife or the mistress of a peculiar
old guy who hardly ever leaves the villa. I've seen
him once or twice; he rides horseback. Has two or
three magnificent horses that look as out of place
on this island as his girl friend does. Who and
what he is I don't know. He never comes to
town."

"You don't know much," I said critically. "If I
talked Greek the way you do, I'd have found out
lots more. You don't even know whether she's his
wife or his mistress?"

"I'm pretty sure she's not his wife."

"Pretty sure! Don't tell me the men in this town
don't gossip about her."

"Oddly enough, they don't." Jim gestured at
the woman, who stood stock-still in the center of
the plaza, gazing off into space. "Notice that
there's quite a crowd around the outskirts, but
not a soul within ten feet of her. Nobody talks to

her. And nobody talks about her. I admit I'm just as nosy as the next guy. The first time I saw her she fascinated me; she was wearing slacks and some kind of fancy blouse, with loads of jewelry. The outfit was absolutely ridiculous in this little place. So I naturally asked who she was. Everybody clammed up. I finally pried out the information I've just given you, but it took me days. They don't want to talk about her. It's as if she didn't exist."

"What's her name?"

"They don't call her anything. I keep telling you, they don't talk about her. I overheard a sentence or two, one time, that I'm pretty sure referred to her, and they mentioned the word 'Potnia.' That's not a name, though. It's a title."

The word was vaguely familiar. Then I remembered where I had seen it. Jim didn't pronounce it as I would have expected.

"But that's the old word for the Minoan goddess," I said. "It means 'the Lady,' or 'the Mistress.' Not that kind of mistress. . . ."

"No. Not that kind."

I looked again at the motionless figure in the plaza. The eerie light of dusk was gathering, dimming the outlines of her face and body. The evening breeze lifted the fragile folds of fabric so that their edges blended with the shadows. A little shiver ran through me. Jim's hand tightened on mine.

"Are you cold?"

"No." I shook myself mentally. I was getting fey, and I didn't like the feeling. It reminded me of the moments in the museum at Herakleion. Greece was an eerie place, there were too many old traditions lingering. I forced a pragmatic tone into my voice.

"I wonder what she's doing. Why doesn't she go into the church, or to one of the shops?"

"I expect she's come to see the procession," Jim said. "After all, that's why we're sitting here."

As he spoke, the church doors burst open. Light poured out of the entrance. The inside of the church was ablaze with light, quite unlike the gloomy cave I had seen; then I realized that a number of the men were carrying torches. I wouldn't have allowed them to be used in that age-dried structure, but then I wasn't the priest. The effect was certainly theatrical.

The torchbearers formed an aisle down the stairs and then the procession appeared, headed by the priest. He was a swarthy young man with a handsome black beard, wearing green-and-gold vestments. Following him came the shrine, supported by four husky villagers. The doors of the carved, gilded box were open, and I assumed that the saint's statue was inside, but I couldn't see at that distance. The villagers genuflected and knelt as the priest led the procession down the stairs. A crowd of spectators followed, forming a rough line. It wound down the stairs and around the plaza.

The priest was absorbed in his singing; he was about a quarter of the way around the circuit before he saw the woman in the center. He stopped; for a minute I was afraid the procession was going to pile up behind him like a multiple collision. But he collected himself and went on, taking a few quick skipping steps to get out of the way of the shrine, which was bearing down on him. It might have looked comical, but it didn't. There was something rather ugly about the incident. I can't explain why it struck me that way. Maybe it was the way the priest started, as if he were recoiling from something dirty or dangerous; or the fact that the woman was the only one in the plaza who didn't acknowledge the saint's passage, not even by the slightest inclination of her head. She stood there unmoving, and as the procession went on its way it almost seemed as if they were paying homage to her, the central figure in the drama.

After circling the plaza three times, the priest led the crowd off into one of the side streets. Gradually the singing died away; but the twinkling lights, twining in and out like a luminous snake, marked the saint's passage through the fields.

I looked at Jim. He was still staring fixedly at the unmoving figure in the plaza.

"Hey," I said. "Now that the excitement is over, how about some food? Or is it too early?"

"It's too early." Jim turned his head. "But if you're hungry, maybe I can. . . . Oh, oh. What was that you said about the excitement being over?"

I turned to see what he was staring at with that apprehensive expression. Frederick was heading straight for our table.

"Oh, hell," I said.

"Don't worry." Jim lowered his voice. "I'm not going to lose my temper. Whatever he says, I am not going to lose my temper. You have a right to have dinner with me. Greece is the home of democracy, isn't it?"

"Uh-huh," I said gloomily.

But our fears were groundless. As Frederick approached, I realized that he was going to be pleasant—for him. He greeted us with a nod and, without waiting for an invitation, pulled out a chair and sat down.

I thought of asking him how he felt and decided I had better not. He looked okay.

"I presume your workmen insisted on a holiday too?" he said to Jim.

Jim's face brightened. Poor boy, he was an ingenuous soul; the slightest gesture of goodwill brought out all his kindly nature.

"That's right, sir. All these holidays and church festivals are a nuisance, but I guess there's no use fighting them."

"None whatsoever. How is your work progressing?"

There was nothing ingenuous about Frederick. He wasn't subtle, but he wasn't ingenuous. I could see what had prompted his affability. I suppose Jim could too. He gave me an amused sidelong look, and answered without reserve. He had no reason to be secretive.

"Pretty well, considering. The site seems to be a villa of considerable size. Sir Christopher is hoping for frescoes, but we haven't hit any yet. Of course we haven't been at it long. Tunneling is slow work."

"And what," said my father, with his usual indirection, "is your background?"

Poor Jim. It reminded me of the old days, when a prospective suitor was quizzed by Papa on his prospects—past, present, and future. Of course Frederick didn't give a damn about Jim as a matrimonial prize; he cross-examined him about his training. He forgot himself once or twice, making rude comments about Jim's professors, but on the whole he was reasonably courteous.

Finally he said, "Yes, your training is not bad. Not too bad. But you are without experience. How did you persuade Sir Christopher to hire you? He has graduate students of his own. You aren't even British."

Jim had kept his temper quite well. He got a little red at this last comment, but managed to smile.

"Personal connections. My mother is English. Oh, I agree, sir, I'm not especially highly qualified, but how can I become qualified without experience? I'm working my—that is, I'm working damn hard. I may have used a little pull to get the job, but I intend to deserve it."

These noble sentiments did not impress Frederick, not so you could notice.

"As I remember Chris, he is not that difficult a taskmaster. What made him select that site? There is nothing for him there. The palace is in my area. He'll find a few houses, that's all."

"You'll have to ask him that," said Jim politely. "I just work here."

Frederick didn't answer. Apparently he had found out what he wanted to know, and he was not the man to indulge in idle chitchat. I exchanged a glance with Jim. He grinned at me. The quirky eyebrows had a cocky look, as if he were saying, "See, I didn't lose my temper, did I?"

It was almost dark now. The woman was still standing by the tree. The center of the plaza was heavily shadowed, but I could see her silhouette, shapeless as a pillar or one of those archaic Greek statues. All the café tables were filled and people were sitting in chairs in front of many of the shops. They were all men; Greek women don't lounge around public places. I recognized one of the men; it was Nicholas, our foreman. I waved. He waved back.

"Who are you waving at?" Frederick asked suspiciously.

"Nicholas. He's sitting over there."

"With all the other lazy louts," Frederick grumbled. "They had better be on the dig early tomorrow, after wasting a day."

He turned in his chair so he could glare at Nicholas. The glare was wasted. Nicholas wasn't paying attention. He and most of the other men were casting sidelong glances at the silent figure by the tree. It was no longer motionless. Slowly, with a majestic stride, it advanced toward the hotel and the terrace where we were sitting.

Frederick continued to grumble.

"Come along, Sandy. There is a good deal of work to do tonight, and I mean to start early tomorrow. It was inconsiderate of you to run off this way. I had no idea where you had gone, and—"

It was as if somebody had chopped him across the throat. His voice caught in a painful grunt.

The woman had stopped a few yards away. The lights on the facade of the hotel shone directly on her, as if she stood in the center of a brilliantly lighted stage. She was looking at Frederick.

If the two of them had been professional actors they could not have communicated emotion more effectively. In fact, there was something decidedly theatrical about the woman's performance. Her head was thrown back, in the gesture adopted by aging ladies who want a smooth, youthful throat line. Frederick wasn't putting anything on, though. His face had gone a queer sickly gray. He looked his full age and older. The bones in his cheeks and forehead stood out, skull-like.

Finally, as if some signal had passed between them, they both moved at once. The woman turned, her draperies whirling out around her, and walked away. Frederick shoved his chair back so abruptly that it toppled over. He headed blindly across the plaza, in the opposite direction from that which the woman had taken—away from the street that led to our house. I thought he was going to bump into the tree, but at the last minute he swerved, exaggeratedly, like a drunk, and vanished into the darkness.

Chapter

5

"WHAT THE HELL WAS THAT ALL ABOUT?" JIM ASKED blankly.

"I—" My voice cracked. I cleared my throat and went on. "I would say that they recognized each other."

"That was more than recognition, Sandy. It was like some old-fashioned farce. You know what I mean: 'Good God, it is my husband, back from the dead, the man I thought I murdered thirty years ago!' Bette Davis and Ronald Colman."

"Joan Crawford," I corrected. "Only she didn't murder him. It was the other way around."

"Not Ronald Colman, then. He was too noble to murder wives. Broderick Crawford?"

"Robert Montgomery, maybe. He was a smooth murderer in one old movie."

"Night Must Fall?"

"I don't remember. Jim, it really isn't funny."

"Neither of them seemed to be amused."

"But—"

"But that's no reason why we have to get up-tight. It's not our problem. Listen, I don't even brood about my own past sins. Why should I stew about other people's? The present—the here and now—is complicated enough without going out of your way to find additional worries."

He leaned forward, his elbows on the table, his face serious.

"What is that?" I asked. "Some kind of creed? Your philosophy of life?"

"I guess it is."

"Keep out of other people's lives," I repeated. "Don't get involved."

Jim frowned. His eyebrows made an elongated, flattened capital M.

"I didn't mean it that way. Sure you should get involved. You have to get involved; people don't live in a vacuum, their lives get wound up with other people's. But why go out looking for trouble? Both these people are strangers to you. You'll never be a friend of Frederick. He doesn't have friends. And he sure as hell wouldn't thank you for worrying about him."

I sat back in my chair, hoping I didn't look as startled as I felt. I kept forgetting Jim didn't know I was Frederick's daughter. To him I was a casual acquaintance of Frederick; there certainly was no excuse for my concern about him. There was no excuse in any case. He was right. I would never be a friend of Frederick. I didn't want to be one.

"So I'm nosy," I said. "People interest me."

"So be interested. From a safe distance. The farther away from him, the safer."

"Are you trying to tell me something?"

"I'm trying to tell you that Frederick is bad news. Maybe you ought to find some other place for a vacation."

"Thanks a lot."

"Oh, hell, I didn't mean I want you to leave." Jim gestured helplessly. "I don't know why I keep saying the wrong things to you. Normally I'm considered a very smooth conversationalist. Let's change the subject. Have some more wine."

"No, thanks. I really had better get back to the house. If I remember my guidebooks, they don't eat dinner in these parts till nine or ten o'clock. Usually I'm tucked into my little sleeping bag at that hour, reading heavy tomes about Minoan archaeology."

"Stick around, please. Angelos will have some food ready pretty soon. I want you to meet Chris."

"Why?" I had started to rise. Now I sat down again. "So he can give me some more dire warnings about Frederick?"

"I don't like your being up there alone with him," Jim said.

I stared at him for a minute. Then I laughed.

"You don't really think—"

"No! Listen, I'd worry less if that *were* what I thought. The man doesn't have a spark of normal warmth in him. Chris says he's been on the ragged edge of sanity for years. He may slip over anytime and decide you're his hated mother or the reincarnation of Helen of Troy, or something."

He reached for my hand. I pulled it away and stood up.

"I never heard of anything so ridiculous in my life," I said coldly. "Who was it who was giving me that line about noninvolvement?"

Jim's eyebrows made alphabetic convolutions. Then they went back to their normal shape and he grinned sheepishly.

" 'Consistency is the hobgoblin of little minds,' " he said.

How can you stay mad at a man like that? I grinned back at him.

"Okay," I said. "No hard feelings, but I really had better go. I'll have dinner another night. Please?"

"Sure. What about that swimming date? We don't work on Sunday."

"Sunday at ten. I'll meet you here."

Before leaving the plaza, I stopped at one of the shops and bought some tomatoes and a fish. The woman cleaned and gutted the fish for me and wrapped it in a piece of newspaper.

There was no moon, and it was dark as pitch once I had left the lighted windows of the village behind. I kept stubbing my toes, and I cursed myself for not having thought to bring a flashlight. Frederick had several. But I hadn't expected to be gone so long.

Finally I saw the light ahead. A candle in the window, to guide the wandering child. . . . No, Frederick wouldn't light a candle for me. He was probably reading.

Now that I could see where I was going and did not have to concentrate on walking, a wild confusion of ideas crowded into my mind, all the new facts and impressions the day had brought. I stopped a few feet from the house. Before I went inside, I had some things to sort out with myself.

Most of them were disturbing things. Frederick's strange reaction to the woman—his incredible news about the sunken ships. . . . For the first time the enormity of that idea engulfed me. Either he was crazy, or there really were wrecked Minoan ships down in the bay. No, but he was insane either way, because he would have to be out of his mind to tackle a project like that with just me. Even I knew that a trained archaeologist doesn't grab with both hands when he excavates. And that was all I could do. I didn't know how to map a site or keep proper records. I didn't even know what to look for. Minoan ships were about three thousand years earlier than my Spanish galleon. Did they carry anchors? If so, what kind? How about ballast—masts. . . . And there was the problem of equipment. A camera was an absolute necessity. Did Frederick have an underwater camera? I doubted it. The customs officials would have checked his equipment carefully, and an item like that would have been a dead giveaway. I couldn't have used such a camera in any case. I didn't even know how. The more I thought about what I didn't know, the more I felt like groaning out loud.

Then an idea hit me. I was dazzled by the brilliant simplicity of it. It made a sort of syllogism. Frederick was a first-rate archaeologist. No first-rate archaeologist would mess up a discovery as big as this one. Ergo—no discovery.

So it wasn't a very good syllogism. It made sense to me. Frederick was fantasizing, the result of years of frustration in his field. He didn't really believe in his dream ships, but the dream was so glorious he couldn't give it up. And if there were no ships, there was nothing for me to do except swim around for a couple of hours a day and report no results. I wouldn't say there was nothing down there, I would just say I couldn't find it. In a few weeks we would pack up and go home. At least I would go home. Frederick could go to— wherever he was going.

Somewhat cheered by this reasoning, I went on to the next problem. Frederick and . . . Medea.

That was a good name for that dark, ruined beauty. She looked like a Medea—quite capable, in my estimation, of killing her children to get back at a man who had betrayed her. As Medea had slaughtered her sons to revenge herself on their father.

Medea was a born constitutional psychopathic inferior. At the very beginning of her career, when she fled from her father's court with Jason, after helping him steal the Golden Fleece, she had committed a horrendous crime, chopping up her young brother and throwing the pieces overboard to delay the pursuing galleys of her father. The poor old king had stopped to collect the fragments and Medea had escaped with her lover. The story had given me a chuckle at the time, it was so corny and melodramatic, like the Tom Lehrer song:

> *One day when she had nothing to do*
> *She cut her baby brother in two*
> *And served him up as an Irish stew. . . .*

In the pitch-black night of a far-off Greek island, the story wasn't funny. It was horrible. No wonder Freud got the names of his classic psychoses out of Greek legends. Maybe I was getting a little psychotic myself, seeing ancient Greeks all over the place. . . . Medea wasn't Greek, though, any more than Theseus and Ariadne were. They came from further back in time, back in the dark abysses of prehistory when people still believed in human sacrifice and killed the king every nine years and sprinkled his blood around to bring back the spring.

I said a word out loud, a vulgar four-letter word. This was not the time, and it was certainly not the place for gruesome fantasies like the ones that had seized my mind. The point was that Frederick and Medea—yes, use the name, use it and go on—had nothing to do with me. Maybe she was an old girl friend. Maybe she was an old mistress. The key word was "old." It was all in the past and it had nothing to do with me.

So that took care of two worries. The third one wasn't so easy to solve. It had to do with Jim.

Not that Jim was a depressing thought. Far from it; he was the only bright spot in a dark world. The worrisome part was my relationship with him. I had lied to him, and I hated having lied. I took it for granted that he would find out. I always get caught when I try to lie, that's why I gave it up years ago . . . till I met Frederick. Mostly I was in the habit of being honest. And if I didn't break down and confess, he was sure to find out some other way. Sir Christopher, for instance—if he knew Frederick, he must know that Frederick had a daughter. Maybe he had dandled me on his knee when I was an infant and he and Frederick were bright young beginners in the field.

I had a feeling that Jim wouldn't like it if he found out I had lied to him. His eyebrows might be crooked, but his mind wasn't.

Off in the blackness behind me something made an odd moaning sound. It was probably a goat or a bird or some other equally natural phenomenon, but it made my hackles rise. There was no solution to the third problem, none that I could think of at any rate, and in spite of my resolution to forget the Greek myths, the night was beginning to swarm with monsters. I stumbled on toward the house. I had mashed one of the tomatoes and it was dripping down the front of my fancy dress, which, I suspected, would not wash very well. The fish was leaking too.

By the time I reached the kitchen I was in a rotten mood. The sight of Frederick hunched over his book and the remains of some awful-looking mess in a saucepan did not improve my humor. I dumped the fish in a pan along with some olive oil and started peeling tomatoes. No point in changing my dress, it was a wreck anyhow.

The smell of the frying fish made me realize how hungry I was, so I opened a can of baked beans and ate that, cold, while the fish cooked. It improved my disposition slightly. I looked at Frederick and for a second I almost felt sorry for him. Not that he wasn't perfectly happy with his cold stew and his boring book, but he looked so alone.

"Want some fish?" I asked.

"I have eaten." He didn't look up from his book.

"Nothing that did you any good. It's ridiculous the way we've been living on this canned junk. The bay is full of sea food and there are some nice-looking vegetables in the shops. From now on I'm going to the village every afternoon and buy stuff to cook for supper."

He didn't answer, but his nose quivered a little when I pushed a plate of fish and tomatoes under it. He reached for a fork.

I grabbed the book out of his hand. He started to expostulate. I said severely, "I refuse to waste good food on a man who isn't giving it its full attention. Anyhow, I want to talk to you."

"Mph," said Frederick, or words to that effect. He took a bite of fish and burned his mouth and swore.

"Tsk, tsk," I said. "Such language."

"You might have mentioned—"

"That it was hot? You're a brilliant scholar; I assumed you could figure that out yourself."

Frederick blew on the next bite. He managed to look dignified and disagreeable even when performing this homely act.

"What do you want to talk about?"

"Lots of things. For a starter, who was that woman?"

"Woman?" He frowned. For a minute I thought

he was putting on an act. Then I realized he wasn't that good an actor.

"Oh," he said, his brow clearing. "That woman. I have no idea. She reminded me momentarily of someone I knew—briefly—many years ago. It could not possibly be the same person."

He fell silent, staring at the fish poised on his fork. Whatever his relationship with that someone he had known years ago, the memory of it was not a happy one. His face looked almost human; there was pain and regret in its lines. Then he shook his head and went on eating.

"Even if she were the same," he said, as if to himself, "it would not matter. It was in the past. Over. Finished."

"You sound like Jim," I said, watching him curiously. "He was telling me tonight how people have to forget the past."

"An unorthodox attitude for an archaeologist," said Frederick dryly.

"You know what he means."

"Quite possibly I do. The past is a subject for scholarly study, not for emotion. Now—is there any other topic you wish to discuss? I am anxious to finish my chapter. Vermeule's arguments are so puerile—"

"Don't you want to talk about the—the underwater business? We have a lot of plans to make, seems to me."

"I have made plans. For the time being you will

continue to work at the dig in the morning. After lunch, while the men take their infernal siesta, you will dive. If you are late in returning, I will complain to Nicholas about the irresponsibility of modern youth. That will hide our real intent."

He looked so pleased at this childish stratagem that I almost laughed.

"No," I said patiently. "I told you, I won't dive alone. Especially not right after lunch! These are strange waters to me. I don't know what the hell is out there."

"I see. In that case we will have to get in a few hours before we go to the dig. The sun rises before six—"

I groaned. Frederick ignored me.

"And all day Sunday," he went on. "Perhaps in a few days you will feel more competent and can continue alone."

There was no point in arguing with him. I shrugged.

"Okay. You'll have to wake me up; I don't get up before dawn willingly. Now suppose you tell me what I'm supposed to be looking for."

"Anything that is not a natural formation."

"That's a lot of help. Jars, I suppose. What about anchors?"

"The question of anchors is interesting." Frederick's face brightened. "It has been claimed that before the seventh century B.C. ships did not carry anchors. That seems to be extremely poor reasoning. There must have been some method of stopping a ship, and the pierced stone, tied to a cable or rope, would seem an obvious solution that would occur to the most primitive mind. A triangular stone, with a hole in the center, has been identified by one authority as a Minoan anchor. Certainly metal anchors were not used until—"

I sighed ostentatiously and interrupted.

"Pierced stones. They are not going to be very conspicuous. How about masts?"

"They used them, of course. Whether they would survive—"

"These amphorae you talked about. Would they be the same shape as the ones we found on the dig?"

"Yes. Long, two-handled, with a narrow neck and a pointed base."

"What else?"

"There could be," said Frederick, "anything down there."

"Well, I guess that gives me something to go on with. Suppose I do find something. How do I mark the spot so I can find it the next time I dive?"

"I have given that matter some thought. An inflatable globule of some sort is the obvious answer; yet I am reluctant to leave a marker that might alert others. The process of triangulation . . ."

He went on talking, but I stopped listening.

The conversation had become pointless and rather pathetic. We were like a couple of kids making solemn plans to build a rocket ship. Neither of us knew the first thing about what we were doing.

"We'll start tomorrow, then," I said, collecting the dishes. There was no use being Women's Lib about the housework; if I had been a man, Frederick would still have expected me to do it.

I had my back turned when he said unexpectedly, "You don't believe you will find anything, do you?"

"Huh?" I turned. "I didn't say—"

"Your conviction is implicit in every word you have said." His eyes narrowed. "Nor can I blame you. You seem to have the rudiments of a logical mind; a pity it hasn't been trained. I suppose I must show you this. It was found in the bay."

He held out his hand.

The light wasn't good. For a second I had the horrible impression that his palm had turned hard and shiny. Midas? Then I saw that he was holding something, a flat, irregular object that covered his palm from the wrist to the base of his fingers. It shone with the glint of gold—the one substance that does not corrode, in soil or seawater.

I snatched at it. He snarled a warning, but there was no need, it wasn't as fragile as it looked. The underlying metal was badly corroded; it showed green and rotten around the ragged edges, but the flat top surface was covered with a hard, shiny substance like black plastic. Into this black surface tiny golden figures of animals and flowers and men had been set. There was a cat, with a bird in its mouth; two lotus blossoms; and a man, a hunter, with a long spear and one of the man-tall, figure-eight Minoan shields. The tiny figures were done with such delicacy and vigor that you could sense the agonized struggle of the bird and the lithe ferocity of the cat.

Frederick didn't have to tell me what it was. I had seen the daggers from the Shaft Graves at Mycenae in the Athens Museum. This was part of the blade of another such inlaid dagger. The daggers in Athens had been found on the mainland, but they were believed to be of Cretan workmanship. They had been found only in royal graves—rare imports, so highly prized that they were buried with their dead owners.

"Okay," I said, with a long breath. "I don't know whether I believe in your ships. But you've convinced me; there's something down there."

Chapter
6

BY FOLLOWING A PATH ACROSS THE HEADLAND WE were able to reach the bay of the villa and save swimming time. I was thinking about Frederick when I proposed the land route, but I was also remembering Jim's warning. I could at least minimize the time I spent in the water under Frederick's unreliable supervision.

As we walked along the path, the roof of the villa came into sight on our left.

"I wonder if we're trespassing," I said. "Maybe that's their private bay down there."

"The sea is open to all," said Frederick vaguely.

"Well, we can but try. If we get warned off, or shot at, it's your problem."

Frederick didn't answer; the question didn't seem to concern him. We turned toward the cliff, which was lower here than it was on our section of the coast, and climbed down to the water.

I hadn't slept too well the night before. I had lain awake for a long time, thinking about what Frederick had told me. In spite of my doubts and reservations, the lure of hidden treasure had infected me. The description of the ships, tumbled and scattered across the ocean floor like bones in a marine graveyard, was so fantastic it sounded like a scene out of Jules Verne. Yet Frederick's theories made sense. The southern coast of Thera, the nearest part of the island to the motherland of Crete, would be the logical place for a major port. Some archaeologists believed that the capital city must have been in the center of the island, which had collapsed into the caldera. But this assumption seemed to be based on the Atlantis legend, as recorded by Plato; and with all due respect to Plato, the details of his story were highly questionable. It simply didn't make sense to have a big city in the middle of an island when the sea was the main highroad of communication. In Crete the cities were on the coast or within easy reach of the coastline. I didn't believe Plato's account of a man-made channel three hundred feet wide and a hundred feet deep that allowed ships to reach a central harbor.

The central part of the island wasn't the only part that had subsided. There was another caldera on the south coast, according to maps I had seen. That's where the main harbors must have been, on the lee side of the island, the part nearest to Crete.

So when I slid into the water I wouldn't have been surprised to see submerged towers and mammoth walls, with fish swimming in and out of the empty window frames. I knew better—but I wouldn't have been surprised.

I was using a snorkel but no air tanks, because I didn't have them or any means of filling them. I couldn't bring my own tanks; they were too bulky to carry and they would have been useless anyway, without a compressor to refill them.

Frederick had done nothing about supplying these necessary items, and his vagueness on the subject was a point against his claims. It was almost as if he were afraid to give me the equipment that would prove or disprove his story. I could see the difficulty; as soon as he started making inquiries about scuba gear, the port authorities in Phira would learn about it. Frederick claimed "they" were suspicious and antagonistic already. He might be exaggerating, but I had read about divers in Greece and Turkey having trouble with government officials. And there was no use telling him he should have thought about these things before he planned the project.

However, my preliminary survey had convinced me that I could do a lot of exploring without scuba gear. The water was fairly shallow and warm. In fact it felt warmer than the cool morning air, and it closed around me like welcoming arms.

The beauty of it hit me first, the way it always does. This sea floor didn't have the luxuriant junglelike vegetation of the reefs off Florida, but the translucence of the water gave objects a pristine, shimmery look, as if they were encased in clear plastic. Sunlight sifted down through the cool green depths and danced on the sandy bottom. It was surprisingly clean; there was almost no marine growth and no mud. Not that the bottom was level—far from it. There were patches of relatively smooth sand, black or white, the black being lava sand. But most of the surface was a jumble of rocks and stones. With a little imagination you could believe you were seeing the ruins of a city strewn across the acres of the bay. Tumbled heaps might have been fallen towers; rock ridges looked like the remains of walls, with gaping holes for doors and windows. But I knew that what I saw was not man-made. The rubble consisted of pumice and magma ejected from the volcano, mixed with fragments of broken lava flow and stones from the collapsed cliffs. Some of them, worn smooth by water, resembled worked stones to an astonishing degree. There had been reports of sunken quays in another part of the island—long strips of stone so straight it was hard to believe they had been shaped by nature.

But they were beach rock, natural concrete formed by water running over limestone and the silica of lava and pumice.

There was only one way of searching the area systematically, and that was to swim a sort of grid pattern, back and forth. It would take a long time because I would have to check every suspicious-looking formation.

The sun was fully up by that time, and the eastern sky was a tapestry of blazing colors. I waved at Frederick, who was sitting hunched up on a rock looking like an irritated albatross. He gave me a limp flap of the hand, and I went down again. I struck out for the mouth of the bay, keeping fairly close to the south coastline. The water got deeper as I went on; at the mouth of the bay it was about fifty feet. I could work down there, but not for long. The rock walls came down sheer into the water, but they were uneven; I could climb out if I had to. I decided to go on out a little farther.

I was swimming with my face in the water watching the scene below. There was considerable activity, fish of all sizes scuttling around. The visibility was excellent.

All of a sudden there was nothing down there. A few fish, yes. But no bottom, only a gaping black gulf. The edge was as sharp as the rim of the Grand Canyon, and I had a feeling the bottom was almost as far down.

There aren't too many things in the water that scare me, but that did. I went flapping back from the edge like a kitten on a glass-topped table. When I could see bottom under me I floated for a minute or two, getting my breath back.

Then I went back to the chasm and dived.

Not down into it, of course, but near the rim. I had to do it to compensate for that attack of nerves. I'm not ashamed of being afraid; caution is a sign of good sense. But this wasn't a rational fear. It was fear of the lightless depths, fear of the dark; peering down into the abyss I half expected to see some monstrous bulk heave itself out of the water, trailing tentacles and staring with big evil eyes full of a cruel intelligence. . . . It was ridiculous. I could drown just as fast in five feet of water as in five hundred; and the Kraken is an imaginary monster.

There was no way I was ever going to get down into those depths. This was part of the outer caldera, and if it was anything like the central bay, it was hundreds of feet deep. Nothing less than a specially designed submarine would ever penetrate the abyss.

I'd had enough. I wasn't nervous anymore, but I'd had enough for one day. I went back to the place where Frederick was waiting, and rose up out of the water at his feet, spitting out my mouthpiece and pushing my mask up.

"Well?" he demanded. "What did you find?"

"Nothing." I pulled myself up onto the rocks and reached for a towel. "If you mean ruins or wrecks. But there sure is a hell of a big hole out there."

"Ah, yes, the outer caldera. Nothing would have survived down there. The pressure must be enormous."

I stood up.

"Let's go. I'm cold and hungry."

As we crossed the plateau back toward the house, I was surprised to find my eyes pricking, almost as if I wanted to cry. I decided it must be fatigue. I had come to terms with my father a long time before, there was no excuse for feeling hurt because he thought of his antiquities first and me second. No, that was a misstatement. He didn't think of me at all.

II

I started the search next morning. It took two hours to make the first crossing of the bay and I was bushed when I finished. The nervous strain was what wore me out; I was so painfully conscious of my ignorance and so afraid I would miss something. The following day I started the second crossing, ten feet beyond the first. Since the bay got wider and the water got deeper, I wasn't able to finish in two hours.

The job would have been much easier with proper scuba gear. Even though the water wasn't deep, only about thirty feet, I had to spend a lot of time on the bottom. I could see why Frederick was unwilling to ask about a compressor, but one thing we had to have, and soon, was a boat, or even an inflatable raft—something I could anchor out in the middle of the bay, in case I needed to get out of the water in a hurry. If I did get into trouble, Frederick wasn't going to be much help perched on a rock fifty yards away.

So, when he tried to haul me out of the sack on Sunday morning I refused to budge. I had to meet Jim at ten anyhow. Frederick was annoyed when I told him of the appointment, which I had seen no reason to mention earlier. I told him Jim might come looking for me if I didn't show up, and finally Frederick gave in. He promised to see what he could do about a boat.

I put on my best flowered shift over my bathing suit, got my mask and flippers, and started for town. I hadn't gone ten yards before I was dripping with sweat. It was unseasonably hot, even for the Mediterranean. The air was close and breathless, and the sky had a queer hazy look. I was looking forward to getting into the water, and that wasn't all I was looking forward to. When I saw Jim at one of the tables on the hotel terrace my heart gave a jump.

He was fully dressed, in old jeans and a blue

shirt, and as soon as I was within hailing distance I called out, "I thought we were going swimming."

"Have some coffee and we'll talk about it."

"Hot," I said, mopping my brow.

"Earthquake weather," said Jim.

I gave him a startled look. He grinned.

"That's what the men are saying. It's possible. This area is seismically unstable."

"I know all about the history of Thera," I said. "But I didn't think—"

"No problem," Jim said smugly. "We have quakes all the time in California. Only I've never been in the water when the earth shook, and I'm not sure I want to try it."

Angelos, the owner of the hotel, waited on us personally. Jim introduced us. I greeted him in my best Greek, which made him smile broadly, but I thought I had never seen anyone who looked less like an angel. He was a big, hulking man, one of the few Greeks I had met who really did look greasy—the result of his trade, perhaps, for Jim explained that he and his wife ran the small hotel together. I assumed he had shaved, since it was Sunday, but his jowls were heavily shadowed. He and Jim talked for a while, and then Jim interpreted.

"He says it's okay to swim. There may be some minor tremors but they won't amount to much."

I studied Angelos skeptically. He smiled at me, his white teeth gleaming against the dark stubble.

"How does he know?" I asked.

"He says he feels it. It's possible, you know. Some of the island people claim to be sensitive to it. They get nauseated, headachy—"

"You sound like a TV commercial for cold remedies," I interrupted. "I've read about that. One of Mary Renault's books, wasn't it? The hero could feel earthquakes before they happened. It would be a useful skill in those days. People would think you had divine connections. But that was fiction."

Angelos seemed to know what we were talking about. He nodded vigorously, and spoke. Then he slapped Jim on the back, with a roll of his eyes at me and a remark that made Jim look self-conscious.

"Let's go," he said.

As we walked down the street toward the beach, I asked, "What did Angelos say about me?"

"You can probably guess."

"Hmmm."

Jim seemed anxious to change the subject.

"I hope you don't mind, but I made a lunch date for you. My boss wants to meet you."

"Why?"

"What are you so prickly about? Why shouldn't he want to meet you?"

"Okay, okay," I said. "It will be jolly lunching with Sir Christopher."

When we reached the pier, there were a lot of men hanging around. Greek men hang around a lot—on street corners, in cafés, around piers. They greeted Jim with enthusiasm.

"The fishing boats are out," he said, glancing around. "I guess that means it's okay. Let's go down the beach a way."

The sea was as flat as a pond on a windless day. We found a nice smooth spot, with a few rocks between us and the pier. It was pleasant and private. I peeled off my dress and shoes and adjusted my flippers. Then I looked up.

For a second I knew how the ancient Greek hero felt when the earthquake was imminent. The ground seemed to dip, and my stomach went down with it.

Jim was standing a few feet away, watching me. His build was on the lean side, but his shoulders were good and the bands of muscle across his chest were hard and smooth. He was nicely tanned. But for that one eerie second he looked like the man in my dream. The breathless stillness of the air, the oily smooth surface of the sea against which he stood added to the strangeness of the atmosphere.

The impression came and was gone. I jumped up, forgetting I had the flippers on. I tripped, and Jim reached out an arm and caught me.

"I hope you swim better than you walk," he said, with a smile.

After that challenge I had to excel. I forgot my half-formed plan of flapping around and pretending to be only a mediocre swimmer. I swam rings around him. He was good but not in my class. I can brag about my swimming because it's the only thing I can brag about. Most of the other things I did that summer were disasters.

When we were ready to quit I raced him in and got there quite a distance ahead of him. He was winded when he joined me. His chest was pumping in and out like a bellows. And of course, damn him, he said just the right thing.

"My God, you're good. How about giving me lessons?"

It was then that I remembered my subtle, crafty scheme for pretending I was a lousy swimmer. I looked at Jim's smiling face. His eyelashes were stuck together in spiky points and his eyes were wide with admiration and pleasure. There wasn't a mean bone in his body. He was as candid and open as . . . as I was not. It never entered his head that my expertise might be turned to illegal ends. That was the first thing that would have occurred to Frederick.

"Oh, well," I mumbled. "You're pretty good yourself."

"Not in your class."

He was still watching me with beaming approval, not a trace of wounded vanity or crushed male ego; and I knew that if I didn't speak up I would never be able to look him in the eye again. I had actually opened my mouth to start the confession when the earth shook.

I mean, it really shook. The sinking feeling wasn't inside me, it was in the ground. It felt like a plane hitting an air pocket, a swoop and then a lift. When the movement stopped, Jim and I were lying flat on the ground. His arms were around me and I was clutching him like a drowning man. In one lovely smooth movement he stood up, lifting me with him.

"Nice little earthquake," he said, and kissed me.

It is a testimonial to Jim's kisses that for a little while I wasn't sure whether the ground was really rocking under my feet or whether it just felt that way. When he finally lifted his head I saw that he was smiling.

"We'd better get back," he said casually, and scooped up our discarded clothing.

Another shock hit. I staggered, and Jim put his arm around me again. My teeth began to chatter.

"Oh, God," I groaned. "This is awful."

"I can see you aren't used to quakes. This was a baby quake, just a tremor. Come on, now, be a big girl."

We walked a few steps, but I was still shaking and I kept tripping over my fins. Jim picked me up in his arms. He was a lot stronger than he looked. As we approached the pier a ragged cheer went up. I lifted my head from Jim's shoulder and saw the men standing along the pier watching us.

"Put me down," I said.

"You sure?"

"Yes. . . . Are there going to be any more earthquakes?"

"How would I know? Maybe we shouldn't take any chances."

He kissed me again. I had not intended to respond, but I couldn't help it. Finally the roaring in my ears subsided and I realized the men on the pier were cheering again.

"Put me down, damn it," I said. "I'm not going to put on a free show for those peeping toms."

"They aren't peeping, they're standing right out in the open."

But he put me down. I took off my fins and stalked toward the steps with what dignity I could manage. I walked past the grinning audience with my nose in the air. Jim was behind me. He said something to the men; there was a laughing chorus of response.

Then Jim caught up with me, and I demanded, "What did you say?"

"I told them you were my girl."

"What do you mean, your girl?"

"I should have said 'woman.' "

I started to object; he cut me short by handing me my dress. I put it on. When my head emerged I saw that Jim was studying me soberly.

"Better understand something," he said. "Insofar as sexual morality is concerned, these people are still in the nineteenth century. There are two kinds of women here—good, respectable ladies, who stay at home and tend their cook pots, and—the other kind. Western women confuse these guys. They still think of women as property. Okay, so I told them you were my property. You may not like it. I don't like it either. But they are more likely to respect my property rights than your feelings. Not that I'm trying to curtail your extracurricular activities, but—"

"That's okay," I said. "I have no—"

That was when it happened. I could pinpoint the exact second; between "no" and the next word, which was going to be "plans." I never said it. I was looking straight at him. Our eyes met, as it says in the old books. It was a meeting, more significant than any physical touch.

Neither of us spoke. Words weren't necessary. We walked up the sloping street toward the plaza, holding hands.

Church was letting out and people were standing around, talking and drinking coffee and relaxing. This was their one day of rest, and they were enjoying it. At one of the tables on the terrace a man was sitting. I picked him out of the crowd right away, because he was the only man who was wearing a hat. It was an expensive-looking tweed cap, and it struck an incongruous note on such a hot day.

I nudged Jim and pointed. "Sir Christopher?"

"Right."

He saw us coming; when we reached the terrace he was on his feet, holding a chair for me and smiling. The cap came off with a gallant sweep. Then I understood why he wore it. He was as bald as an egg, and, without protection, that pink skin would have fried like an egg. As if to compensate for the hairlessness on top, he had cultivated a handsome handlebar moustache that curved like a buffalo's black horns. I was reminded of Hercule Poirot, but Sir Christopher wasn't short and tubby like Agatha Christie's detective. He was tall and lean and rather handsome in a bony, big-nosed way. He had a nice smile and an air of understated elegance that made me feel grubby, with my salt-soaked hair and damp dress.

"How do you do, Miss Bishop," he said. "I hope our little earthquake didn't alarm you."

"It did," I admitted.

"There's no danger, unless you happen to be in a ravine or under a cliff when loose rock is shaken down. You may have noticed the arched construction prevalent here. It is quite well adapted to quakes; I've seen these houses swaying to and fro, but they don't often collapse."

I assumed the speech was meant to be reassuring. It did not affect me that way. Sir Christopher's smile broadened.

"You'll become accustomed to earth tremors if you spend much time in this part of the world," he said consolingly.

"I guess they have lots of earthquakes," I said. "I knew it, from my reading, but until you've experienced it. . . . How about the volcano?"

"Quite active," said Sir Christopher cheerily. "But don't fret, you'll not see anything like the great eruption of 1450, the one that has preserved so much for us. The only other disaster of that magnitude occurred in approximately 25,000 B.C."

He chuckled as he saw me surreptitiously counting on my fingers.

"An interval of almost twenty-five thousand years, my dear," he said. "There has never been anything like the fifteenth-century eruption in recorded history—except for Krakatoa, of course, and that was probably not as great as the Thera eruption."

"Krakatoa was bad enough," Jim said. "The descriptions of eyewitnesses are strikingly reminiscent of certain legends that have come down to us from early times."

He glanced at Sir Christopher, who laughed lightly.

"Jim and I enjoy arguing about his theories. Atlantis, the Greek flood legend, the Exodus story—"

"Then you don't believe in the idea that Thera is—was—Atlantis?" I asked.

"Oh, I think the majority of scholars agree that the eruption and the consequent destruction of the Cretan cities may have furnished the kernel of Plato's story," Sir Christopher said disinterestedly. "But I am unable to go along with the enthusiasts who want to connect every myth with that single event."

"Not all of them," Jim admitted, looking a little flustered as Sir Christopher turned to regard him with a humorous smile. "But there has to be a connection between the eruption and the story of the Exodus; it's just too circumstantial to be a coincidence. We know, from the Krakatoa eruption, that volcanic action of that magnitude is accompanied by earthquakes, rain, hail, lightning—side effects that could explain all the plagues mentioned in the Bible. Areas a hundred and fifty miles from Krakatoa experienced total darkness; and as you said, the Thera eruption was considerably greater than that of Krakatoa. As for the parting of the waters, it's generally agreed that the Hebrews didn't cross the Red Sea, but rather a Sea of Reeds in the northern part of the Egyptian Delta, along a well-known ancient route into Sinai and Palestine. The receding of the sea along the coast, followed by a tremendous tsunami wave, has been observed many times as a result of seismic action. Even the death of the first-born could have resulted from crop failure and disease after—"

" 'Could,' " Sir Christopher repeated. His smile, which I had found so pleasant, was beginning to get on my nerves. "We will never know, will we? Speculation of that sort is entertaining, but not very profitable, my boy."

"Let's talk about something else besides earthquakes," I said.

"Certainly." Sir Christopher continued to smile. "How is my old friend Frederick?"

"Fine," I said. "Just fine."

"I'm happy to hear it. I saw him recently, and I didn't think he looked well. He never took proper care of himself. Is he still eating out of tins?"

"Yes," I said. "I mean, no, not all the time. I buy fish and things for supper sometimes."

"I'm glad he has someone to look after him."

"I thought you didn't like him," I said.

Sir Christopher raised one eyebrow. He must have practiced, it moved so smoothly.

"Now where did you get that impression? I feel sorry for the poor chap, actually. There was a time when I considered him the most fortunate of men. He had success in his field, good health, good looks, a pretty, devoted young wife, and a child. . . ." The pause was, I thought, quite deliberate. Then he went on. "Frederick destroyed himself. Or rather, his one failing destroyed his success. It was a tragedy in the classic Greek sense, one flaw in an otherwise noble character—"

Jim had been increasingly uncomfortable as

this speech unrolled. Now he interrupted, "Not quite the classic Greek tragedy, Chris. The Greek heroes failed because they incurred the displeasure of some fickle god or other."

"If Frederick were a religious man, he might consider himself cursed," Sir Christopher said gently. "I'm sure that to this day he doesn't understand why he failed. He is incapable of understanding emotion. That constitutes both his flaw and his inability to recognize it as such."

"Where did you know him?" I asked.

Sir Christopher glanced at Jim. It was one of those meaningful glances.

"It is a rather painful story," he said softly.

I felt like some poor savage who goes to a fancy party and commits an unwitting faux pas.

Jim got red. "I've told you, Chris, that it doesn't pain me one damn bit. I wish you wouldn't—"

"I'm sorry, my boy. I was being overly sensitive. It is painful to *me*, even after all these years."

Jim was now the color of a nice ripe tomato.

"I'm sorry," he mumbled. "I didn't mean—"

"Oh, for God's sake," I said. "Either tell me or change the subject. And if you think I'm going to join in the chorus of apologies, forget it."

I wasn't embarrassed any longer, I was mad. I can't stand that kind of hassling, the gentle, prickly kind. Especially when it was directed at Jim.

"There is no need for you to apologize," said Sir Christopher, with a forgiving smile. "You had

no idea that the subject might be. . . . You see, my
dear, your . . . employer and I were at Oxford together before the war. Frederick was a Rhodes
scholar. We became friends—we two and another
young student named Durkheim. They called us
the Three Musketeers, of course. We were drawn
together because of our interest in pre-classical
Greek culture. Durkheim was the oldest; I think
perhaps he was also the most brilliant. He had
been studying the Linear B script, and if he had
lived. . . . But I anticipate.

"When World War Two broke out, Durkheim
was assigned to Crete—a rare example of the military's actually using a man where he could be
most useful. I went with him. We hadn't been
there long when who should appear but your—
but Frederick. We couldn't imagine how he had
managed it. This was in the early months of 1941,
before America entered the war, and your government was not precisely encouraging its citi-
zens to travel abroad. Yet there he was,
imperturbable as ever, and in a frightful state
about his precious antiquities. You would have
thought the ruins of Knossos were the only things
threatened by a possible German invasion.

"As you know—or perhaps you don't, all this
is ancient history to you young creatures—the invasion came. It was airborne, and quite overwhelming. Our troops fought on for a short time,
but eventually we were forced to withdraw, and

the Germans occupied the island. Because Durkheim knew the language and the terrain, he stayed on as liaison officer with the underground; and I stayed as well. So did Frederick. In his peculiar fashion he was more effective than any of us. He had spent only one short season in Crete before the war, yet he knew the country as well as Durkheim did.

"It was a frightful existence. We were constantly on the move, eating scraps, sleeping where and when we could, constantly anticipating discovery and death. But we were young and healthy and fired up with patriotism. I remember the night when we got the news of America's entry into the war. We were staying in a remote village in the eastern mountains, and we got roaring drunk on retsina. Even Frederick got drunk. It was the only time I ever saw him display a human weakness.

"That was the high point. From then on, everything went wrong. Crete is a splendid place for guerrilla warfare—mountainous, rugged, primitive; and the men were superb. But the Germans were inhumanly efficient. They rounded up the resistance fighters group by group. Durkheim was the prize catch, of course, they wanted him badly. I don't know precisely how it happened. Everyone who was with him that night is dead. Frederick and I were not in his group, we were off on errands of our own.

"I met Frederick next day, at the rendezvous we had arranged, and it was he who informed me of Durkheim's capture. We were making futile plans for freeing him when one of the men from the village found us and told us he had been executed."

I paid Sir Christopher the tribute of a moment of silence before I turned to Jim.

"Who was he, your father?"

"Your arithmetic is terrible," Jim said. "He was my uncle. My mother's older brother. Look, let's not pull out all the stops, shall we? I never even saw him. I wasn't born till after he died."

I had never heard him sound like that—like a sulky little boy saying something deliberately naughty and waiting to be scolded. Sir Christopher said nothing, and after a moment Jim went on.

"It's different for you, Chris. You knew him. He was your friend. I mean—"

"Quite all right, my boy. Don't give it another thought. I understand your point of view thoroughly."

Oh, he was an expert, that man; he had both of us speechless and feeling obscurely guilty. I knew what he was doing, but I couldn't seem to prevent it. He looked from me to Jim, as if waiting for us to speak, and then offered a change of subject.

"Did you enjoy your dip? You are a splendid swimmer, young lady. I was almost moved to join you."

"Oh," I said. "You saw us. Where were you?"

"I was taking a stroll on the bluff above the beach. You ought to consider marine archaeology, my dear. It's a new and expanding field. One day I hope to investigate some of the sunken harbor sites in Crete. Perhaps I can induce you to join me."

There was no question about it. He knew. The cat-and-mouse hints were beginning to annoy me. Maybe he didn't mean them as threats, maybe he was trying to warn me. He was beaming benevolently, like Jupiter without his beard or hair. Jim looked puzzled. He knew something was going on, but, bless his honest heart, he didn't know what.

Sir Christopher turned to him. "Jim, you had better get some clothes on. It's a bit breezy here in the shade."

"Okay. Back in a minute, Sandy."

As soon as he was out of sight, I turned to Sir Christopher. I knew I had to take the initiative, or the man would continue to intimidate me with that soft voice and gentle smile.

"Okay," I said. "How did you find out?"

"Find out what?" That damned eyebrow slipped up again.

"That I am Frederick's daughter."

It was out, and I had an instant feeling of relief, like lancing a boil.

"You are a direct young person, aren't you?" Sir Christopher said, looking amused.

I winced. "Usually I am. I sort of got roped into this lie. You haven't told Jim. Why not?"

"But, my dear girl, that's your affair. If you don't choose to tell him, why should I interfere?"

"I'm going to tell him," I said. "I'd appreciate it if you would let me do it."

"If I had meant to betray your secret, I would have done so by now, surely."

I let my breath out with a big whoosh of air. His smile faded as he watched me.

"My dear child," he exclaimed. "You surely don't think I would hold this over your head? I'm not that sort of person. Deal with the situation as you see fit."

I started to say I was sorry and caught myself just in time. Maybe I had misjudged him. Apparently I had. But I still wasn't going to apologize. He waited for a minute and then went on.

"Only do be careful about your diving, won't you? If I know Frederick—and I think I do—he will be inclined to urge you on rather than caution you. You mustn't take careless chances."

"What diving?" I asked.

"Now, now," Sir Christopher said indulgently. "That isn't worthy of you, Sandy."

"I suppose you saw the article in *Geographic*," I said resignedly.

"No; but I knew Frederick had a daughter, and when a lovely young lady of precisely the right age joined him here, I made inquiries."

"You could report him," I said. "I mean, if you think I'm going to do any diving—"

"I have no intention of reporting anyone," Sir Christopher interrupted, sounding annoyed. "I felt obliged to warn you; even to do that violates my cherished habit of noninterference."

"And you won't tell Jim?"

"I won't tell him. And don't you tell him I knew," he added, with a flash of wry humor. "He would murder me if you injured yourself and he learned that I had been aware of your activities."

"I won't injure myself."

"I certainly hope not." He glanced up. "And here he comes," he said calmly. "Just in time to order. Jim, I think we ought to introduce our young friend to the gourmet flavor of octopus, don't you?"

Octopus tastes a little like old automobile tire. It's good exercise for the jaws. We had a big fattening lunch, with plenty of retsina, and we talked of this and that. Sir Christopher was a fascinating conversationalist, when he put his rapier away. After lunch he rose.

"Back to the job. Paper work is the curse of excavation. Laymen don't realize that it takes ten times as long as the actual digging. No"—putting his hand on Jim's shoulder as Jim started to rise— "I don't want to see you until tomorrow morning, Jim. Enjoy your day of rest."

He walked toward the door of the hotel. Sunlight slipping through the vines cast a pattern of weaving shadows across his back and shoulders.

"He must like you," Jim said ingenuously. "This is the first time he's told me to run off and play. What'll we do?"

"I could take a nap," I said, yawning. "I'm not used to all that heavy food."

"Let's walk some of it off."

I knew what he had in mind. It was in my mind too. But the walk did me in. It was awfully hot. We climbed the hill behind the town and wandered around the slopes for a while, looking for a shady spot. There were vines on the terraced hillsides, but they didn't provide much shade. Finally we followed a goat trail up into an area that was too steep and rocky for cultivation, and found a tree. It was scrawny and bent, but it was a tree, and that's rare on Thera. We lay down in the shade and Jim put his arms around me. . . . And in five minutes we were both asleep.

I woke with a start, after dreaming that a dog was licking my feet. The sun was warm on my legs, and Jim was tickling my toes with a stalk of grass. As soon as I opened my eyes he leaned over me.

"And now," he said, "let's get back to what we were doing when you copped out on me. I've never been so insulted in my life."

He kissed me before I could think of an answer, and I stopped trying to think.

There's something exciting about making love in the open air, a suggestion of innocence and freedom. The air was hot and sweet; no smog, no gasoline fumes, only the scent of wild thyme and sun on clean dust, and the smell of the sea. But one of the reasons why those moments stand out in my memory is that they ended so soon, and so dreadfully.

It started with a rhythmic pounding. I thought at first it was the beat of my heart, or Jim's, but the pounding grew louder, faster, fiercer. A shower of pebbles rained down. They weren't big, but they stung, and the sound seemed right on top of us, like wild horses charging, intent on riding us down.

I understood then what the Greeks meant by the word panic, an attribute of Pan, who was another of those monstrous Greek mixtures, half man, half goat. Wildly I struggled to sit up. The rain of stones trickled out. I looked up; and I would not have been surprised to see the god himself, immense and shadowy, thundering past on his cloven hooves.

I saw a man on horseback—presumably the same man I had seen once before. He was motionless for a moment; then he turned in the saddle and the horse broke into a trot. In a few seconds they were out of sight. The hoofbeats faded into silence.

"Damn," said Jim. "Of all the times . . ."

I let my head fall onto his shoulder. I felt foolish, remembering my reasonless terror, but some of it lingered.

"Good old Pan," I mumbled. "Riding around to chaperone the heedless maiden. . . ."

As usual, Jim followed my train of thought without difficulty.

"Wrong god," he said, with a little laugh. "Wrong religion, in fact. The Greek gods didn't chaperone maidens. Neither did the goddesses, except when their husbands went astray after human girls."

"And then they turned the girls into spiders or something," I said dreamily. His lips were against my hair, moving down in search of my mouth, and I was losing interest in gods and goddesses, Greek or otherwise.

All of a sudden he pushed me down flat and threw himself on top of me. Shock and physical pain brought a cry to my throat, but I couldn't let it out because my face was mashed against his shoulder. I couldn't breathe. There was a jagged rock digging into the small of my back, and his weight on my chest reminded me of an old medieval torture, the one where they pressed people to death. Then something hit me on the left ear, the only part of me, except my feet, that was exposed, and I understood. For a few minutes I thought the whole damned hillside was falling down on us.

The rattle and crash of falling rock finally stopped, and Jim lifted himself up. I took in a lovely deep breath, and let it out faster than I intended, as Jim collapsed on me again.

I squawked out a few useless questions, like "Are you hurt?" It was obvious that he was. He managed to roll off me, though, and sprawled onto his back, limp as a rag doll. There was blood trickling down his face from half a dozen places, most of them above the hairline.

I grabbed my dress—I had been lying on it—and started tearing it up.

"My God," I said. "That was close. What happened?"

"I would say that was obvious," said Jim.

"Rockslide. I know. But why then? The horse was long gone."

"Who cares?" Jim's voice was weaker. "A minor quake, maybe. I wouldn't have noticed. . . ."

I mopped the blood off his face. Most of the cuts were small ones. I thought it was shock that made his face such a funny color till I noticed the puddle of blood under his head.

He yelped when my fingers probed and found a long gash at the back of his head. The blood was coming out in a thick, steady stream. His hair was already soaked. I tore off another wad of cloth and held it against the wound. I was scared, but I don't think it showed in my voice.

"Look, you lie still. I'll go for help."

"I can walk. Let's get going, before I get any weaker."

I helped him up. His back, which had taken most of the punishment, was a mess, all scraped and bloody.

"There's a house down there," I said, pointing.

"No, thanks. They'll slap some goat dung on it and say a prayer. Chris has medical supplies."

We started down the hill, but we hadn't gone far before I knew he'd never make it to the village, not on his feet.

"We're not far from our house," I said, panting. "If you can get that far—"

He didn't have to get that far. A few minutes later Frederick appeared around a curve in the path. I had never been so glad to see him.

Frederick didn't seem to share my feelings. His brows drew together in a scowl, and he exclaimed, "Must you go about the countryside embracing like a pair of cheap hippies? Not only is it in poor taste—"

Jim chose that moment to fold up. We went down together, our knees buckling in perfect harmony, and it dawned on Frederick that things were not quite as they seemed.

"What happened?" he asked. His voice was only slightly less irritated.

"Can't you see he's hurt?" I snarled. "Don't stand there, give me a hand."

Frederick hauled Jim to his feet and draped a limp arm over his shoulders. I took the other arm and we started walking.

"Where are you planning to take him?" Frederick asked.

"Our place; it's the closest. You can go for the doctor while I—"

"There is no doctor," said Frederick distantly. "Not in the village. What happened to him?"

"Rockslide. I suppose part of the cliff was weakened by the quake."

"Ah. And may I inquire how it happens that you are unmarked, whereas he has cuts only on his back?"

It wasn't what he said, it was the way he said it.

"I am unmarked because he shielded me," I said shortly. "If it's any of your damn business."

"Hmph," said Frederick. "Save your breath. You'll need it, this stretch is rough."

It was rough, and steep; but I couldn't help noticing that it showed no signs of fresh disturbance. There had been no falls of rock anywhere—except right above where we happened to be lying.

I put the idea out of my mind. Living with Frederick was infecting me with his delusions of persecution.

Frederick had an extensive collection of medical supplies, including antibiotics, which you can buy in Europe without a prescription. He got to work on Jim with ruthless efficiency, ignoring Jim's groans and curses. The big cut wasn't as deep as I had feared, and after an examination that made Jim rise to new heights of profane comment, Frederick announced that there didn't seem to be a fracture or concussion. He then jabbed a hypodermic needle into a little sealed bottle of penicillin, and ordered me out of the room.

I stared at him. I was standing there holding bloody bandages and a basin of bloody water. My hands were bloodstained. I had watched the whole process without any signs of squeamishness. I couldn't understand why he was suddenly so considerate of my nonexistent sensitivities. Then Jim, who was lying on his stomach with his chin propped on his folded arms, turned his head painfully and winked at me.

"Oh, for God's sake," I said, catching on. "Really, Frederick, you are archaic."

I slammed the door behind me; but when I was outside I couldn't help laughing. This was a side of Frederick I had never seen. He was behaving like a stuffy, old-fashioned . . . Father.

I didn't feel like laughing anymore. But don't get me wrong, I didn't feel teary and sentimental either. I wasn't anxious for Frederick to develop paternal feelings about me—especially when the feelings all seemed to be negative.

I invited Jim to stay, realizing there was nothing for supper except those everlasting tin cans, but he insisted on going back to the hotel. Frederick agreed with him, pointing out that the path was tricky after dark, and that Jim shouldn't risk falling on his head a second time. I gave my kindly old father a long, thoughtful look. He returned it with interest.

The three of us started out. Jim was walking with the careful steadiness of a drunk who is not certain his head is tightly anchored to his neck. Frederick hadn't offered him any pain pills, not while I was around, anyway. We talked stiltedly— God knows what about, I wasn't listening, not even to myself. I was wondering what would happen when we ran into Sir Christopher, Frederick's old war buddy.

He was sitting on the hotel terrace when we reached the plaza. His bald head shone in the light of the lanterns Angelos had strung along the arbor. I rather expected Frederick to turn back then. But he didn't, he marched on, holding Jim by the arm, like a keeper returning an escaped lunatic. And it was in that spirit that he addressed Sir Christopher.

"Better keep an eye on him tonight," he remarked, without a word of greeting. "There is always the possibility of concussion."

Sir Christopher, always the perfect gent, had risen. He stared down at Jim's bowed head in understandable surprise, and then looked at Frederick.

"Hello, Frederick. Good of you to look after my young friend. What happened to him?"

All in order, you see—the greeting, the polite thank-you, the pertinent question. He even managed to nod and smile at me during the speech.

I explained about the rockslide, with a little tribute to Jim's quick-thinking courage, which had saved me from injury. It was now Frederick's turn to make a graceful comment acknowledging Jim's kindness to *his* young friend. He didn't, and I suppose nobody expected him to.

Sir Christopher shook his head. "I did warn you, I believe, about being in a ravine or under a cliff during a tremor."

"I don't think it was a quake," I said. "The rider dislodged some stones when he went by. Maybe others were loosened."

"Rider?" Sir Christopher repeated.

Jim sat up straight. He was looking better.

"You know, the old guy who rides, back in the hills. The one who lives in the villa on the headland." He turned to me. "I found out who he is, did I tell you? At least I found out *what* he is. German. They call him the Colonel."

Frederick was sitting to my right, balancing on two legs of the chair and staring at the darkening sky, as if to express his boredom with the lot of us. I wasn't looking at him when Jim spoke, but his reaction would have been hard to miss. The legs of the chair hit the ground with a crash. As I whirled around I saw that his face had gone gray. He tried to speak, but only a gurgle emerged from his gaping mouth. Then he fell forward onto the table, smashing Sir Christopher's coffee cup.

Chapter
7

MONDAY MORNING. THE USUAL ROUTINE. AWAKENED in the cold gray dawn by Frederick shaking my shoulder. . . .

I blinked at him. Then I sat up, which is not easy when you're zipped into a sleeping bag.

"What are you doing out of bed? I thought I told you—"

"Don't be ridiculous," said Frederick. "It's getting light. Hurry." He walked out of the room.

It had been too dark for me to see his face. His voice and his walk seemed to be normal; and yet I could have sworn that he had a light heart attack the previous night. I had a hell of a time getting him back to the house after he collapsed on the hotel terrace. He refused help, and anyway, Sir Christopher was too busy fussing over Jim to insist on accompanying us. Frederick was still shaky when I sent him off to bed; the fact that he let me order him around proved how shaken he was. Now the old rat was himself again, and I didn't know what I was going to do about him.

I figured he might have another heart attack if I frustrated him, so I dragged myself out of the sack and went to the kitchen. Frederick had boiled water, so I had a cup of coffee, watching him all the while.

I didn't like what I saw. He was moving with forced briskness, as if he were trying to prove something. I had not questioned him the night before; I couldn't third-degree a man in his condition. Now I decided I had to know.

"Do you feel all right?" I asked.

"Certainly."

"What made you pass out the way you did?"

"I have attacks now and then. The result of that lung condition, perhaps. Nothing to worry about."

"Then it wasn't what Jim said, about the German officer?"

Frederick made a sound that was probably supposed to be a light laugh. It was more like a sick hen cackling.

"What sort of trashy novels have you been reading?"

"I haven't read anything but books on archaeology for days," I said indignantly. "You don't even have a murder mystery in your library.

Look, Frederick, I can't go ahead with my work if I'm worrying about you. Sir Christopher told me about Crete—"

"Indeed. What did he say?"

"Just what happened. About your friend, the one who was killed."

"Vince." Frederick sat down at the table and reached for a jar of marmalade. "What about him?"

"Jim is his nephew," I said.

"I thought he might be. There is a distinct resemblance."

I looked at him incredulously. He sat there stolidly eating bread and marmalade. He had a passion for marmalade; it was the only food he really seemed to enjoy.

"Sir Christopher knows who I am," I said, forgetting about his presumed weak heart in my desire to jar his smug impassivity.

"That was to be expected. I suppose he guessed—challenged you—and you fell for it."

"Uh," I said, taken aback. It had been rather like that.

Frederick went on. "That doesn't matter, so long as he has no suspicions about your diving."

"Oh, but he does," I said. "He warned me to be careful. He said *you* wouldn't give a damn."

That got him. He started to speak, choked on a mouthful of bread, and had quite a struggle before he got it down.

"Damn his impudence," he exclaimed, still sputtering. "I hope you weren't fool enough to admit that too?"

"Oh, I denied it. I doubt that he believed me. But he said he wasn't planning to do anything about it."

"There is nothing he can do at this moment." Frederick brushed crumbs off his hands and stood up. "There is no law against swimming. The trouble will begin when you start using scuba gear. When do you think that will be?"

He was halfway to the door when he finished this speech; if I wanted to reply I had to follow him, so I did.

"What do you mean, when do *I* think? I can't begin till I get air tanks and the use of a compressor. The air in those tanks is only good for—"

"I know, I know. We'll have to go to Phira for them. One day this week, perhaps."

"And a boat," I went on. "I'm working some distance from shore now, and the distance will increase as I go on. If I do get in trouble, I want something to hold on to."

"Certainly, certainly," said Frederick agreeably. "I wonder. . . . How much can you accomplish without the scuba gear? I have heard of divers descending to almost two hundred feet without a self-contained air supply."

"I heard of it too," I said. "I also heard that the

diver spent considerable time in the hospital afterward."

The sun was up by the time we started for the bay of the villa. The bright rays dazzled my eyes. I was still seething. Frederick was being unusually obtuse this morning, and his remarks were more than normally provocative. Was he trying to keep my mind off certain subjects? If he thought I intended to nag him about his health he was mistaken. Right then I wouldn't have cared if he had fallen down and breathed his last at my feet.

He could keep me from talking about the other subject, but he couldn't prevent me from thinking. I could see the pattern. It was pretty clear—and pretty queer, too. Wasn't it a coincidence that all these people should have gathered in the same remote spot at the same time? Two of the Three Musketeers, the heroes of the Cretan underground—and the surviving relative of the third hero? I might have accepted that as coincidence, or rather as the consequence of the interests and specialties of these men. But Frederick's reaction to the news that the mystery man in the villa was a former German officer stretched coincidence to the breaking point.

I got that far in my reasoning and then my common sense rebelled. I mean, it was like the plot of one of those trashy novels, as Frederick called them. It would really be too much if the man in the villa turned out to be one of Frederick's former enemies from Crete.

We had reached the bay by the time I reached this point in my thinking, so I gave it up. I didn't have enough facts to make sensible deductions anyway.

Frederick perched himself on a rock, with an air of exaggerated patience. I passed him without speaking, adjusted my mask and fins, and went into the water.

As always, it cooled me off in more senses than one. It was too beautiful and too peaceful down there for rancor to last. Nor could I pursue the train of thought that had occupied me on the way to the beach. I had to concentrate on what I was doing. The farther out I went, the more jumble there was on the bottom. Once my heart leaped at the sight of a long, straight ridge of tumbled stone that could have been a wall. Examination proved I was wrong. I disturbed my first octopus, though. He came boiling out of a hole in the stone, exuding ink. He was about a foot across, tentacles included, and he was as cute as could be. I wondered how you went about making friends with an octopus. I had already found one buddy, a big fat blue-and-white-striped fish of a species I didn't recognize. He had been following me with an air of inquisitive interest, probably hoping I would stir up some food for him.

I finished my crossing and pulled myself out

on the rocks at the far side to rest. Frederick was still sitting in the same spot. When I waved, he flapped a limp arm at me.

I hadn't gone far on my way back before my friend the fish joined me. I decided to call him Alice; his facial markings gave him a distinct resemblance to Alice Cooper. We went down together to look at a clump of unusually luxuriant anemones; plants will often cluster on decayed wood. This time they had not. When I surfaced I saw that Frederick had disappeared.

I guess I had been half expecting some such development, because I wasn't surprised. I wasn't even very angry, just disgusted.

I was hanging there, treading water and cursing, when something made me look around. I don't know why I should have looked in the direction of the villa. I had almost forgotten it was there; I had seen no signs of life. Now, however, there was a figure standing on the cliff looking down.

It was a man. I could see his shape but not his features. Naturally I connected his appearance with the disappearance of Frederick. The villainous German officer.

I might or might not be trespassing, but my best move was to hope he hadn't seen me and get out as fast as I could. I swam underwater most of the way and got out in the shelter of a rock. He was halfway down the cliff when I looked back;

the darkness of his body stood out against the chalk-white ash.

Rather than risk being seen climbing the cliff I swam around the headland and headed for our own bay. I lingered deliberately at the house, eating a huge breakfast, taking my time. It must have been almost noon before I got to the excavation.

Frederick was in a terrible mood. I would have liked to believe that he was worried about my late arrival, but I knew him well enough to doubt that. The men were visibly amused at my tardiness; Nicholas gave me a grin and a wink when I joined his crew.

We were still digging up pots. Frederick thought that the area we were working in had been a storeroom, with another such room above. The reason why the pots we found were so badly shattered was that they had fallen when the upper floor collapsed. Since all I had to look forward to when these scraps were cleared was another layer of pots, I was not working with much enthusiasm. It was a warm, sleepy day, and everyone was moving slowly.

All of a sudden Nicholas stood up. I stared at him from my squatting position and saw that his face had gone queer and pale. He screamed out something I didn't understand, although I had been picking up some Greek. Then he took off at full speed, followed by the other men.

I ran too. Mine not to reason why. But it took me a few seconds to get myself together, so I was still within the confines of the ravine when I heard the roaring. That was what it sounded like, the bellowing roar of a huge animal. Then the ground heaved.

The tremor was more severe than the ones I had felt the day before. It knocked me flat. That's a good place to be during an earthquake, flat on the ground, although I would have preferred a more open area. A few rocks fell, but not many.

I continued to lie there even after the movement stopped. I didn't stir until someone shook me.

"Get up," said Frederick.

"No."

"Why not?"

"I feel good here."

"Don't be a fool," Frederick said impatiently. "There may be another shock. We must get out into the open."

We went back to the house. Frederick was grumbling all the way; he seemed to feel a personal resentment against the earth for interfering with his work.

"The men won't be back today," he complained. "Another wasted afternoon. Perhaps you might spend a few more hours—"

"Oh, no," I said firmly. "In fact, I'm not going in again unless you get a boat. If you're going to walk out on me the way you did this morning. . . . Did you run away because that man showed up?"

"What man?"

"The one in the villa. The Colonel. Don't tell me you didn't see him."

"I did not. More important, did he see you? On no account must you allow him to—"

"Why not?"

Frederick shrugged. "Why, legally, I suppose we are trespassing."

"That's the only reason?"

"What other reason could there be?" inquired Frederick.

I decided there was no point in going on with this sort of thing, so I went to the village.

The church was open, and people were going in and out. A sizable crowd had collected. People clustered together, talking in low voices. When I passed they looked up and smiled in response to my "hello," but the smiles were stiff and the eyes avoided mine.

I figured they were worried about the quakes, and I didn't blame them. I headed for the hotel to see how Jim was doing.

It was the first time I had been inside the place, and the appearance of the lobby made me glad I wasn't staying there. Chickens were roosting on the chairs, and my sandals stuck to the floor. Nobody was at the desk, so I banged on the bell and shouted. Finally a woman came out of the back, wiping her hands on her apron.

I had heard Jim speak of Angelos' wife. He said she did most of the work, acting as cook, chambermaid, and bellboy. Her name was Helena. I had felt sorry for her because Angelos struck me as a typical peasant-type male, the kind that expects a wife to work all day and lie still all night; but when I saw Helena I decided she was probably a match for her burly husband. She was a massively built woman who had weathered middle age better than women usually do when they work like mules. Her hair was streaked with gray, but it was still thick and shiny, and the black hairs on her upper lip added to her charm.

After I had tried to explain what I wanted and had received no response except a blank stare, I began to wonder if all her strength had gone to her biceps. I was about to give up when Jim came down the stairs.

"I thought I heard your dulcet tones," he said, with a smile. "Are you calling on the sick and wounded? How nice."

I looked him over. Except for the white bump of bandage on top of his head, he appeared normal.

"I see you're okay, so I'll leave," I said.

"Have some coffee or something. No more work today. I suppose your crew departed too?"

I nodded. Jim spoke to Helena, asking her if she

could bring us some coffee, out on the terrace. He got a much livelier reaction than I had. She rolled her eyes at Jim and giggled. I studied Jim with a new interest. He had somewhat the same effect on me—although I knew better than to giggle and bat my eyelashes—but it hadn't occurred to me that he might affect most women that way.

We sat down at one of the tables on the terrace. The crowd was still moving, in little restless eddies, like water in a pond after it has been disturbed. From where we sat I could see the lights inside the dark cavern of the church.

"Lots of candles being lit today," Jim said. "I wonder who the patron saint of earthquakes is."

"Is that why they seem so queer and restless?"

"I guess so. They seem to be unusually disturbed. I mean, tremors aren't all that unusual around here."

"There's Nicholas," I said, pointing. "He felt the quake coming, Jim. At least he started to run before I heard or felt anything."

Nicholas turned, as people will when you are looking at them and talking about them. I beckoned. He came toward us, and Jim invited him to sit down. He gave me a rather sheepish grin. Like many of the men he had beautiful white teeth. He spoke to Jim, gesticulating.

"He wants to apologize," Jim translated. "He says he should have warned you, but when the—

damn, the word is hard to translate—the queasiness, I guess, comes over him, he can't think."

"Queasiness? Ask him what it feels like."

Nicholas was watching me anxiously. I patted him on the arm and smiled, and he smiled back, looking relieved.

He and Jim talked for a while, and then Nicholas rose. He turned to me and said, speaking slowly and clearly, "Not more. All gone now, today. All right?"

"Good," I said heartily.

He understood that. We bobbed our heads and grinned at each other, and then he walked off, with the hip-swinging swagger characteristic of the men of the island.

"You got that," Jim said.

"No more quakes today. How does he know, Jim?"

"He says it's an inherited talent. Lots of the islanders have it. He can't describe the feeling very well, but apparently he starts to feel sick. Like a migraine, I guess. Frankly, I find it hard to believe."

"But it happened. He yelled something and started to run long before I heard the rumbling. I didn't hear it yesterday, by the way."

"Yesterday's shocks were milder. When it's a bad quake the sound is quite loud. You can understand why the ancients thought of Poseidon as the Earthshaker and compared the noise with the roaring of the sacred bulls."

"Yes, that's what it sounded like."

I shivered. The concept was disturbing, now that I had actually heard the sound.

"Did Nicholas say why this quake bothers the villagers so much?"

"He was evasive," Jim said, frowning. "I gather they expect more action. A new vent has opened on Nea Kaimeni."

"Nea—oh, the island out in the bay?"

"Yes. It's the cone of the new volcano that arose after the old one blew itself up. Hell, Sandy, don't look so apprehensive. Volcanoes smoke all the time."

"They erupt all the time too," I said. "How can anybody live in a place like this?"

"People live in the craziest places," Jim said cheerfully. "The peasants go right back to the slopes of Vesuvius after each eruption. And what about Californians? Scientists have been predicting for years that San Francisco is about to collapse into the Bay."

"I think Californians are crazy too," I said.

"How's Dr. Frederick?" Jim asked.

"Trying to change the subject? He's okay."

"He sure looked bad last night."

"I asked him, this morning, about the man in the villa."

"What did he say?"

"As usual, nothing. He laughed at me when I suggested your remark had brought on his attack."

"It is pretty farfetched," Jim muttered.

"Aha. You are thinking what I am thinking."

"It's because we were raised on bad melodrama," Jim said, with a wry smile. "TV crime series, James Bond. In a thriller the guy at the villa would turn out to be the Gestapo officer who pursued your boss across the mountains of Crete, yelling *'Achtung,'* or *'Gotterdämmerung,'* or whatever TV German villains yell. . . ."

"What does your boss say about it? He was in Crete too."

"Why should he have anything to say? Our cast of characters is purely hypothetical, love. The man in the villa is probably some retired merchant who has never even set foot on Crete. He may not be a colonel or even an army officer."

"True." I felt the same relaxation, the same sense of security I always felt with Jim. I wondered if this was the time to tell him that Frederick wasn't only my employer but my father. But it was so peaceful, I hated to disturb the mood. The crowd in the plaza was thinning. People were returning to their normal pursuits, as if the danger was over. I leaned back in my chair. Neither of us spoke for a while, and the silence was comfortable, the way it is when two people who know each other so well they don't have to make idle conversation.

Jim saw her first. He sat up with a start.

She came into the plaza, and, as before, the people scattered before her. She was wearing beautifully tailored white slacks and a printed blouse that strained across her bosom. She jangled with jewelry. A scarf of fiery mustard yellow held her black hair. She was walking so fast the ends of the scarf blew out.

She came straight toward us. Jim got to his feet as she stopped at our table, but she didn't look at him, she was staring at me.

"Ariadne," she said. "Yes. It is true. I could not believe when they told me. But, as always, they are right. Welcome back."

Chapter
8

I THINK MOST PEOPLE WOULD HAVE FOUND THAT speech disconcerting. For me the effect was absolutely devastating. It was not only what she said, it was the way she was looking at me, with the queerest mixture of longing and hostility. I had heard of devouring eyes, but I had always thought it was a figure of speech, till then, when her black eyes fastened on my face like claws.

Jim pulled out a chair.

"Won't you join us?" he said. "My name is Jim Sanchez. This is Sandy Bishop. Madame . . . ?"

"Kore." She didn't look at him.

"Will you have coffee, madame? Ouzo? Wine?"

His insistent courtesy finally won her attention. When she turned those eyes away I felt as if an actual physical restraint had been removed.

She wasn't as tall as I had thought. Next to Jim she appeared quite short. She looked up at him with her head tilted. It might have been instinctive coquetry, for, as I had noticed, he was that sort of man. Or it might have been appraisal.

"Coffee," she said. "Thank you. You forgive the informality, yes? In this small place we outsiders must be allies."

The smile she gave him held a hint of the sexual allure she must have possessed once upon a time. She had lost most of it. Her figure was still good, if you like the Junoesque type, but at close range her face was a sad ruin. The fiery black eyes were her only remaining beauty; her cheeks and forehead were a map of wrinkles. Instead of camouflaging the disaster, her heavy makeup merely emphasized its marks.

Jim held the chair for her and then seated himself.

"Allies?" he repeated. "Against what enemy, madame?"

"Is not the enemy always the same?"

"I think not." Jim was watching her curiously. "The age-old struggle between evil and good is eternal, but the definitions vary, depending on which side you happen to be."

She laughed. She had a pretty, tinkling laugh.

"But what an absurd conversation. I do not mean to be so serious. I express only my pleasure to find a breath of the outside world. The world of fashion, newspapers, reason. These people talk only of fish and their foolish superstitions."

"What kind of superstitions?" Jim was carrying the conversation. I was still tongue-tied.

"Every kind. Thera is the home of the *vrykolas*, the vampire. Sometimes the men do not work the fields because there are ghosts. And you have seen"—she opened her eyes wide—"how they are afraid of me. Perhaps they think I am *vrykolas*, an old harmless woman like me."

"You could never be old, Madame Kore," Jim said. "And no beautiful woman is ever harmless."

"And they say Americans are without gallantry." She smiled at him. "That, too, I miss. The men of Zoa run from me as if I were a demon. Not that a woman would wish their compliments. . . ."

"Without offense, madame, may I suggest that you encourage their fear? Even your name. . . ."

"Kore, the maiden," she said dreamily. "The mother, in one of her many aspects. Persephone, bride of Hell. . . . But of course it is not my real name! My real name I have forgotten, it is so dull." She swung on me, so suddenly that I shrank back. "A woman may choose her name to suit herself, is that not true?"

Before I could answer, Jim intervened again. He was frowning, aware of the strain between us, although he didn't understand it—any more than I did—and was doing his best to intercept Kore's verbal thrusts.

"You chose an ominous name," he said. "Especially in view of the superstitions you mention. And do you always wear those ornaments?"

He indicated the bracelets she wore, one on each arm. I hadn't noticed them before. They were not simple circles around her wrists, but coils of gold that went halfway up her forearms and ended in serpents' heads. The eyes were tiny rubies.

"I am fond of jewelry." She toyed with the chains on her breast. The ruby eyes of the golden serpents flashed.

A movement in the doorway attracted my attention, and I saw Sir Christopher standing there. I wondered how long he had been watching us. When he caught my eye he came toward us. Jim started to perform introductions.

"I know Madame," Sir Christopher said, bowing over her hand.

"You never mentioned her to me," Jim said.

Sir Christopher looked surprised at his belligerent tone.

"I don't believe the subject ever came up."

"You do not talk of me?" Kore laughed. "How unflattering."

"Archaeologists are a dull lot," Sir Christopher said with a smile. "But I'm sure the subject would have arisen sooner or later. You are a prominent citizen, madame."

"So prominent it makes me wonder what you are doing here," Jim said. "A woman like you burying herself in this remote place."

"But you do not know my circumstances."

"No," Jim said encouragingly.

"Someday I will tell you. When I know you better. How long do you stay on the island?"

Sir Christopher answered.

"Another month, perhaps. I have commitments in England."

"An Honors List, perhaps?" She smiled at him.

Sir Christopher became the image of the well-bred Englishman expressing modesty.

Jim laughed. "There have been rumors," he said, smiling at his boss.

"Only rumors," said Sir Christopher. "Actually, I must prepare for a lecture tour in the States and Canada. It was arranged some time ago."

"And you?" She turned to me. "How long do you stay?"

"I don't know." Damn the woman; I was actually stammering. "A few weeks, maybe. . . ."

"Longer, I think." She stood up, in a sudden decisive movement that caught Sir Christopher with a half-spoken comment on his lips. "I must go now, I cannot stay," she said. But she didn't leave. She stood there looking down at me with the same avid fascination that had marked the first moments of our meeting.

"The sea king's daughter," she said softly. "It is

fitting. I came to warn you to go away, but now. . . . Yes, I think you will stay longer than you meant, Ariadne. Give my greeting to Minos."

And away she went.

"She knows," Sir Christopher exclaimed, staring after her. "How does she know?"

"Know what?" Jim demanded.

Sir Christopher appeared not to hear him. I had never seen the man so shaken. His lean cheeks were flushed with anger or embarrassment.

"Our old code names," he said, addressing me. "They were a conceit of Frederick's. Taken from Cretan legend. I was Daedalus, Durkheim was Poseidon; and Minos was your—"

He stopped, shooting Jim a guilty look. I think Jim was beginning to catch on anyway, but that look and halt, as explicit as a hand clapped over the mouth, finished the job. Jim's face reddened, and I had no doubt as to the emotion that caused the flow of blood to his cheeks.

"Is your name really Ariadne?" he demanded.

"Yes," I mumbled, staring at the tablecloth as if I were trying to memorize its varied stains. "But I never use the name, I hate it. Jim, I want to tell you—"

"You don't have to tell me." Jim's voice was flat with controlled anger. "If I hadn't been so damn stupid I would have seen it right away. Who else but the bastard's daughter would come out here to work for him? What the hell kind of mother do you have that she would let you do it?"

It was such an absurd question that it would have made me laugh under any other circumstances. Now it served as an excuse to turn my anger into outrage.

"You leave my mother out of this!" I shouted.

"Children, children," Sir Christopher began.

"Children, hell," Jim yelled—only he didn't say "hell." "You shut up! I'm sorry, Chris, I shouldn't have said that, but that is really adding insult to injury. You knew, and you didn't tell me, and now you've got the nerve to—"

"If you were too stupid to figure it out, why should he tell you?" I interrupted. I rose, with my chin in the air. "I apologize, Sir Christopher, for this boorish outburst. You have behaved like a gentleman throughout. Good night."

I stalked off into the gathering darkness. My chin was still in the air and I kept stumbling over the cobblestones. It wasn't until I reached the edge of the plaza that I realized I had succumbed. I had apologized to Sir Christopher.

II

Frederick and I had our dinner out of cans after all. I was so upset I didn't stop to buy food in the village. The long, bumpy walk back to the house gave me time to regret my rudeness to Jim. Remorse demanded a scapegoat, and it wasn't hard to find someone toward whom my self-anger could be turned. I burst into the house, slamming doors, and confronted Frederick, who was in his usual chair in the kitchen. He looked up, his eyes widening, as I stormed in.

"You," I said, panting with anger. I added a few epithets no nice daughter should apply to a parent. "What kind of game are you playing? How could you drag me into this? Give me one good reason why I shouldn't pack my bags tomorrow morning and leave."

I had to stop to breathe, and Frederick, who had been waiting for his chance, said coldly,

"I haven't the faintest idea what you are raving about. If you will calm yourself and speak coherently, perhaps I can—"

"Damn coherence!" I shouted—only I didn't say "damn."

Frederick looked severe.

"Such language is disgusting from a young girl. Sit down and hold your tongue. If you don't, I will assume you are hysterical and deal with you accordingly."

I think he would have slapped me, at that; but it wasn't fear of the threat that made me subside. My rage had blown itself out. I have a hasty temper, but it is short-lived. I sat down in the nearest chair and glowered at him.

"That woman," I said. "Don't tell me she doesn't know you. She knows my name. She called me Ariadne. And she sends her greeting to you, Minos. Is that really what you called yourself? If you ask me, it was pretty corny."

"So it was Kore," Frederick said coolly. "She has changed a great deal. I had hoped—"

"You'd hoped it wasn't. Why? Who is she? Or rather, what was she—to you?"

"Nothing that concerns you," Frederick said. "I knew her for a short time many years ago—yes, in Crete. And yes, we were corny, if that is the word you prefer. We were young. The names seemed appropriate."

"Minos, the sea king," I said. "So that's why you named me Ariadne. I'm surprised, Frederick. I wouldn't have expected such a poetic touch from you."

"You know nothing about me," Frederick said, in a queer, flat voice. "But you are ready to judge me. The cruelty and intolerance of youth—"

"I'm not judging you for what you did. I don't care about that, it's over and done with. I question what you are doing now. I'm afraid. . . . No, not afraid; I'm apprehensive, because I don't understand what is happening. I don't understand that woman. Is she crazy? She said the strangest things."

"What things?"

I repeated some of Kore's remarks. Frederick listened with interest.

"She does sound a bit mad," he agreed. "She was an ignorant, superstitious peasant girl when I knew her. Astonishingly beautiful, of course, but virtually illiterate. Now her beauty is gone, and although she has acquired a veneer of sophistication, the peasant girl is basically unchanged. Quite understandable. I don't see why such nonsense should make you apprehensive."

"You didn't hear her. And what was the point of the snake bracelets? Jim seemed to think there was something meaningful about them."

"Ah, did he? Interesting." Frederick got up and began opening cans. It was the first time he had ever offered to do any of the menial chores around the house, but after he had opened a can of peaches and one of tomato paste, I took the can opener away from him and started putting together a halfway balanced meal. Frederick went on talking.

"Yes, it would be interesting if Kore's mania has taken that form. The roots of it go quite far back; she called herself Kore when I knew her. It seemed to suit that dark beauty of hers, and the position she had chosen, in defiance of custom and loyalty. . . . Kore, as you know, was one of the names of Persephone, the daughter of Demeter, who was stolen away by Pluto, king of Hell. The grieving mother, who was goddess of grain and vegetation, refused to fertilize the new crops unless the gods intervened and restored her child. They did so; but Pluto tricked his young bride into eating a pomegranate, and by virtue of its magic she was forced to spend half the year in the Underworld—thus accounting for the drear winter months. In the spring the maiden returns to her mother, and the rejoicing goddess allows the new shoots to appear."

He took a big bite of the tuna fish I shoved in front of him.

I said impatiently, "I know all that, I had to study Greek legends in school. What about the snakes?"

Frederick put down his fork and looked at me critically.

"After all I have taught you you ought to know the answer to that. Kore and Demeter are two aspects of the same Cretan goddess, the mother and maiden, mistress of life and death. Surely you have seen the statuettes of the Cretan mother goddess, with the serpents twining around her arms. It appears that Kore, in her mature years, has very properly assumed the role of mother rather than maiden—a title to which she lost the right long before I knew her."

I decided to overlook the cattiness in the last sentence.

"You mean she thinks she's a snake goddess?" I demanded.

"The crudity of youth," Frederick muttered. "Actually, her fantasy seems to be fairly consistent. No doubt she is terrorizing these simple peasants by pretending to have occult powers. Many of them still worship the old gods in their hearts, although they call them by the names of the saints."

"Jim said he'd heard someone refer to her as Potnia. That's a Greek title; at least it appears in the Linear B tablets, which are Greek. I thought you said the goddess was Minoan."

"Minoan-Mycenean connections are well known," Frederick said. "The Myceneans were certainly Greek, but they derived a certain amount of their culture from the Minoans. After Knossos and the other Cretan centers were destroyed by the explosion at Thera, a Mycenean dynasty ruled at Knossos for a time. The last Minos—the word is a title, like the Egyptian Pharaoh, not a name—was Greek. Like his predecessors he worshiped the mother goddess, and his daughter—your namesake—was priestess of the goddess. Your name means 'Most Holy'; were you aware of that?"

"No," I said unenthusiastically.

"You might read Levy's study of Stone Age religion and its effect on later religious beliefs," Frederick went on, in his lecturing voice. "It seems obvious that—"

"Never mind," I interrupted. "You've already

told me more than I wanted to know. How about answering some more important questions? The man in the villa—"

"His identity is irrelevant," Frederick said. He rose, closing his book. "If you choose to leave, I can't prevent you. Assuming, of course, that you have enough money for a return ticket . . ."

I stared at him in unwilling admiration.

"My god, you are an unscrupulous rat," I said.

"I'm going to bed," said Frederick.

If there had been a rack or thumbscrew handy, I would have considered applying them. Nothing short of torture could make him talk when he didn't want to. And, knowing Frederick, I suspected even the rack wouldn't do much good.

I was awakened in the cold gray dawn by someone shaking me.

"Hurry, it is getting light," said Frederick.

I got up. What can you do with a man like that?

Chapter
9

FOR THE NEXT FEW DAYS FREDERICK STAYED ON WATCH while I swam. He still hadn't done anything about a boat, and I didn't push. The man at the villa was watching me. I had seen him on the cliff top, and once a flash of reflected light indicated he was using binoculars. I was pretty sure he had not noticed Frederick, who always chose a perch where he could not be seen from the villa. There seemed to be no objection to my presence, but I was afraid that if I brought a boat or dinghy to the bay, the watcher would suspect that I was not swimming for pleasure.

Why was I going on with a pursuit I considered both dangerous and futile? I can see now that the answer is a lot more complicated than I realized at the time. For one thing, I didn't really believe it was all that dangerous. I was young enough then to have a child's faith in my own invulnerability. As for my feelings about Frederick—well, psychiatrists use the word ambivalent. That's putting it mildly. I was never conscious of it at the time, but what I really wanted was to find his treasure for him single-handed. Then I could walk away, free. I suppose it sounds silly, but that's how I felt.

However, I had a more practical reason for continuing. I had found a pot.

You might think, from the way I have been sneering at pots, that this would not be an exciting discovery. This wasn't an ordinary pot, though. It was an amphora, a whole one, and it was a beauty.

I found it on Tuesday, almost as soon as I got into the water. It was half sunk in the sand at the base of the cliff. My friend Alice the fish actually found it. He and I had become quite matey. In fact, he was a nuisance; I had to push him out of the way when I investigated objects on the bottom, and he was waiting for me every morning when I went in. That morning—Tuesday—he nudged me and flipped away as if he wanted to play tag. I went after him and there it was—a symmetrical black hole, too round to be anything but man-made. It was the mouth of the amphora.

I scraped the sand away with my hands. In the translucent water the painted designs stood out as if they had been freshly retouched—spirals

and bands of orange and black, and a row of nau-
tilus shells circling the shoulder of the pot. Two of
the handles were still intact.

I had a coil of nylon line with me, but I didn't
dare use it for fear that any strain on the handles
might snap them off. Nor could I empty the pot;
there might be something inside, buried under
the sand that had drifted in. I just about killed
myself lifting it. Frederick came running to help
when I neared the shore. He was incoherent with
excitement. This was not an ordinary storage vessel, but a luxury item, one that might have been
used in a nobleman's home.

For the next two days I found nothing, but the
infection had seized me. I would have spent all
day in the water if I could.

I think it was Thursday afternoon when I went
to the village again. I was getting sick of canned
food. At least that's what I told myself. Actually, I
was hoping to see Jim.

I hung around the plaza for a while, but he was
nowhere in sight. The shops were just reopening
from the long siesta. I bought fish and tomatoes
and lentils and onions and olives, and then I
bought a straw bag to put everything in, since the
newspapers in which my purchases were
wrapped were getting soggy. I bought some postcards, too—and then realized there was nobody I
could send them to.

I had written to Betsy when I first arrived,

telling her to forward mail to the hotel in Zoa. So far nothing had come, but that wasn't surprising. Jim had told me that mail sometimes took weeks to get here from the States. I hadn't thought about it then, but as I looked foolishly at the brightly colored pictures of Phira perched on the multicolored cliff, I realized that I was truly cut off from my family and home. A wave of homesickness washed over me. How could I find out if anything happened to Dad or Mother? How could they reach me? It was that thought that made me determined to see Jim if I had to wait all day. I wasn't going to let pride cut me off from the sole source of warmth I had found in this faraway place.

It was still early. He probably had not left work yet. I sat down on the terrace to wait for him.

I waited for quite a while. At first I was too preoccupied with my mournful thoughts to notice anything else, but finally I realized that nobody had come to take my order. Eventually Angelos came out; I ordered coffee, and he brought it, but he didn't linger, as he usually did, and he didn't smile, either.

His behavior brought into focus something I had been too distracted to notice earlier—the behavior of the other villagers whom I had encountered while shopping. Now that I thought about it, they had seemed unusually sober and uncommunicative. Usually they were very friendly people; I would try out my new Greek vocabulary, which was always received with cries of admiration, no matter how bad the pronunciation. But today . . .

I forgot about it then. Jim was coming across the plaza.

He came straight toward me, his face serious. I felt the way I had the first time I was in a school play. Butterflies were ricocheting around in my insides.

Jim sat down. "Hi," he said.

"Hi," I said.

Then both of us started to talk at once.

"Jim, I'm sorry about—"

"Sandy, I want to apologize for—"

We both burst out laughing, and Jim took hold of my hand.

"I acted like a jerk," he said.

"Right," I agreed.

"How about you? Nancy Drew on a case. Why all the mystery?"

"It's a long story."

"I've got all day," Jim said, smiling.

He looked tired and hot and dusty. Dark patches of perspiration stained his crumpled shirt, and chalk dust whitened his brown hair like premature gray streaks.

"No, you don't," I said repentantly. "I bet you want to shower and change."

He laughed. "Shower! You know not whereof

you speak, spoiled child of civilization. That bowl of lukewarm water can wait. Talk."

"My mother left Frederick when I was about two," I said. "I hadn't seen him since, until last winter. She married again. I've got a sensational stepfather, whom I adore. Neither one of them knows where I am, incidentally. They think I'm touring Europe."

"I'm sorry I said that about your mother," Jim said.

"You were upset."

"Yeah. Well, that's very enlightening. When you decide to open up, you don't stall around, do you?"

"I hate lying," I said vehemently. "I felt rotten about having had to lie to you."

"Then why did you? No, don't tell me; Frederick insisted."

I nodded.

"For a supposedly brilliant scholar he's singularly stupid about some things," Jim said. "Did either of you think you could keep your activities a secret? Small towns are all alike. Everybody in the village knows you're diving."

"Oh, damn," I said. "Everybody?"

"Yes, and it's lucky for you you weren't around when I found out. I was so mad I almost came calling on you with a club. I may yet. If you broke an arm or a leg, you'd have to stop this nonsense."

"It's not nonsense," I said defensively. "Frederick thinks—"

I stopped just in time—but it wouldn't have mattered. Jim was laughing.

"Frederick thinks there are ruins out in the bay. So do a lot of other people, you little turkey. But nobody else is fool enough to risk his neck looking for them without proper equipment, not to mention official sanction."

"I'm not doing anything wrong. Not until I— My God, what's the matter with me? I keep blurting out all these things."

"It's me," Jim said proudly. "I bring out your true, honest nature, and you can't lie to me." He sobered. "Sandy, I know all. Your old man was down on the pier the other day talking to one of the men about air tanks and compressors. Platon is an honest crook, he'll supply you and keep his mouth shut if he's bribed well enough. But you can't hope to keep it a secret from the others. Promise me you won't use that gear. In fact, I want your promise that you'll stop diving altogether unless I'm around."

"You?"

"Frederick is no damn good; he's got a weak heart or something. If you got in trouble he couldn't possibly rescue you. In fact, if what Chris says about him is true, he might not even try."

I should have resented that, but I couldn't. My

expression reflected my memories of the times Frederick had simply walked off and left me alone in the water. Jim, watching my face, swore.

"I thought so," he said. "Look, Sandy, I'll spend as much time diving with you as I can spare. Not only will I not horn in on anything you find, but I won't even tell Chris what we're doing. I can't be any fairer than that, can I?"

It was not only a fair offer, it was magnificently generous. I knew how uncomfortable his position would be if we did make a major discovery and Sir Christopher learned that Jim had helped, unbeknown to him. I was so tempted I felt dizzy. But I realized what Frederick would say if I proposed the scheme to him. I knew Jim was trustworthy. Frederick wouldn't trust his own mother.

"What will you do if I say 'no thanks'?" I asked.

Jim's smile faded. "Report you to the port officer in Phira."

"You wouldn't."

"Don't make me, Sandy. I'd like to see you away from here. Oh, don't give me that hurt look, you know I'm crazy about you. I want to see you and go on seeing you. Only not here. There's something peculiar going on around here; your stupid diving is only part of the problem."

"What do you mean?"

"Haven't you noticed the way the villagers are acting? Don't worry, I'm not going to say 'the natives are restless.' They aren't restless. They're afraid. It can't be the quakes or the volcanic activity out in the bay, they're used to that."

"What, then?"

"It's that woman—Kore, or whatever she calls herself. I managed to worm a few more confidences out of some of the men after our conversation with her. The picture I'm building up is somewhat disconcerting. Her boyfriend at the villa *is* a former German officer. Sure, it's been a long time since that particular war; but the older people still remember the occupation, and German military types are resented. And the Greeks have several words for women like Kore, who went over to the enemy. Her position, and her lover's, would be difficult here if she didn't have some hold over the villagers. That hold is fear. She's playing on their superstitions and doing a hell of a good job of it."

"They think she's a witch? That woman in her Dior slacks?"

"It's more complicated than that," Jim said soberly. "They believe she has magical powers, yes; but they don't regard her as a witch. She's something much more dangerous. I don't know precisely how she convinced them. It can't only be the way she talks, although that's disturbing enough. You heard her the other night, rambling on about the bride of Hell."

"But why should the raving of a half-crazy old woman worry you?"

Jim shook his head. "Never mind Kore's fantasies. There are enough solid facts to worry me. How did she know who you were?"

"Oh, hell, let's not beat around the bush," I said. "We're both thinking the same thing. It's unavoidable. She was in Crete when your uncle and Sir Christopher and Frederick were there. Frederick admitted as much the other night."

"He did? What did you do, tie him up and burn his feet?"

I had to laugh, the question was so in line with my appraisal of my father.

"No, he talked freely, but that was about all he said. How about your boss?"

"I haven't asked him."

"It's possible he didn't know her. You're really jumping to conclusions if you think the man in the villa was in Crete during the occupation, and that Kore was his mistress even then. Obviously she knew Frederick in his secret-agent days or she wouldn't know his alias. That suggests she was a member of the Cretan underground. She might have been in contact with Frederick but not with either of the others."

"It's possible," Jim said.

"Well, it's useless to speculate about it. Weren't you the one who was telling me we shouldn't dwell on the dead past?" I glanced toward the bay, where the first star of evening was now visible. "Geez, it's late. I've got to get this fish home before it goes bad."

"I'll walk you home." Jim rose.

I stared at him in surprise. "Why, sir, I do believe your intentions are serious! I'd ask you to supper, only Frederick—"

"I couldn't. Chris is really cracking down; I've got eight hours of work ahead of me tonight. But I've got time to see you get home all right."

He looked taller than usual, standing so close to me; I had to tilt my head back to look up into his face.

"You never offered to walk me home before," I reminded him. "Jim, you're being silly. I'm a lot safer on that back road than I would be on the streets of an American city."

We stared at one another for a moment. Neither of us was smiling. Finally Jim shook himself, like a dog coming out of the water.

"I'm fey," he muttered. "Or getting senile, or something. You're right, of course. See you, Sandy."

He took me by the shoulder and kissed me, quickly but thoroughly.

I was in a pleasant daze as I threaded my way through the steep back streets and onto the road above the village. The view toward the west was sensational, with the black bulk of the mountain outlined against a sunset of garish crimson and copper. Such sunsets are caused by dust in the air; and a faint unease shadowed my mood as I remembered the steaming volcano out in the bay.

But nothing could mar my happiness for long. Jim and I were on good terms again, and I had nothing more to hide from him.

I was almost at the house when I heard the hoofbeats. This time I knew what they were, and except for making sure I was a good safe distance from the cliff I didn't worry about them. The crescendo of thundering hooves increased and then I saw them, on the upper trail. The man was bent low over the horse's neck and they were going hell for leather. For an instant I saw the flying forms black against the sunset, and then they were gone, down the hill into the gathering night.

I walked on, but my euphoric mood was gone. It was a funny time of night to go riding, especially at such a breakneck pace. The man rode as if pursued. I wondered what Furies were on his trail. The ghastly hags who had pursued Orestes after he murdered his mother were symbols of guilt, so psychologists say. Maybe they weren't symbols to the Greeks, though. The Greeks believed in monsters. My imagination re-created the flying figures of horse and rider, and added shadowy snake-haired forms, flapping black bat wings.

I broke into a trot. The shadow of the mountain lay dark across the ground.

II

When Frederick and I left the house the next morning, we found Jim waiting for us. He was wearing swimming trunks, a guileless smile, and a fine assortment of goose pimples.

The look he got from Frederick should have made him hot enough. I said hastily, before Frederick could turn the look on me,

"Why, Jim, what a surprise. What are you doing here?"

Jim turned the guileless smile on Frederick.

"I know how busy you are, sir; thought maybe you might like someone to relieve you while Sandy gets her daily exercise. It would be a pleasure. Nothing I enjoy more than a brisk morning dip."

He didn't look as if he were enjoying the brisk-morning part of it.

"You can't swim with that cut on your head," I said.

"I'll just dabble my toes," said Jim.

"Foolishness," Frederick muttered. "Very well, since you are here, I may as well. . . . Don't be more than an hour, Sandy, I will need you on the dig. And don't leave this cove."

He strode off without waiting for an answer.

"Lousy actor," Jim said, lowering his voice. "I can't imagine how he ever survived as a spy."

"Maybe he was more flexible in his younger days. Come on, let's go before you catch cold."

"Not that way." He caught my arm. "How do you get to the next bay overland?"

There was no point in being coy; he obviously knew exactly what I was doing.

"I don't want to go there today," I said.

"Well, I do. I'd like to get a closer look at Kore's haunts anyhow."

The early-morning chill disappeared as the sun rose higher. It was going to be another warm day. Before long we saw the white walls and red-tiled roofs of the villa ahead. I indicated the path that led toward thĕ bay.

"Let's go a little closer to the house first," Jim said.

"I don't want—"

"What can they do, shoot us?"

I didn't need much persuasion. I was curious too.

After all, we didn't see much. The house was enclosed by high walls. We traced their outline at a respectful distance and saw no signs of life except for a stray goat or two on the slopes above.

"They sure like their privacy, don't they?" Jim said. "That looks like ground glass on top of the wall."

"Kore's acting may not be enough to keep the villagers at a respectful distance."

"Ground glass is surer," Jim agreed.

We retraced our steps and descended the cliff. Then Jim produced a bathing cap from the folds of his towel and solemnly pulled it on. I couldn't help laughing; it was a gaudy purple-and-pink cap with a clump of plastic orchids on top. He grinned at me.

"This is the best Antonia's souvenir shop could come up with," he said. "I didn't bring one with me, believe it or not. Fetching, isn't it?"

He posed, one hand on his hips, and rolled his eyes at me.

"No," I said, between gasps of laughter. "It's no use, Jim, you couldn't look anything but one hundred percent male, even in that cap."

"I'm glad to hear it. It inhibits me a little, though. I have an overwhelming urge to kiss you when you laugh that way, but I don't think I can do it while I'm wearing this hat."

We swam for about an hour and then I insisted that we quit. Jim couldn't do much, since he had to keep his head out of the water, and I suspected Sir Christopher would have plenty to say to him if he were late. Before we started back, he took off his bathing cap and his inhibitions and kissed me. His kisses got better all the time; we might have lingered on the sun-warmed rock if I hadn't been so conscious of the silent white house on the cliff. I told Jim about seeing the man watching me. His face lengthened, but he made no comment.

When he left me, at the house, he went down the path at a run. So he was late, and worried about it.

Next morning he was there again. Frederick's face was absolutely thunderous. We had had an acrimonious argument the day before, and I had to swear on everything sacred that I had not let Jim in on the secret. I don't think Frederick believed me. He paid no attention to my statement that the whole village knew what we were doing, and that it was only a matter of time before the port authorities landed on us. He was almost beyond reason on this point. And when he saw Jim the second time, he didn't even speak to him, he just went back into the house and slammed the door.

"We can't go on meeting this way," I said, as we walked along the path.

"I'm afraid you're right," said Jim. "Chris had a few things to say to me this morning."

"Go back then." I stopped. "This is silly."

"On one condition. You go back too."

"Oh, all right. I can't have you lose your job on my account."

We parted at the house.

"I may be here tomorrow and I may not," Jim said. "I won't ask you to promise—"

"I can't promise. I'll do my best."

"Then so will I. You like honesty, Sandy. I'll be honest. I intend to stop this somehow."

"You mean, report Frederick?"

"I'll do whatever I have to do."

"So will I," I said.

He didn't kiss me good-bye.

Frederick and I had a little talk that evening. It was a humdinger. My voice must have been audible several hundred yards away. Frederick didn't shout, he just got colder and meaner with every word. Losing my temper meant that I'd lost control of the argument. It took a direction I had not expected.

"What do you mean, betrayal?" I demanded at one point. "That's a rather melodramatic word to use for a—"

"It is accurate. Your loyalty should have been to me, if for no other reason than because you promised me. The first adolescent male that comes along pawing at you—"

"Pawing!"

"I've seen him kiss you, put his arms around you. Disgusting, promiscuous—"

"That's enough," I said. I wasn't angry anymore, I was appalled. "My God, is that the way you think? Is that the way you were with—"

I stopped just in time. There are some things you can't say. Of course Frederick knew what I meant. It had an unexpected effect. Instead of getting madder, he calmed down. We were like two people whose furious combat has brought them to the edge of a cliff; we had to agree to a truce to keep from falling over.

"All right," I said. "Let's try to stick to the subject, shall we? Jim is worried about my swimming alone, and he has every right to worry. All I want from you is your word that you won't leave me alone. You aren't a lot of help, but you're better than nothing."

"Very well," said Frederick. "I will agree to be present while you are in the water. Is that what you want?"

"That's all. I want to be reasonable—"

"Then I must agree. I have no choice." Frederick rose. "Have you any other demands?"

"I'm not making demands. I just—"

"Then we are agreed. Good night."

It wasn't a good night. I slept badly. There was no reason why I should have felt guilty. His attitude was completely unreasonable. But I did feel guilty—and upset. Mother had said she left Frederick because he cared only for his work. I had been pretty naïve to accept that. Had he hurled words like that at her every time she flirted a little or let a friend hold her hand longer than was strictly necessary?

When I finally fell asleep I dreamed, and a Freudian would have found the subject matter of the dream perfectly predictable. I was back in the foul den where the Minotaur waited, and Theseus stood ready to face him. Only Theseus wasn't an anonymous Greek hero. He was Jim. I saw the sweaty pallor of his face and the way his eyebrows were drawn together, in a capital M. I was myself, and I was Ariadne, the Most Holy, sick with a complex of terrors no modern woman could wholly comprehend. Not only had I betrayed my father for the love of a stranger, an enemy; I had betrayed the goddess, whose priestess I was. The stranger would end the old worship. His barbaric people preferred male gods, and he was the son of Poseidon himself. The Earthshaker would do battle for his son; but which of his sons would he support? The Minotaur was born of the sacred bull, which was Poseidon's incarnation. . . . Then the stinking darkness in the heart of the maze moved, and the bull roar shattered the silence and shook the ground.

I woke with a shriek, to find Frederick shaking my shoulder. I shrank away from him, because he was the sea king, whom I had betrayed.

"What is the matter with you?" he asked irritably.

I swallowed.

"Bad dream," I mumbled.

"Oh. Hurry and get up."

We made our way along the path in a silence that was passive, if not amicable. I could tell by Frederick's expression and his occasional sidelong glances that he had gotten over his anger and would have apologized, if he had been that sort of man. I let my eyes travel along the slope of the hill, with its multicolored strata of rock and gray-green veils of vegetation. The sky was a deep, cloudless blue and the sea below a pale emerald, deepening to sapphire farther out. It was a beautiful morning. I realized, with surprise, that I was going to miss some of this when I got home.

For the first time in days my buddy Alice wasn't waiting for me. I looked around, and finally I saw the familiar blue-and-white shape. We went on together. I was almost in the exact center of the bay when I found the second amphora.

I was investigating a pile of fallen rock—lava fragments, by the look of them—when I saw the rounded curve of the side and a flash of brilliant color. The orange-red band was like the decoration on the first pot I had found. I brushed away drifted sand and the ornament of the lower part appeared—an octopus, sprawling brown-black tentacles around the flank.

The pot was wedged in by stones. It was a marvel it hadn't broken, but so far as I could see, it appeared to be intact. The strain in my chest reminded me I was getting short of breath. I had been so excited by the discovery I had stayed down a little too long. I came up and blew the water out of my snorkel. When I looked for Frederick, he was gone.

I didn't swear because I didn't want to waste my breath. But I thought of a lot of bad words. I looked up toward the house and saw what I expected to see—the flash of light on a pair of binoculars. There was no doubt in my mind that

Frederick knew the identity of the man in the villa and was reluctant to be seen by him.

Watcher or no watcher, Frederick or no Frederick, I had to dive once more. I had no intention of trying to remove the amphora, but I had to mark the site; you'd be surprised how easy it is to misplace an object the size of a jar in all that water. I had my nylon line and an inflatable buoy, which is rather like a balloon, only heavier, so I took a deep breath and went down. I should have attached the line and left; but I couldn't go without seeing what else was down here. The amphora might be another isolated find, or it might be the most visible of a cache of treasures.

Alice hung around, peering myopically at me, while I pulled the stones away. I was in a hurry, I admit it. I wanted to see what was what, and get out of there. Careless haste causes accidents. But I know now that this accident would have happened sooner or later anyhow.

I had lifted one of the larger stones when it happened. I saw the flash and felt the sting at the same moment. That was what it felt like, just a sharp tingling sensation; it wasn't very painful. Then the water started to cloud up.

I couldn't believe it. I stared stupidly at the dark stain in the water. It was small at first, spreading out slow tentacles like a little octopus. But it wasn't an animal, it was liquid, darker and heavier than the water. It was blood.

It wasn't the first time I had cut myself. In my own coastal waters coral is omnipresent, and sometimes the damned stuff almost seems to reach out for you. I knew what to do and I did it, moving by pure instinct—a sharp kick that brought me straight up to the surface. I spit out my mouthpiece and headed for shore with my fastest crawl, and I didn't worry about being seen. I had to get out of the water before the blood attracted some predator. I hadn't gone ten yards before I knew there was a more pressing danger. Already I felt myself weakening. The cut must have been deeper than I realized. I was losing blood too fast, and shock was having its effect. The water no longer felt warm.

I was still some distance out when I knew I wasn't going to make it.

Everything had slowed down, like a broken movie film. One picture after another flashed through my mind. Not my whole life, in chronological order, just disconnected pictures. The piece of metal, coiled like a spring, that had flashed out and slashed my arm. The empty rock where Frederick should have been. Jim's smiling face, under that absurd cap with its topknot of plastic flowers. The side of the amphora and the painted octopus, like the spreading shape of blood in the water.

Then another face, thin and lined, with brown eyes and black hair streaked with white. The face

of a man I had never seen before. I recognized
him, though. His face and hair were streaming
with water, so he had to be Poseidon, come to finish me off. I had invaded his domain and threatened his sovereignty, and now, because I was
taking too long to die, he had come to finish the
job. A long, sinewy arm reached for my throat. I
made a last convulsive effort, trying to avoid that
grip, and water closed over my head and invaded
my lungs.

Chapter
10

WHEN I WOKE UP I THOUGHT AT FIRST I WAS STILL UN-
derwater. Space swam in a clear, cool, green light.
Then I saw that there were sea-green curtains at
the windows. The shades were drawn against the
sunlight. I was lying in a bed; the softness, the
smoothness of the sheets added to the illusion. I
hadn't slept in a decent bed for weeks.

I felt pretty good, except for the ache in my
arm. I turned my head. My right arm was bandaged from wrist to elbow. I remembered quite
clearly what had happened; I could even reinter-
pret the facts that had been clouded, toward the
end, by my growing weakness.

The rustle of linen as I turned my head caught
the attention of the woman standing by the window. She came toward me. I had already recog-

nized her; the shape was unmistakable. She was wearing a long embroidered robe, slit at the sides.

"Madame," I said, with difficulty. My tongue felt as drugged and lazy as the rest of my body.

"But surely you must call me Kore." Smiling, she sat down on the edge of the bed. "You are better; that is good. Jürgen has said you would take no harm. He is an amateur doctor. More amateur than doctor, I tell him."

Her smile was no longer aimed at me. I rolled my eyes toward the other side of the bed.

I had a moment of panic, then; between the two of them I felt imprisoned. But the face of the man who stood looking down at me, though severe and unsmiling, was not frightening. It was, of course, familiar.

"You brought me in," I said. "Thank you . . ."

"Should I allow you to drown?" He didn't exactly smile, but the corners of his long, rigid lips relaxed a trifle. At one time he must have been a strikingly handsome man, if you like the military type. He was still lean and broad-shouldered; the streaks of white in his hair only made him appear more interesting. Yet the face was forbidding. His dark eyes fled from mine. He looked at my hands, at the wall, anywhere except directly at me.

"I was trespassing," I said weakly. "My fault . . ."

"Don't talk. You are still weak, you have lost much blood. There is no way of giving a transfusion here, but I think there is no need to carry you to a hospital. You are young and strong. Rest is all you require."

"But . . ."

"What worries you?"

He took my wrist. His touch was professionally cool; the long fingers, resting lightly on the beating pulse, barely touched me.

"My . . . employer. He will worry about me."

"Minos," said Kore. She emitted a tinkle of laughter. "I will inform him. And the other, the young hero, him too I will see. I think he will be the one to worry. Do not fret, child, all will be in order."

My eyelids were so heavy; I had to close them, but I didn't sleep for a while.

So this man was the mysterious occupant of the villa—the Colonel. Kore had called him Jürgen. A good German name, that one. He was rather intimidating, but his withdrawn manner seemed to be caused by reserve rather than ill will. Certainly I couldn't complain. He had undoubtedly saved my life.

He must have had some trouble doing it, too. I had a vague recollection of hitting out, the way I had been trained never, ever, to do when someone was trying to rescue you. I wondered what had brought him to the shore in time to see my floundering progress. Had he been on his way down the cliff?

Or had he known that an accident might happen?

I had to dismiss that idea. I couldn't be sure that the coiled metal spring had been planted. It was an extremely inefficient method of attack; I might have been quick enough to avoid the cutting edge or received a glancing blow. It seemed much more likely that the accident had been just that. Certainly no villain would rush out to rescue his intended victim. If there was a villain, it couldn't be the Colonel.

Sleep began to overcome me. My last waking thought could not have invaded a wholly conscious mind; I would have fought to keep it from surfacing.

If someone wanted to stop my diving, a minor accident would do the job. It was just bad luck that the cut had been so deep and that Frederick had chosen that time to absent himself. And Jim had said, only a few days ago, that he would do whatever he had to do to stop me.

When I awoke the second time it was evening. Lamplight cast a yellow glow, and the windows were dark squares behind the draperies. As soon as I stirred, Kore came into view.

"Ah, you are awake. And hungry, perhaps?"

I was ravenous, and I said as much. Kore beamed.

"Good, that is good." She clapped her hands.

The woman who entered, carrying a tray, wore

a neat maid's uniform. She was middle-aged, with iron-gray hair. Her nationality was questionable, but I thought she was Greek. Obeying Kore's imperious gesture she placed the tray on a small table, moved it close to the bed, and left.

Kore pulled up a chair. She had changed clothes again. This outfit was the most gorgeous I had seen yet, a kind of caftan of gold brocade that twinkled with rainbow-colored jewels.

"Now I feed you," she said, smiling. "I am a good nurse, I tell you. I do it neatly."

"I think I can feed myself," I said. "In fact, there's no reason why I should stay in bed."

"No, no, you must rest. But you may sit up, if it does not make you faint."

She hadn't been kidding about her talents as a nurse. Deftly she arranged the pillows behind me and helped me raise myself up. Then she spread a linen towel across my lap and lifted the tray into position.

I don't remember what the food was, except that there was some kind of soup, thick with barley and lentils, the inevitable fish—and wine. It tasted good, but I had to eat left-handed, which was awkward.

"He has taken twelve stitches," said Kore, patting my bandaged arm. "Twelve! It is terrible! No wonder it is hurting. How could you be so clumsy? Always you seem like a . . . what is the word? A mermaiden, yes; at home in the world of water."

"Things happen," I said vaguely, and put down my fork. The effort had tired me more than I would have believed possible. Kore whisked the tray away and then settled down in a chair by the bed.

"Did you see Frederick?" I asked.

"Oh, yes." Kore giggled. The sound was quite unlike her normal laugh, and for an instant I could almost see her as the young girl she had once been.

"He has not changed," she went on. "He said you are to come home. Home! That terrible place, with him to be your nurse! I have told him no, you stay here till you are well."

"That's very kind of you, but I don't want to impose."

"You do not impose." She leaned forward and put her hand over mine. Like the rest of her, her hands were a little too plump, but I was suddenly conscious of the hard bones in her fingers. "You do not impose," she repeated, holding my eyes with hers. "It is for me to enjoy you."

I knew she didn't speak English too well, but that phrase struck me unpleasantly. She must have been aware of my distaste; she released my hand and leaned back, the picture of relaxed sophistication.

"Also I have spoken to Jim," she went on. "I have been busy today! It was as I said, he was the one who was angry for you. I tell him he may come tomorrow. Not tonight, because you do not look yet so pretty. Tomorrow I make you beautiful for him."

"I feel very beautiful," I said, glancing down at the folds of fabric that—barely—concealed my torso. It was the sort of nightgown I would have expected Kore to wear, pale chiffon, like drifts of cloud.

"Ah, that—it is old, I throw it away. Tomorrow you will have a better."

"You are kind," I said again. "You make me feel guilty, madame. I had no right to swim in your private bay. And I didn't thank—the Colonel—for saving me. How did he happen to come when he did?"

She accepted my name for him without comment.

"But he watches you often. He is a man; he likes to see a pretty girl, there is no harm in that." She made a comical face. "I do not look so in a swimming costume, not now. Once. . . . But that was long ago. So Jürgen watches you; he says, that is a pretty girl; she swims well. Let her enjoy our water, I will not go for my swim till she finishes, I would not make her think I am bad old man. But today he sees you are hurt. He sees you swim slowly. He rushes down. . . ." Her eyes flashed; she waved her hands excitedly. "It is romantic, is it not? But poor Jürgen is not romantic, he is too old. You do not have to be afraid of him, not when you have a handsome young lover."

She had a lot of charm. The story was told with such verve and humor I couldn't help smiling.

It was a little unbelievable, though. Her Jürgen must have been on his way down the cliff when he saw I was in trouble; he couldn't have reached me in time otherwise. And strain my imagination as I might, I couldn't hear him saying the words she had so gaily attributed to him, or drooling through his binoculars over a girl's figure.

But I didn't really care. I didn't care about anything; I felt drowsy and warm, and so comfortable. . . . I had forgotten how pleasant it was to enjoy the commonplace comforts of civilization. There was even a plump, smiling mother type sitting by me, patting my hand.

The thought of Kore as a motherly type made me want to laugh. And yet there was something maternal about her, under the glittering clothes and expert maquillage.

"You are sleepy, yes?" She put her hand on my forehead. "Good," she murmured. "It is good; there is no fever."

But her hand did not leave my brow. The fingers moved slowly; I thought of little snakes, squirming. But there was nothing repellent about the idea. I'm not afraid of snakes. I used to have a garter snake whose name was Herman. Snakes aren't slimy, they are cool and hard and a little rough. Bundles of living muscle, moving . . . but quickly, not like those white fingers with their gentle, rhythmic caress. . . .

The pillow under my head was lowered. I lay flat, staring up at a shadowy ceiling. Somewhere a voice was whispering.

"You are drowsy . . . you will sleep. And when you sleep, she will awaken, she who has slept so long and found a vessel of rebirth. O Most Holy, guardian of the dancing floor, daughter and maiden, awaken to your ancient heritage and live again!"

I heard the words. I understood what they meant and knew them for the half-pathetic, half-menacing nonsense that they were. But I was sinking down, down into green watery depths, sinking as if a stone had been tied to my feet; and as the darkness of the deep wrapped around me it was as if I, sinking, passed Another who was rising up out of the sea floor into sunlight.

II

Drugged.

I woke with that word floating on the surface of my mind. Sunlight was bright at the windows. The room was no longer like subaqueous space, it glowed like the green of a forest in broad daylight. My mouth felt dry, but otherwise I was in good shape. I flexed my arm experimentally and got a stab of pain for reward, but it wasn't as bad as I had expected.

There had been some drug in the food or the wine. I had no doubts about that; my physical sensations just before I fell asleep had been typical. No worry, no concern, only an illusion of clarity and comfort and understanding. That's what grass does for some people, at least so they tell me. It didn't do anything for me except make my mouth taste foul. But I could get addicted to this stuff, whatever it was.

Looking back now on that episode, it seems incredible to me that I could have accepted it with such blind complacency. For it was a sign of what was to come, and not until the very end was I able to break free and reject what was happening to me. But it's easy to be wise after the event. Each separate incident could be explained, and I was only too eager to explain them. The personal weaknesses that made me vulnerable also made me blind.

And surely that first incident was easy to understand. People get all uptight about the word "drugs," but drugs have medicinal purposes too. No doubt I had been given a sedative or painkiller. Any kind of drug can affect the mind. I couldn't even be sure I had really heard the eerie whispering. It fit only too well with previous outpourings of my subconscious.

Besides, the villa was such a pretty, comfortable place. If there had been gothic arches and moldering castle walls, or a few bats. . . . Who could imagine demons in a room furnished with French antiques and linen sheets?

I felt so good I decided I would get up. That was a mistake. The bed was a lot higher than I had expected. My feet didn't quite reach the floor, and as soon as I sat up my head started to spin. Then the whole room began to heave slowly up and down, just like an earthquake. I slid off the bed and hit the floor with a thud. Luckily I fell on my left side, but the impact jarred my arm, and it hurt so badly I must have fainted. I wasn't out very long. The crash alerted Kore and the maid; they came running in and put me back to bed. Kore was clucking like a mother hen.

"See, how foolish! You have hurt yourself. You are bad! I must call Jürgen to look at you."

Jürgen duly appeared. In the unflattering light of day he appeared much older than he had the night before, but he had the strong, elegant bone structure that triumphs over wrinkles and sagging flesh. His eyes continued to avoid me, while he checked my pulse and temperature and unwound the bandages to look at the wound.

"Already it heals," he said with satisfaction. "That is what it is to be strong and young! But no more foolishness about leaving the bed. Rest and sleep and eat, that is what you need."

He smiled in my general direction and started backing away.

"How soon can I leave?" I asked, and then felt my face grow warm as the ungraciousness of the question struck me. "I didn't mean that; I just meant—"

"Of course you meant it. You are young, and already you are bored. I can offer you only books. My selection of English volumes is not great, I fear. Shall I bring you what I have?"

"Yes, please," I said resignedly. He hadn't answered me, which indicated that I had a couple of days of boredom ahead of me. He might not be a doctor, but he had a physician's reticence.

"Bah," said Kore. "Bring your dull books. There is nothing else. No television, no theater, no music. Such a place! How do I endure it?" She waved her hand. The jewels on her fingers flashed, and one sleeve slid back, showing the coils of the golden serpent.

The Colonel had taken advantage of her speech to retire noiselessly, and the maid appeared with my breakfast. It was an English- or American-type meal, not the European *petit dé jeuner* I had expected. The bacon was thicker and fatter than the kind I was used to, and rather too salty, but the eggs were fresh and well cooked. Kore sat watching me, nodding with satisfaction at every bite.

"I cannot eat so," she announced blithely. "It makes too fat, you see. But you are needing the food, Jürgen says. He is clever, Jürgen."

"He is a very good man," I said. "I'm grateful."

"Yes," she said soberly. "He is a good man."

After the tray had been removed, Kore went into action. She hadn't been kidding when she announced her intention of making me beautiful. I didn't like it. I felt like a life-sized doll, or one of those cult statues, the Virgin or a female saint, being re-robed by devout peasant women. But I hated to complain when she was being so kind, and enjoying herself so much. She twisted my hair up and tied it with ribbons, and the fresh nightgown she produced had obviously been altered to fit my measurements. It was a stunning gown, layer on layer of chiffon that ran the gamut of greens and blues and blended into a heavenly aquamarine. When she came at me waving brushes and lipsticks, I protested. She looked so hurt I gave in, but I hated it. I don't know how movie and TV stars stand being made up; I felt like a thing.

Finally Kore stepped back, clapping her hands, and exclaimed with joy. I started to smile, but stopped; my face felt as if something were going to crack. I asked for a mirror. While Kore was flapping around looking for one, the maid came in and said something. Kore answered her and then turned to me, her eyes glowing.

"It is Jim," she announced—she pronounced it "Jeem." "We are just in time. Now sit up—let me make the pillow straight. . . . Ah, he will be drunken with love, you are so beautiful!"

I heard him coming from a long way off. Even the sound of his footsteps was unique. My heart was beating faster, and not only with pleasant anticipation. Jim would have a few things to say about my carelessness.

He must have come straight from the dig, without stopping to change clothes. They were his usual garb, un-pressed cotton work clothes, but he looked marvelous in them, and I thought, with unaccustomed sentimentality, of the couriers who had reported to the king in their travel-stained garments, in token of their zeal.

Jim took one look at me and stopped short. "My God," he said.

"Well, that's really sweet," I said. "That's a nice way to greet someone in my condition."

"What condition are you referring to?" Jim inquired politely.

Kore giggled. "Ah, the lovers' quarrel," she exclaimed, beaming. "I go. I leave you alone, to make it up. See, Jim, she is beautiful for you. Only for you."

She slipped away, closing the door with exaggerated care and giving me a wink before she went. Jim sat down on the chair by the bed and stared at me.

"How do you like it?" I asked self-consciously.

"I like you better the way you were."

"Men," I said.

"Did Kore dress you up that way?"

"She was just trying to be nice."

"Have you seen yourself?"

"No."

"Do you want to know what you look like?"

"No."

"Then I won't tell you. . . . Oh, you look beautiful. But you look beautiful to me with your wet hair all over your face and your nose peeling. And," he added, while I was still gulping over that tender declaration, "if you weren't in a delicate condition I'd take you by the throat and squeeze till your face turned blue. How could you have been so stupid? What happened?"

I sighed with relief. That took care of the lecture. At least he wasn't the sort of man who said "I told you so."

"Didn't Kore tell you?" I asked.

"She gave me some wild story. I can't believe half of what she says. What did you cut yourself on?"

"I didn't get a good look at it. Metal of some kind. It sort of jumped out at me when I lifted a rock."

"You ought to know better than to stick your hands into some place you can't see clearly. What were you looking for?"

I told him about the amphora. At first he wasn't visibly impressed, but as I went on to describe it in detail he listened with increasing interest and asked several questions. The answers didn't seem to please him; he fell into a frowning silence.

"Well?" I said. "It was a Minoan amphora, don't you think?"

"What? Oh—oh, yes, it sounds like it. Late Minoan IB. But I don't understand why. . . . You couldn't describe the location, I suppose?"

"Not accurately. I was about to mark it with a buoy when I got hurt. Maybe I can find it again."

"Oh, no. That's the silver lining to the cloud, my girl. No more diving for you. I'd feel better if a doctor looked at that arm. Suppose I borrow a car and drive you to Phira tomorrow."

"I don't think that's necessary, Jim. Jürgen seems to know what he's doing."

"So it's Jürgen, is it?"

"That's what Kore calls him."

"What's he like?" Jim pulled his chair closer.

"Oh—sixty-ish; tall; military bearing and all that. He's nice. Withdrawn but nice. He must be pretty good in the water. I was in bad shape when he reached me, and I struggled some."

"Are you sure he hasn't got a horrible scar? Or that he doesn't bear an uncanny resemblance to the late Adolf Hitler?"

"Of course I'm sure. What are you talking about?"

"Trying to find an explanation for his retiring habits."

"Maybe he's just shy."

Jim snorted.

"Never mind Jürgen," I said impatiently.

"What about Frederick? I suppose he's mad at me."

"I'm not sure who he's mad at," Jim said. "I saw him last night, and I will frankly admit I went up there looking for trouble. We had—er—words."

"Why waste your time? He'll never admit he's made a mistake. I've failed him. You're right, I can't do any more diving, not for a while. He'll blame me, not himself."

"That's about the gist of it."

I smoothed the sheet that lay over my lap and avoided looking at Jim.

"I don't suppose he said anything about coming to see me."

"Well . . ." Jim's voice was very gentle.

"It's okay," I said.

"Chris sent you his regards," Jim went on. "He was concerned when I told him what had happened; he didn't even object when I took time off to come and see you. In fact, he reiterated his offer of a job next summer. He likes you, Sandy."

"Big deal," I muttered. I regretted my rudeness immediately. Jim was trying to make me feel better, and it was nice of Sir Christopher to offer me a job. I said so, and Jim brightened.

There was a tap on the door. I assumed it was Kore, coming back to see how the lovers' quarrel was progressing, and I said, "Come in." Instead of Kore, I saw Jürgen with a pile of books. He hesitated in the doorway.

"I am sorry I intrude," he said. "I have brought the books. I did not know you had—"

"This is Jim Sanchez," I said, as Jim turned. "I'm afraid I don't know—"

My next words were lost in the sound of the heavy books hitting the floor. Jürgen's face looked like a faded papier-mâché mask, except for his eyes, which had widened until the whites showed all around the pupils. He said something in a strangled voice and then he disappeared. The footsteps that echoed back along the hallway were the steps of a man in mindless, headlong flight.

Chapter
11

I TURNED MY OPENMOUTHED STARE ON JIM. HE WAS standing, one hand on the back of the chair. His face wore its thoughtful expression—lips tight, eyebrows emphatic.

"What was that all about?" I asked.

Jim took his time about answering. He walked to the window and stood looking out, his hands clasped behind his back.

"Didn't you hear what he said?"

"I don't understand German, if that's what it was. It sounded pretty incoherent."

"It was. I only caught a couple of words. Something about returning from the dead."

"He and Kore must be members of the same weird religion," I said.

"Kore's obsession is with the ancient past," Jim

said slowly. "This guy has a more recent incident in mind."

"What do you mean?"

Jim came back to the bed and stood there looking down at me. "I'm told I bear quite a resemblance to my late uncle."

I suppose I had been expecting something of the sort. The evidence had been there all along; I just had not wanted to recognize it.

"So we were right after all," I said.

"I don't know about that. As I recall, we avoided coming to a conclusion. But it can't be avoided any longer. Your Jürgen is the man who was in Crete during the war. The man who killed my uncle."

"It was duty!"

The voice echoed in the high-ceilinged chamber. I started. I hadn't heard them approach, but there they stood, both of them. Kore had both hands clasped tightly around the man's arm. He was still pale, but it was not he who had spoken.

Kore went on passionately.

"He did what he must do. It was war, it was his duty—"

"I remember reading about the case," Jim interrupted. His eyes were fixed on the older man's face. "My mother corresponded with various people after the war—she kept the letters. There was some talk of a trial. But the military authorities decided—"

"It was his duty," Kore said again.

"More or less," Jim said quietly. "My uncle was out of uniform. You"—he nodded at Jürgen—"you were a captain at the time. You made colonel before the war ended. A real hot-shot officer, weren't you? I've forgotten your name. . . ."

"Keller." The word was clipped.

"That's right, I remember now," Jim said.

"You told me you never thought about it," I said. "You told me—"

Keller stepped forward, shaking Kore's hands from his arm.

"You look just as he did, over thirty years ago," he said, staring at Jim. "He was then twenty-eight years of age. Can you wonder that when I saw your face. . . . I know it well. I have seen it every night for over thirty years."

"Why?" Jim asked. His voice was cool, his body relaxed; only his hands, gripping the back of the chair in a hold that whitened his knuckles, betrayed the underlying strain. "Why should he haunt your sleep if you were only doing your duty?"

"Because I knew him," Keller said. He was moving slowly forward, one step at a time, like a horrible parody of a wedding march. "I knew his work. We had met at Oxford before the war. He was a fine scholar. He had a splendid career ahead of him."

"And you killed him," Jim said.

"And I killed him." Keller continued to move forward until he stood face to face with Jim. They were almost the same height—tall men, both of them. "And now," Keller went on, "he has come back. No, no, don't look at me as if I were mad; I am not mad, I know who you are. But I believe in Nemesis—retribution. There is still a debt to be paid. It is fitting that you should be the one to collect it. When I saw you, I knew the time had come."

His voice got louder and more excited as he spoke. When he raised his clenched fists, I thought he was going to attack Jim. The movement broke the paralysis that had held the rest of us motionless. Jim jumped back; Kore, who had been standing stock-still, her hands pressed to her mouth, cried out and ran toward Keller. She flung her arms around him.

"No, Jürgen, no. It is time for your medicine. Come with me."

Keller stood quietly. "Time for medicine," he repeated like a child.

"Yes. Come, come now with Kore." She tugged at him. He went docilely. Neither of them looked at us as they went out, her arms around him.

Jim came out from behind the bedpost. "Wow," he said.

"Sit down," I gasped, reaching for him. "No, here on the bed. Don't go away."

"I won't. Quite a scene, wasn't it?"

"Oh, don't pretend to be so cool. You're sweating. I thought he was going to go for your throat."

"No," Jim said thoughtfully. "He wasn't going to do that."

"What was he doing, then?"

"Something worse." Jim mopped his wet forehead with his sleeve. "I had the feeling he was going to kneel. Bare his neck to the knife, if you know what I mean."

"God."

"Yeah."

"I feel kind of sorry for him," I said.

"My God, do you think I'm inhuman? So do I. The man is off his rocker. There must have been some mental instability to begin with, or this wouldn't have hit him so hard. There are people who have worse crimes on their consciences and who sleep quite well at night."

"Jim, you told me you didn't know anything about the case."

"No, I did not. I told you I wanted to forget about it. I do. My mother . . . well, you could say she never got over it. He was her big brother; she idolized him. She's okay now, I mean she doesn't go around trailing black veils or anything; but she still has the file of the correspondence about his death. I read it when I was—oh, in my teens. I was looking for a hero about that time, and he was pretty impressive. I suppose that's what got me interested in archaeology to begin with, but honestly, Sandy, I'm not—I mean, I haven't thought about the man for years. I used his name, sure, when I applied to Chris for this job. Maybe that wasn't strictly kosher, but it's a rough field, there's a lot of competition. . . ."

"I don't see why you should feel bad about it," I said.

"I don't. I mean, I'm doing a good job. Chris wouldn't have hired me if I hadn't been qualified, no matter who my uncle was."

I decided a change of subject was in order. His finicky conscience was obviously bothering him, no matter how ever he might deny it. And it seemed to me we had more important things to talk about.

"Does Sir Christopher know that Keller is here, I wonder?"

"I hadn't thought about that. I wonder too."

"Not to mention Frederick," I said. "Jim, this is too much, all of them converging on this place."

"There's something behind it," Jim agreed. "I'm pretty sure your father does know about Keller. Chris is another matter. He might not."

"Well, I sure as hell would ask him if I were you."

Jim nodded thoughtfully. Then a look of impatience crossed his face and the nod turned into a shake of negation.

"No, damn it. I'm not going to get all involved

in some long-dead tragedy. I'm here to do a job, and that's all that concerns me."

"You don't think the tragedy concerns us? Jim, I tell you, these people aren't here by accident. Something is going on, and I want to know what it is."

"You're hopelessly inquisitive," Jim said remotely.

"It's all very well to forget the past," I argued. "But if the past is still affecting people's lives—our lives—"

"How can it, if we don't let it?"

"You don't want to question your precious boss," I said. "Afraid you'll lose your job?"

Jim flushed angrily. "I refuse to poke my nose into other people's business."

We'd have had a nice, air-clearing fight, right then, if Kore had not returned. She marched up to Jim.

"You have upset him," she said belligerently. "He has not been so upset for years."

"*I* upset him? Oh, well, hell. All right. I'm sorry."

"I don't see any need for you to apologize," I said. It was all right for me to yell at Jim, but when someone else attacked him I was on his side.

"No," Kore said. Her shoulders sagged. "I am angry, I speak unfair words. I had hoped he

would not see you. You are so like your uncle.
The first time I see you I am struck dumb."

"The night of the festival?" I asked. "So that's
why you stood there in the plaza so long."

"Yes. I am dumb," said Kore softly. "I try to understand why this has happened. So many
years. . . . Then She makes it clear to me. When
She comes, at evening, with the women singing
her praises."

She bowed her head. All her movements had a
touch of the theatrical, but the gesture, and her
words, made me ashamed. She was a religious
woman after all. The prejudices of the villagers
had prevented her from attending church on the
saint's day, but she had cared enough to come to
the plaza to pay her devotions.

I glanced at Jim. He was trying to look blasé,
and was not succeeding very well.

"Look," he said awkwardly. "As far as I'm concerned, we can forget the whole thing. It happened a long time ago. I'm not judging anybody.
In fact, I'm sorry your—your friend has had such
a bad time. He seems to have punished himself
for what he did. I'm certainly not going to do anything, if you know what I mean."

Kore completed his discomfort by snatching
his hand and kissing it.

"Hey," he mumbled. "Please don't. . . . That's
not necessary."

"You are a good man," said Kore emotionally.

"He is good, too. That is why I stay with him all these years. He is so good. Only a good man would suffer as he has."

"I guess that's true," Jim muttered. "Why did he come here? Why didn't he change his name and go to South America or someplace?"

"He is not criminal. He does not have to hide."

"I know, but—Greece, of all places! It's not the same island, but I would think it would bring back unpleasant memories all the same. Why not—"

Kore released his hand. She dabbed at her eyes with a dainty handkerchief. I couldn't see any traces of tears, though. They would have showed, with that heavy mascara.

"I thank you," she said. "And now I think the patient should rest."

"About that," Jim said. "I was thinking—I mean, Sandy shouldn't be imposing on you."

"She cannot go back to that house," Kore said sharply. "I have seen; it is terrible, dirty, no comfort—"

"I agree. I thought I would get her a room at the hotel. I'm sure she'd feel better not imposing—"

"Impose, impose!" Kore's eyes flashed. She drew herself up. "In that filthy hotel she will get infection just from touching. No; you do not think impose, you think we are evil here. You fear my poor Jürgen."

"Oh, damn," Jim said uncomfortably. "That isn't the point."

"You do not think he would harm her? He has saved her life!"

"I know, I know. I just thought—"

"I wish you would both stop fighting about me," I interrupted. "I feel like a bone between two dogs. Don't I have anything to say about what becomes of me?"

They both looked at me as if I'd said something rude. Then Kore smiled.

"You see, she is better. But not well yet; she cannot go anywhere today. Will you carry her to the village on your back? We talk tomorrow, yes? We must think before we act. And now it is time for her to sleep. I will wait outside while you say good-bye."

She closed the door after her, but I was sure she would hang around till Jim left. I lowered my voice.

"I do feel pretty groggy, Jim. And I've got to think about what I plan to do. You're not worried about that poor old man, are you?"

"I don't think he's homicidal, no. And I must admit the hotel doesn't have much to offer. I just don't like the situation here."

"What bugs you? She's been charming to me."

"Too charming."

"Oh, stop it. You sound like an old village witch croaking. Jim, I need a few days to think about what I'm going to do. I ought to talk to Frederick."

"Why? It seems to me he's forfeited his rights—if he ever had any to begin with."

"It isn't that simple."

"It sure isn't. Your feelings about him are the most ambivalent—"

"When I want a psychiatrist, I'll hire a pro," I said sharply. "All I meant was that I don't have any money. Frederick owes me a plane ticket."

"If you want to go home, I'll see you have a ticket," Jim said.

"I don't know what I want to do. I need time to think."

"Okay. I guess I'd better go, before Kore comes in here and throws me out."

"Good-bye," I said.

"See you later." He leaned over me.

Kore chose that moment to open the door. Jim glanced at her over his shoulder and then went on with what he had been doing. If Kore's soft laughter bothered him, his technique was not noticeably affected.

"Mmmm," I said dreamily. "That was the best yet."

"The best is yet to come." Jim straightened. "I'll see you tomorrow."

Still laughing, Kore took his arm. They might have been two old friends, or mother and son, as they went out together.

I was supposed to take a nap after lunch. I didn't plan to sleep, but I looked forward to being alone and uninterrupted. I had a lot of thinking to do.

I should have been thinking about my future plans, but there really wasn't much to think about. I knew what I ought to do. I ought to go home. I didn't want to. It was as simple as that, and there didn't seem to be any compromise.

The main reason I was reluctant to leave was Jim. Sure, he seemed to be interested, but. . . . It's a long way from California to Florida. Maybe I could get a job in California.

I knew that was impossible. I had already signed a contract for fall. I also knew that my concern about Jim was probably a pretense. The way we felt about each other was too strong to be stretched by distance. I was as sure of that as I was sure of my own name. . . .

I decided to abandon that analogy. There were times when I wasn't sure of my own name.

But Jim was wrong about the past. It cannot be ignored. It sends out runners, like crabgrass. The roots grow underground, unseen, until suddenly a new shoot springs up. What was happening here and now was the result of that thirty-year-old tragedy. Something had drawn the protagonists of the drama together here on Thera—the German officer and his mistress, two of the three who had fought him—and Jim.

Thinking is tiring, and thinking when you are curled up in a nice comfortable bed is even more difficult. I had gotten that far in my meditations when I fell asleep. I woke up to find Keller sitting by the bed.

I must have recoiled. His face changed; he put out his hand and then pulled it back.

"Don't be afraid," he said quickly. "I did not— I was waiting for you to wake."

"You startled me," I said.

"I am sorry. I have brought the books. . . ."

He held them out, like a peace offering. I couldn't be afraid of him.

"Thank you," I said.

"I would like to talk. Are you strong enough?"

"I'm fine. I could run down the hill right now."

"No, you must not do that," he said seriously. "That is what I wish to talk about. First, to say we hope you will stay here until you are ready to leave Thera. It is a favor to us, you must think of it so."

"That is very kind," I said noncommittally.

"I say this first, so you will understand that your presence is no trouble, but a pleasure. Because otherwise you may interpret what I am about to say wrongly."

He hesitated, staring at me with wide eyes. His pupils were dilated, more so than the fading light would explain.

"Yes?" I said.

"You must leave Thera. As soon as you are able to travel, you must go. It is not—"

He stopped speaking and turned his head, as if he had heard some sound at the door.

"It isn't what?" I asked urgently. "Go on . . . please!"

"Safe." The word was whispered. "You are not safe in this place. You are like a fly in a web, caught by forces you cannot control. For your own safety—"

The door opened.

"So she wakes," said Kore gaily. "Ha—do I interrupt a tête-à-tête? Shall I return later?"

Keller leaned back in the chair. "I am telling her she must not leave us until she is ready to go back to her family," he said calmly. "You *have* interrupted, *Liebchen*; I was about to offer, if she should need money—"

"Oh, no," I said.

"But certainly." Kore sauntered across the room. The woman had an incredible wardrobe; every time I saw her she was wearing a new outfit. This was a pant suit of mustard-colored raw silk. Not many women could have worn such a shrieking shade, but Kore carried it off superbly.

"As a loan," she continued. "That is understood. But we hope you will not go soon. It is pleasure for me to have you. Another woman of my own kind, you understand. I am often lonely."

It was a pretty picture; but I was unconvinced. No one could have looked less pathetic than

Kore, with her jewels—she wore them with everything—and her Paris clothes and her arrogant, experienced face.

"So now you see," she went on, when I didn't answer. "You understand. Jürgen, you have examined the patient? You are ready to dress for dinner?"

The hand she placed on Keller's arm suggested the grip of a warder rather than that of a lover. I couldn't figure out whose side she was on. I couldn't even figure out what the different sides were. He urged me to leave, she begged me to stay. I couldn't accept his concern as meaningful. What danger could there be for me here?

However, I decided that I had better start getting myself back into shape. Kore's motives for keeping me in bed might be entirely charitable, but inactivity would weaken me as much as loss of blood. I wasn't worried or afraid. I just didn't like the idea of being helpless.

As soon as they had left, I got out of bed. I was dizzy at first, but after I had walked a little, holding on to the edge of the bed, my wobbly legs felt stronger. I got back into the bed with a feeling of childish triumph, and when Kore came back I was innocently reading one of Keller's books. It was a volume of Shakespeare.

Kore stayed with me most of the evening. She could be very entertaining, when she tried; her stories about people she had known, their weaknesses and foibles, were quite funny. I didn't like it so well when she started fussing with me again, arranging my hair and polishing my nails. I was getting used to it, though. It didn't bother me as much as it had the first time. In fact, there was something luxurious about being waited on.

"It seems a shame to waste all this," I said lightly, after she had tied my hair up with pale-green ribbons. "I'm just going to bed, you know. Or are we going to a party?"

"No, no," said Kore, tucking in a stray curl. "You must sleep. It is late; I have stayed too long. Here. Take your pill and sleep soundly."

She couldn't have anticipated my reaction. I hate pills. I won't even take aspirin unless someone makes me. The little white ball looked harmless enough, on a plate with a glass of water beside it. But I had no intention of taking that pill—or of arguing with Kore about it.

I had had a lot of practice in handling unwanted medicine. I tongued the pill back into my cheek, holding Kore's eyes with mine so she wouldn't look at my mouth, and swallowed half a glass of water without even wetting the pill. I lay back and made sleepy noises. I said goodnight. I closed my eyes. And Kore sat there.

I could have killed her. I felt the damned pill beginning to dissolve. It wasn't a capsule, just a plain pill like an aspirin tablet. Finally, after what seemed like a year, she tiptoed out, and I spat the fragments of the pill into my hand. But I knew I had swallowed some of the stuff, whatever it was.

The medicine was supposed to knock me out completely; I'm sure of that. Instead it knocked out everything except consciousness. My muscles felt as if they had been cut. I couldn't move. I didn't want to move. I lay in a state of utter relaxation, watching the shadows on the walls through half-closed eyes. Kore had left a lamp burning, and its yellow glow made a bright spot on the outer rim of my vision.

Things got hazy for a while—how long I never could determine. Maybe I slept, but I don't think so. My eyes were almost closed; they must have looked completely closed, but I could see a little through the slitted opening. Then a woman's face came into view.

It wasn't Kore. It wasn't the maid. It wasn't anyone I had ever seen.

Some deep-down rational streak in my mind assured me that I must be dreaming. It was a peculiar dream, unlike any I had ever had, but what I was seeing could not be real. The woman's face was the first of a series of faces, each gliding across my limited field of vision and vanishing, to be replaced by another. In the dim light they looked like the same face—olive-skinned, crowned by black hair, with aquiline features. I could hear a faint far-off sound, like the distant murmur of the sea—or like voices.

Another indeterminate period of drowsiness followed. Then something brought me wide awake. It might have been the sound of my door closing.

When I say I was wide awake, I mean only by comparison to my previous state. I was still awfully sleepy, but somehow I knew I had to move. Dad always said I was as stubborn as a mule. Maybe it was that rocklike stubbornness that got me moving.

I crawled back and forth across the bed for a while. I kept collapsing, flat on my face; it took an enormous effort of will to push myself up off the cradling softness. I slapped myself on the face. At first my slaps felt like the kinds of pats you give a tiny kitten, but gradually my strength increased until a left-handed smack brought tears to my eyes.

I slid down off the bed. I crawled quite a way before I was able to pull myself erect. My arm hurt, not so much that I couldn't use it, but enough to keep me from falling asleep again. Staggering from one piece of furniture to the next, I finally reached the window.

It was closed. No wonder the room felt so stuffy and hot. My arms felt like cooked spaghetti; I didn't think I would ever get that window open, and I craved fresh air the way a starving man craves food.

Well, I did it. Finally the casement gave, and I fell on my knees, with my head on the sill, gulping in the sweet night air. It smelled of thyme and of the sea; the scents blended into a perfume that was the essence of the island.

The cool air cleared my head. As I knelt there I saw that I was looking down into a stone-paved courtyard with a high wall on its far side. To the right, behind the wall, the dark bulk of the mountain cut off a segment of the night sky. There was no moon. I could make out shapes, but not details.

I had just about decided to attempt the return trip to my bed when I heard something below— the sound of a door opening. The faintest murmur of voices reached my ears. Then a dark figure came into the courtyard and moved toward a corner deep in shadow. I wouldn't have seen any more except for a touch of modernity that seemed incongruous in the atmosphere of hushed darkness—a flashlight. The woman switched it on when she reached the dark corner, and the beam showed the shape of a door in the wall. Then the light jumped wildly as a hissing cry came from the part of the house immediately under my window. The cry was one of warning, I suppose; the light went out. But not before I had seen the face of the woman who held it. It was a dark, aquiline face like the ones I had seen in my dreaming vision, but now, with the fumes of the drug almost dissipated, I recognized it. Her name was Sophia, and she ran the store in the village where I bought my fish.

Chapter

12

SOMETHING TOLD ME I HAD BETTER GET BACK TO BED as fast as I could. I closed the window and made a run for it. Then I lay back and willed my pounding heart to calm itself. There wasn't time enough; I could still feel the furious beat when Kore slipped into the room. She came straight to the bed and stood looking down at me.

It seemed to me that she must see the betraying pulse in my bare throat. It felt like a hammer. So I muttered and rolled over, away from her. She said my name softly. I muttered again but didn't move. After a while she went away.

I fell asleep. I wouldn't have believed it possible, I had so much on my mind, but I guess some of the sleeping medicine had been absorbed into my system.

It was good medicine. I felt great the next morning, rested and not at all hung over. I decided I had better pretend to be groggy, though, just to be on the safe side.

Kore came in with breakfast, and the morning proceeded with its now ritual activity. First breakfast, then a formal visit from Keller, to check on the state of my health. He put on a fresh bandage, and I got a look at the cut. It was healing well. Then, after he left, we had the ritual bath. The maid gave me an expert massage, using some kind of scented oil. She dressed me in a pale-blue satin gown that was elegant enough for a party, and Kore did my hair and tied it up with blue satin ribbons.

All morning I had been biting my tongue to keep from dropping a hint about what I had seen the night before. It would have been interesting to hear what Kore had to say about the incident. I figured she would probably tell me I had been dreaming. I knew it had not been a dream. I had dreamed, later; I couldn't remember what about, but I had vague memories of a voice talking, or maybe singing, like the priest performing the service in church.

When Jim appeared I hadn't made up my mind whether to tell him or not, but one look at his face decided me. He had enough worries of his own. He produced an artificial smile when he saw me, but I could tell the smile had been a scowl seconds earlier.

After we had exchanged greetings—and I don't mean just "hello"—I asked him what was bothering him.

"Sssh." He looked over his shoulder like a stage villain. "I think your girl friend listens at doors."

"Probably," I agreed. "She would. So what?"

"Everything okay?" He looked at me a little oddly.

"Great. Now that I know how the other half lives, I think I'll start looking for a millionaire. I could learn to like this kind of life."

Before I knew what he was planning he reached over and tugged at one of my hair ribbons. A whole side section of hair came down.

"God damn it!" I grabbed at my head. "What do you think you're doing?"

"Nothing to get that excited about," Jim said.

"Well, damn it, Kore put in a lot of work on this, and I don't think you ought to mess it up. Of all the dumb, childish—"

"What's happened to my girl with the hair in her face?"

"Oh. . . . Forget it. I guess it's not important."

"No," Jim said. His eyes went over me, from my ribboned hair across my bare shoulders and down to where the sheet lay neatly folded back over my lap. His expression annoyed me. I was showing a lot of healthy-looking skin, and I expected some signs of interest and approval instead of that cold, appraising stare.

"I talked to Chris," Jim said. "He agrees that you ought to leave. The transcontinental flights are pretty full this time of year, but he thinks he can get you on a flight from Athens this weekend. You could catch the boat from Phira on Thursday and be in Athens—"

"Wait just a bloody minute," I said. "What gives your boss the idea he can run my life?"

"It was pretty decent of him to offer. He doesn't like to use his influence—"

"Like hell he doesn't. He adores being Sir Christopher. I bet he can hardly wait for the next title."

When Jim got mad he forgot about eavesdroppers, common courtesy, and care of the wounded.

"God, you're in a bitchy mood," he shouted. "I don't know why I should stick around here and be insulted."

"So leave," I said. My voice wasn't exactly a whisper.

Jim stood up. Then he sat down. He took six deep breaths. I could see his lips move as he counted.

"We'll try again," he said. "If you give me any more lip, I'll belt you one."

"You and what army?" I snapped; and then, because it had sounded so silly, even to me, I laughed.

The door opened and Kore's head came in.

"Ah," she said, grinning. "You laugh. You are friends, that is nice."

The door closed.

Jim stopped laughing. "Damn that woman," he said.

"She's all right," I said tolerantly.

"She's a menace," Jim said. "Sandy, I'm sorry I got off on the wrong foot. I ought to know better than to sound as if I'm trying to give you orders. May I respectfully inquire what your plans are?"

I shrugged. One shoulder strap slipped down. I let it hang. "What's the hurry?"

"No room at the inn," Jim said.

"What?"

"Sorry if I blaspheme. I mean I tried to get you a room at the hotel. Angelos says they're full up."

"Maybe they have a tour coming."

"No. The place is half empty."

"And you think that's significant or something?"

"I know it is. I offered to move in with Chris and give you my room. Angelos practically gibbered trying to think of reasons why that couldn't be done. You are persona non grata in town, love."

"But why?" I asked in bewilderment. "I haven't done anything."

"The only thing I can think of is that you've gotten friendly with Kore."

"What a bunch of superstitious peasants," I said scornfully. "Who cares about the hotel? I'll stay here."

I shrugged again. The other strap started to slide. Jim pulled it up and adjusted the first strap too, scowling like Martin Luther admonishing a harlot. His hands still on my shoulders he shook me, none too gently.

"For God's sake, Sandy, what's happened to you? You're acting like a—like—somebody else. You look like one of those dummies in store windows. Even your face is blanking out. Will you come with me, now? I'll drive you to Phira this afternoon."

"Why bother?" I asked coldly. "For a big blank-faced doll—"

Jim made an exasperated noise. He slid his arm behind my back and pulled me away from the pillows so that my head lay in the curve of his shoulder. His free hand ran roughshod through my carefully arranged hair, till it hung loose. I yelped with the pain and he stopped my mouth with his. I couldn't help responding; but after the first moment or two I began to get angry, not because he was rough but because he didn't seem to care whether I responded or not. I started to struggle. Finally I brought my hand up in a wild swing, and felt it connect.

Jim let me go. I fell back, gasping and disheveled, puzzled and furious. There was a patch of red on Jim's cheek where I had slapped him. He was smiling.

"That's my girl," he said approvingly. "You don't like it, do you—being treated like an inanimate object?"

"Was that the point of that little demonstration?"

"Yes."

He sat on the edge of the bed, his breathing still uneven, his cheek flaming and his eyes anxious. But he didn't say any more.

"Okay," I said. "I'll go. This weekend."

I had forgotten about Kore. Maybe Jim had not; he didn't look startled when the door burst open.

"Now," said Kore, advancing like an infuriated duenna. "What is this? You have hurt her, Jim. Ha! She hit you. That is good, you deserve it. You go now."

"Okay." Jim stood up. "I'll be back tomorrow."

He grinned at Kore. The corners of her mouth quivered.

"Men; they are all the same."

After lunch, when I was left alone, I did my exercises instead of sleeping. Kore had announced I had a big treat coming. I would be allowed to go downstairs for dinner.

Early in the afternoon she started getting me fancied up. She worked on my hair for an hour, and then produced one of her silk caftans for me to wear. It was pale green; apparently she had decided that was my color.

I went downstairs supported by Kore and the silent maid. I felt a little giddy at first, but the feeling soon passed away, and I studied my surroundings with interest. I had not seen the interior of the villa, except for my own room. It was a beautiful place. The floors were made of those smooth shiny tiles that are common in the Mediterranean countries, cool deep blues and soft greens—sea colors. The wide staircase had a handsome wrought-iron balustrade. The drawing room was a large, low-ceilinged chamber, with wide windows opening onto a courtyard; not the one I had seen from my window, but a small space, with a little fountain in the center and exotic trees in big pots. The furniture was a mixture of European antiques and local peasant work.

After I had been settled in an overstuffed chair, the maid left and another woman came in with a tray of drinks and hors d'oeuvres. Her face gave me a start; it was so like the faces that had passed through my field of vision the night before. She was young, probably not much older than I; but it's hard to tell people's ages in the islands, they grow old so fast.

I said, *"Efkaristos,"* and took the glass that had been offered to me. Usually the islanders responded with big grins when I said anything. This girl didn't respond, except to duck her head, as if she were bowing.

My start and my stare had not gone unnoticed by Kore.

"They are so shy, these people," she said, after the girl had left. "Like animals, fearful and silent. *Prosit!*" and she lifted her glass.

The German word, which I always associate with enormous steins of beer, sounded unnatural coming from her. I said "Cheers," or something, and drank. The liquid didn't taste like anything I recognized. It was a sweet, thick substance that made me long for a glass of water. Kore saw my grimace.

"A true antique, this wine," she said. "I have made it as the Greeks and Romans did. Our wines to them would be vinegar, too thin, too sour. Theirs were sweet, so always they mix with water, with honey and herbs. It is interesting, yes?"

The wine was too sweet, but it was potent. Kore kept refilling my glass and urging me to drink up. She continued to talk, at first about Greeks and Romans and antiquities; but then the topic changed. As I listened, I was reminded of some of the nature freaks I had known back at school. I believe in a lot of that sort of thing, actually: the unity of living creatures, the great underlying life force, life and death as part of an unending circle. For what is death but reabsorption into the universe? And if the body is absorbed, what happens to the soul—the spark of life that animates the body and makes it something more than a collection of molecules?

I had heard it all before, from different people. The Hare Krishnas and the back-to-nature types, and my roommate, who was reading Sybil Leek and studying to be a witch—you name it, you can find it on a college campus. I knew about reincarnation, too. That was what Kore was talking about, although she didn't use the word, but kept referring to rebirth. When I was young I used to think the idea made a lot of sense. It explains so many things—the seeming waste of life, only a few short years of enjoyment before you get old and senile and sick; the queer memories of things you couldn't have experienced in your present life; the sudden, unreasoning antipathies and affections you feel for people and food and other things. It's an old, old idea; a lot of people have believed in it.

"I had a boyfriend once, named Joe," I said.

"Yes?" Kore said softly.

"He believed in reincarnation. He used to tell me we had been lovers in medieval Italy." I giggled. "Like Romeo and Juliet."

"But why not?"

"He used to quote me things," I went on dreamily. "From Nietzsche and other people who believed in it too. He made me read that book about Bridey Murphy. I didn't really believe it, but I've had some queer experiences. A couple of weeks ago when I was in Crete . . ."

I stopped. The room was getting hazy as the sun sank lower. Broad streaks of light lay across the floor like a carpet of gold.

"I'm getting drunk," I said distinctly. "What's in this wine?"

"You are not drunk," Kore murmured. "What happened in Crete?"

"Funny," I said. "Funny dreams, about the Minotaur and Theseus. I was there, watching them. And when I went to Knossos. . . . They call it *déjà vu*. I've read about it. Scientists can explain it—"

"Scientists know nothing," Kore said scornfully. "You know Knossos? What is so strange about that? You have lived before, you will live again. Many lives. One of them in ancient Crete. You were Greek, like me. Perhaps we know each other, then. I feel this."

"Ariadne wasn't Greek," I said grumpily. "She was a Minoan, Cretan."

"No. She lived in the last great days of the palace, after the destruction, after the Greeks came from the mainland and made a new palace and new dynasty in the ruins. What you see now in Knossos is the remains of this dynasty—all Greek. It is the Greek Minos who has subjugated Athens; to him are sent the boys and girls for the sacrifice; it is his daughter who loves the stranger prince. Only now are scientists learning this is true. You read, in the books—it is true! But I have known. Always I have known. Why do you shiver? It is not cold here."

"It was horrible," I said. "That slimy, dark, stinking hole. . . . Why did I let him go? He couldn't have found the way if I hadn't helped him."

I had not been aware that Kore had risen, but she was now standing beside me. Her hand was on my forehead.

"The sin," she whispered. "It haunts you, all these years, yes? You must expiate the sin. Soon—"

The door opened with a sound that echoed like a pistol shot. I jumped halfway out of the chair. Kore stepped back.

Keller stood in the doorway. His eyes moved from me to Kore.

"What are you doing?" he demanded.

"She is not feeling well," said Kore calmly. "I have told you, it was not wise for her to come down."

Keller crossed the room with long, angry-looking strides. He reached for my wineglass.

"Why do you give her this? No wonder the child is sick." He turned to a tall cabinet and came back with a glassful of clear liquid. "Drink this."

I drank it. It tasted foul. As soon as I had emptied the glass, Keller dragged me roughly to my feet.

"Come to the window. You need air."

The window was of the French type. It stood

half ajar. Keller kicked it open and pulled me out into the courtyard. I was feeling better, but I was still staggering. We stood by the fountain, his hand tight on my arm.

"Breathe," he said harshly. "Deeply. Again. That is—"

The sound—a blend of *crack* and *whine* and *crash*—cut through the last word. The crash was that of broken glass from the window behind us. Keller went down, dragging me with him. I thought he was hit, and tried to get to my knees; his hand slammed into my back, knocking me down behind the low parapet of the fountain. A fusillade of shots rang out, but these, unlike the first, came from the house. Turning, I saw Kore standing amid a sparkle of broken glass. She was holding a rifle.

Keller shouted at her.

"I cover you," she shouted back. "But I think he has gone."

"Stay here," Keller said to me. He stood up and ran a zigzag course toward the gate on the south wall. My skin crawled, but nothing happened.

I stayed there. Kore stood in the doorway, the rifle at her shoulder. After a few minutes the gate opened again and Keller came back.

"No one," he said.

I stood up, very, very slowly. Kore dropped the gun with a clatter and ran to Keller.

"He has hit you!"

"It is only a scratch," said Keller.

We went back in the house. Keller seemed unconcerned about the reddening slash that had slit his shirt sleeve; he waved Kore away impatiently when she tried to fuss over him. She was as white as a dark-skinned woman can be.

"I kill him," she muttered.

"How do you know it was a man?" Keller asked dryly. "I am not so popular that a woman might not try to shoot at me. Kore, sit down and drink some wine. It is not the first time."

"You mean people go around shooting at you all the time?" I asked curiously. The excitement had cleared my brain; I felt quite alert and inquisitive.

Keller shrugged. "When I first came here, there were a few incidents."

"But not for years," Kore said. "I thought . . ."

"You thought you had learned how to deal with these people," Keller said. "It seems you were mistaken."

"No," Kore said slowly. "I think I was not mistaken."

At Keller's suggestion we had brandy all around. I barely sipped mine, figuring I needed to keep my head clear. And I was right. The fun and games weren't over.

We hadn't been sitting for long when there was a loud knock at the front door. Keller and Kore exchanged startled looks, and Kore reached for the rifle that was leaning hazardously against her chair.

Keller clucked disapprovingly. "You must not be so nervous," he said. "Put the gun away. It was foolish, what you did. You might have been killed, standing in the open."

The knock was repeated. I heard footsteps in the hall as one of the servants went to answer it, and then the sound of voices. I almost dropped my glass. I recognized one of the voices—the louder of the two. Keller stood up, but made no move to go to the door. It was opened by the young Greek girl who had served the wine. She was flushed and distraught. Twisting her hands nervously, she started to speak. Someone pushed her out of the way.

"She did try to keep me out," Frederick said. "I take it you do not encourage visitors."

He looked at each of us in turn, his face registering no particular emotion. I waited curiously to hear what he would say to these ghosts out of his past. In a movie it would have been something like, "So, Herr Kapitan, we meet again!" But Frederick, as I ought to have learned, never wasted his breath on meaningless speeches. Instead, he spoke to me.

"I've come to take you home," he said.

He tossed me a bundle. Reflexively, my hands went out to catch it. It seemed to be a shirt and my sneakers, wrapped in a pair of jeans. One of the sneakers fell out as I caught it.

Keller laughed.

"Is that all you have to say?" he asked.

"What else is there to say? An emotional speech of thanks for saving the girl's life? Consider it said. She has been here long enough. Go and change your clothes, Sandy. You look ridiculous in that—that thing."

I let out my breath in a long sigh.

"You know," I said, "I've missed our fights, Frederick. I can't imagine how I've managed these past few days, living in peace and comfort with kind, civilized people who are trying to make me happy."

Kore clapped her hands. "Very good," she said, smiling broadly. "You know how to deal with him. He has not changed."

Frederick looked her over. "You have," he said brutally.

Kore's face quivered, more in anger than in pain. Keller took a step forward. His face had lost its smile.

"That was unkind and unnecessary," he said. "Sit down—Minos—and let us talk like adults."

"Oh, very well," Frederick said. "But if you want adult conversation, I suggest you avoid nicknames. They were childish in any case, and after all this time—"

"Over thirty years," Keller interrupted. "Kore was right about you, Frederick; you are incredible. You don't even ask me what I am doing here. Can it be that you know the answer?"

"Yes," Frederick said. "There can only be one answer. As soon as I knew you were here, I knew why."

"Then," Keller said, "you have a question to ask me, I think. Ask it."

He put his glass down on the table and straightened, his eyes fixed on Frederick. Arms at his sides, shoulders rigid, he looked like a man facing a firing squad.

"Yes," Frederick said calmly. "I do have a question. What have you done about it?"

"About . . . it?" Keller's mouth dropped open in a ludicrous expression of surprise. "You ask me what I have done? And that is all you—"

Kore sprang to her feet. She put her arms around Keller's heaving shoulders. I couldn't tell whether he was laughing or crying.

"He has done nothing," she cried, glaring at Frederick. "Oh, you have not changed, you are the same cold, unfeeling—"

"For God's sake!" It was my turn to leap up. We stood there like four people in a room without chairs. "I can't stand this oblique conversation any longer. What the hell are you all talking about?"

"None of your business," said Frederick.

"Then I've got a question for you," I said, snorting with rage. "Were you the one who shot at Mr. Keller a while ago?"

"No," Frederick said. "Why should I shoot at him?"

"I don't have the faintest idea," I said wildly. "That's one of the things I'm trying to find out."

Keller gently detached himself from Kore's clinging arms.

"Sit down, *Liebchen*, and calm yourself. I apologize for losing control. She is correct, Frederick. I have done nothing. Nothing at all, except to stay here quietly and watch. You are the one who initiates action. What will you do now?"

"Take my daughter home," Frederick said. "Sandy, go and change."

"No," I said.

"I had anticipated a refusal," Frederick said calmly. "I therefore enlisted an ally, reluctant as I was to do so. In this matter, however, we agree. He should be here presently."

So we sat and waited. I tried to start a conversation, but nobody gave me any help; my leading remarks fell heavily into an abyss of silence. The situation was so bizarre I couldn't think coherently. I had been exaggerating when I said I didn't have the faintest idea what they were talking about. I did have an idea; but it seemed preposterous. Besides, I was preoccupied with the arrival of Frederick's ally, whose identity I thought I knew. Sure enough, before long there was another knock at the door, and the maid showed Jim into the living room. With him was Sir Christopher.

Talk about socially awkward situations. Offhand I can't imagine anything worse than this one. Kore reacted with less than her usual savoir faire. She huddled in her chair, saying nothing and glaring impartially on the entire group. If looks could kill, all three outsiders would have dropped dead.

Men are amazing. Jim was the only one who looked embarrassed. The old enemies merely nodded at one another.

"I hope you don't mind," Jim began, glancing at his boss. "When I told him—"

"I thought I had better come along," Sir Christopher said. "I confess that it was curiosity, in part. We never met, *Herr* Keller; but I saw you many times as you went about your duties."

"I do not speak of those days," said Keller softly.

Sir Christopher smiled. "Very wise. It would be better if we all forgot the past. I came primarily for another purpose: to offer my assistance to Sandy, whatever her plans may be."

He wasn't looking at me, though; he was staring at Keller as if trying to recognize a man he had once known. Keller couldn't keep his eyes off Jim. Jim was looking at me, and I was trying to watch all of them at the same time. Frederick and Kore were the only ones not involved in the staring contest. Neither of them seemed at all interested in what was going on.

"Sandy," Jim said sharply.

"What? Oh. Are you all waiting for me to say

something? How flattering. I haven't made up my mind. Maybe I should take a poll. You all seem to have an opinion."

"There is nothing to discuss," Frederick said in a bored voice. "You promised to spend the summer helping me. I want you back at the house tonight, ready to work tomorrow morning."

"One vote in favor of me leaving here, but staying on Thera," I said brightly. "Jim? But I know what you think. You want me to go far, far away. Sir Christopher wants me to go too. Kore?"

"Stay," said Kore, in a stifled voice. "You cannot go now. You cannot."

"Three to one," I said. "Mr. Keller?"

Keller didn't answer. He was still staring at Jim. His eyes had a vacant glitter.

"I see now," he said, as if to himself. "I see the meaning. Yes, it was meant; or why should you come, with his face, as I remember it? You are the one I have waited for, so that I could tell you."

He advanced on Jim, who stood his ground. The rest of them moved as one man—or one person, including Kore. She made a dash at Keller and put her arms around him. Sir Christopher stepped in front of Jim. Frederick stood up.

"Wait," he said. "Hold on—"

Somehow, I don't know how, Kore got Keller turned around, and out of the room. He calmed down as soon as Jim was out of his sight and went with her like a big puzzled child. When the door had closed behind them, Jim let out a long whistle of relief.

"I'd better get out of here," he said.

"You seem to affect the fellow adversely," Sir Christopher agreed, studying his assistant curiously. "I would not have expected the resemblance to disturb Keller so much."

"His conscience is disturbing him," Jim said.

"No doubt. Well, my boy, I agree that we had better go. Frederick?"

"Not without Sandy," said dear old Daddy, settling himself in his chair.

"Then I stay too," said Sir Christopher grimly. "I'll not have you harassing this girl, Frederick."

"Whose girl is she?" demanded Frederick.

"Not yours," I said. "Frederick, whenever you suggest something, it makes me want to do the exact opposite. Leave. I may come tomorrow—if you get off my back. I certainly don't intend to come now."

"Oh, very well," Frederick grumbled.

I went with them to the door. The maid seemed to have vanished.

Jim hung back. "I've got to talk to you," he said out of the corner of his mouth.

"I would also like to talk to you," I said.

"Can you sneak out of here?"

"Sneak? I'll meet you tomorrow morning. Outside, if that's what you want."

"Make it one o'clock."

Sir Christopher turned. I didn't think he could overhear, but I was taking no chances. I nodded at Jim.

I stood in the doorway watching them as they walked away. Frederick was several paces ahead of the other two. It was getting dark; the soft grayish-blue air closed around the three forms, blurring their outlines. They might have been three young men walking in a Cretan evening in a far-gone year. If Kore's crazy ideas had any foundation, the young man whose life had ended prematurely could find no more suitable place for rebirth than the body of his sister's son.

Who are we, anyway? Combinations of common chemicals that perform mechanical actions for a few years before crumbling back into the original components? Fresh new souls, drawn at random from some celestial cupboard where God keeps an unending supply? Spiritual scrap bags—bits and pieces of everyone we have ever been, from the shambling apelike creatures of the Ice Age to the present?

The tiled floor under my feet swayed just a little. Nothing was stable, not even the solid ground. I closed the door and went back into the darkening room.

Dinner that night was an experience. I can't remember what we ate, I was so interested in watching my host and hostess. To a casual observer they might have seemed normal enough, although Keller's black tie and Kore's glitter of jewels were a little overdone. I decided they must dress for dinner the way the Victorian empire builders did in remote outposts, to keep up their morale. They both talked fluently, but every now and then a silence would fall, and one of them would steal a sidelong glance at the other, as if searching for something he was hoping not to see.

The atmosphere was not lightened by the occasional quiver of the earth. You couldn't even call them minor quakes, they were just enough to make the chandelier sway. Midway through the meal the movements stopped, and we finished dessert and coffee without further disturbances. Kore insisted on putting me to bed immediately afterward. I went without argument. I was tired. It was not so much physical fatigue as mental strain. I thought Kore felt it too. She looked old that night. She didn't fuss over me the way she had before, and when I refused a sleeping pill, she merely shrugged.

"I put it here," she said, and placed the tray, which also held a glass of water, on the table by the bed. "If you need . . ."

"I won't. I'm tired."

She left a light burning, as usual, when she went out.

I didn't take the pill, but I drank the water. The

sticky sweet wine had produced a thirst that was still with me. Though I was tired, I was not really sleepy, so I read for a while. The book was dull enough to put anybody to sleep; Keller's English library consisted mostly of books on archaeology and related fields. This was a sober text on Stone Age religion; I remembered having heard Frederick mention it. There was a footnote on practically every word. I read on, my eyelids getting heavier and heavier, till I came across my own name.

The more I discovered about the origins of that name, the less I liked it. Ariadne was not only the daughter of Minos the sea king, she was also a goddess, a vegetation deity who died in the fall and was reborn in spring. . . . There it was again, that reference to resurrection and reincarnation that was beginning to haunt me. Ariadne was a girl too; she was mentioned by Homer, when he spoke of "the dancing ground which Daedalus wrought in broad Knossos for fair-haired Ariadne." No one had ever really figured out what the dancing ground was, or why the master craftsman of ancient Crete should have directed the construction of a simple dance floor. The author of the book I was reading suggested that the dancing ground was a maze, like the Cretan Labyrinth, and the dance was a twisting, circling survival of an old fertility ritual. The tributary youths and maidens of Athens performed the dance, under pressure, and met the bull-masked

killer who was priest of the goddess. "Only Theseus penetrated to the center, to discover Ariadne . . . with the help of her own clue."

The words blurred. I dropped the book and let
my head fall back on the pillow. The night light was
a dim golden haze somewhere off in the distance.

I had never read this book before. It wasn't exactly my type of literature. How, then, had my
subconscious mind come up with the idea that
Ariadne herself waited in the center of the maze,
the prize of the hero who killed the Minotaur?
The dancing place. . . . An innocuous term, suggesting harmless pleasures. How had I known
that Ariadne's dancing place was a labyrinthine
web of stone, and that the function of the dance
was to deliver a victim to sacrifice?

I fell asleep and dreamed.

There was a period of confused and fragmen-
tary impressions—lights flickering, dank, cool air
against my face, voices murmuring words I could
not understand. Then the mists cleared. I awoke
to darkness, but it was not the foul black of the
Labyrinth. Stars blazed down out of a high night
sky, and the air smelled of wild herbs and of the
sea. A hard, gritty substance stung my bare feet as
they moved, stumbling at first and then more
surely, in a measured rhythm. The music was a
thin, high piping. It was the strangest music,
without a recognizable tune. Even the scale was
unfamiliar. The notes had no ending, no resolu-

tion, they repeated endlessly, and my feet moved with them, moving faster as the beat picked up. I was spinning, moving in a narrow circle, with my arms outflung to keep my balance, and the stars were spinning too, so fast that they looked like coiling, luminous snakes. My moving feet made a pattern, a complex network of force like an invisible cat's-cradle. When the pattern was complete, something would take shape. I could feel it hovering, waiting with a terrible eagerness, like a creature crouching behind a barrier waiting to spring out. The barrier was crumbling, inch by inch. . . .

Then the night was dissected by a rising bar of fire. The ground shook under my moving feet; they stumbled and missed the beat. I lost my balance and grasped vainly at empty air; but as I fell I saw the thing that waited behind the barrier. It had my face, but the green eyes blazed like emeralds and the mouth was curved in the queer, disquieting smile I had first seen on the archaic statue Frederick had sent me. I toppled, screaming soundlessly, into a bottomless hole of darkness.

I awoke to clear morning light and a cool breeze from the open window. The sheet was twisted around my legs and the memory of the dream was still heavy on my mind. But as I came back to full consciousness, I was infinitely relieved to realize that for once I had had a nightmare whose origins could be explained. It was the book I had been reading that had set me off.

Relaxed, I lay on the soft bed and contemplated the day ahead of me. The meeting with Jim was not an unmixed pleasure to anticipate. I wanted to see him, but I knew he was going to lecture me. I was tired of people telling me what to do, as if I were a little child. I wanted to be left alone.

It was an effort to sit up. I was still tired, and my legs felt stiff; the sheet had been wound so tightly around them that red welts showed. Apparently I had done quite a bit of thrashing around in the throes of the dream. And then, as I bent my knees, preparatory to getting out of bed, I caught a glimpse of my feet.

The soles were spotlessly clean. There wasn't even a trace of dust. But from heel to toe they were red and scraped, as if I had run, barefoot, across a rough, hard surface.

Chapter

13

AS I SAT THERE STARING AT THE DAMNING, INCONTRO-
vertible evidence of my scraped soles, I had to
fight down a crazy impulse to run, out of the
room and out of the house, just as I was—bare
feet, gossamer nightgown, and all.

However, after the first moment of panic I realized that the incident had broken the spell Kore
had cast. It was nothing less than that, a combi-
nation of drugs, amateur hypnotism, charisma—
and a normal human reluctance to accept the
incredible. Up to that point I had not been sure
what was real and what was my imagination. But
the marks on my feet were a fact.

Kore spent longer than usual that morning
fussing over me, rubbing oil on my hands and
body, arranging my hair in intricate coils. I had to

set my teeth to keep from shouting at her, but I managed to keep quiet. I didn't know what she would do if I faced her with the truth. She might try to keep me there by force. Kore and Keller, even without the servants, were a match for me. I couldn't count on Keller to help me; the man's motives were a mystery.

So I smiled and chatted and ate my lunch like any polite visitor, and as soon as I was left alone, I got up. The clothes Frederick had brought me were in the wardrobe. The coarse, unpressed denim felt good against my skin; I was sick of clinging softness. Carrying my sneakers, I tiptoed to the door and eased it open.

The corridor was deserted. I couldn't hear a sound. Apparently all the members of the household were resting. I made my way cautiously down the stairs, prepared to make a run for it if anyone tried to stop me.

I met no one. But I didn't draw a deep breath until I was outside the villa, with the high white walls behind me.

Within a few minutes I was sweating. It was a hot, hazy day, and the air had the peculiar stillness I had learned to dread. But I was willing to risk an earthquake—a small one—to be free of the atmosphere of that troubled house.

Jim and I hadn't settled on a specific meeting place, so I walked along the path that led toward the village. I was a little late. I didn't see him, though, so as soon as I was out of sight of the villa I sat down on a big rock to wait for him.

My thoughts were not good company. By now I was fairly sure I had figured out Kore's plans. Jim had been right about her. She had resurrected some antique cult and was playing high priestess, with half the women of the village dancing—literally—to her tune.

In my ignorance I found this knowledge less frightening than one might suppose. Kore had been trying to fit me into the unwanted part of the young goddess, or junior priestess—Ariadne the Most Holy, Persephone to her Demeter—Kore, in fact. I was to be Kore, the maiden, and she was to be. . . . Who? It didn't matter. I had quit the cast, and she would have to put on her play without me.

Keller was the one who worried me, because I didn't understand him. He had warned me to get away. But his apparent concern for my well-being might be a sham, or a delusion born of his feelings of guilt. Perhaps he meant to warn me about Kore's uncanny but harmless activities.

Or did the warning have something to do with the fact that someone had shot at him? I couldn't get over the way they had reacted to that attack, without even trying to investigate it. They assumed the would-be killer was one of the villagers. That seemed implausible to me, after years of peace, and in a year when there were three newcomers on the island who had good reason to resent Keller.

I didn't like the direction my thoughts were taking, but I couldn't completely reject the possibility that Jim had fired that shot.

I was so wrapped up in my depressing thoughts that I jumped convulsively when I heard someone approaching. I had almost forgotten that I was a fugitive. The footsteps were coming, not from the direction of the village, but from up the hill.

When Keller came into view I got to my feet. He was wearing sunglasses; the dark ovals hiding his eyes gave him a sinister look. He might not be young, but he was in excellent physical condition. I wondered how fast he could run.

As soon as he saw me he stopped. "Don't be afraid," he said quickly. "I followed only to be sure you were safe."

"I'm meeting Jim," I said. "He should be here any second."

"Good." He sounded genuinely relieved, and I felt as if a heavy weight had been lifted off my shoulders. Apparently he didn't suspect Jim of shooting at him.

"You must not be alone," he went on. "I will wait."

"Really, you needn't bother," I said politely.

"I wait."

We waited. Keller stood perfectly still, as if he

realized that any advance on his part would start me running. I shifted uneasily from one foot to the other. I wasn't really afraid, but I wished he would take off the dark glasses that masked his expression. His eyes were his most attractive feature; with their warm brown hidden, he looked like a stony-faced stage Nazi. Finally, after what seemed like hours, I heard someone coming, his feet crunching the pebbles of the path. It was Jim.

For a moment I felt as if I were not seeing Jim but another man who strongly resembled him. Presumably that man had also been tall and slender, with unruly brown hair and skin toughened by sun and rough weather. Maybe his eyebrows had had that same upward angle, and his mouth the same warm curve when he smiled. He must have been quite a man to inspire such a fury of repentance in his murderer. Even Frederick's voice had softened, momentarily, when he spoke the name. Vince. No one else had referred to him by his first name, but Frederick remembered him that way.

The impression lasted only for a second; but it was so strong I wondered whether I was receiving Keller's thought waves. The sight of Jim really bothered him, even now, when he was prepared and waiting. Jim wasn't too happy to see Keller either.

"What's going on?" he demanded.

"Herr Keller is acting as my bodyguard," I said lightly.

"That's nice of him," Jim said. "But it would be more to the point if Herr Keller told us what he's guarding you from. And," he added, turning on Keller like a duelist, "don't give me any more of that stuff about my uncle. He's dead and gone. Your guilt feelings don't concern me, Keller. I need information. And not about what happened thirty years ago, that's dead and gone too."

Keller laughed harshly. "The past is never dead. You and this girl think you are free of it? You are wrong. The past shapes the present, and our lives are circumscribed by the acts of others long dead. We are all of us trapped in the labyrinth of time."

The speech might have sounded contrived and theatrical if it had not been for the fact that the man was in deadly earnest. And what had prompted him to select the metaphor of the labyrinth? I shivered. Jim put his arm around me.

"No," he said. "I'm not trapped, and neither is Sandy. At the moment we're inconvenienced, not by your past actions but by your present behavior. Damn it, if you have something to say, why don't you say it? I'm tired of vague hints and wild-eyed warnings."

"I cannot," Keller whispered.

He covered his face with his hands. To me he seemed a very pathetic figure, but Jim was unmoved.

"You said last night there was something you

ought to tell me," he insisted. "I'm not stupid, Keller. It's no accident that your old adversaries came to Thera this summer. Why did they come? What secret do you all share?"

Keller lowered his hands, but he did not speak. After a moment Jim went on.

"I'll start the ball rolling, then. When Sandy was hurt the other day, it was no accident. The amphora she found had been planted, with a booby trap attached. I knew when she described it to me that it couldn't have been underwater for three thousand years. Not only was it free of marine incrustations but it was entire, unbroken. Wave action will shatter a pot that's only twenty-five or thirty feet deep. The amphora had to be a good one, so that Sandy would be moved to dig it out, but it isn't impossible to find vessels of that caliber. The museum at Phira has some, and I would guarantee to rob that place any night of the year, it's so poorly guarded. Or if a man lived here for years, excavating in an amateur fashion, he might discover unbroken amphorae. Why do you want Sandy to stop diving, Keller? What's out there in the bay?"

"Ships," said Keller. "The fleet of the sea king."

His surrender was so complete, so unexpected, that Jim was taken aback.

"What?" he gasped.

"Yes." Keller let out a long, shuddering sigh. "It is yours by right. It was his. I am only the guardian."

Jim's arm tightened around my shoulders.

"He's right," I said. "Frederick knows about it too. That's why he brought me here."

"Wait a minute," Jim said dazedly. "I can't take it in, it's too much. A fleet? One Bronze Age ship was found in Turkey. A trading vessel, fantastically well preserved, but not carrying a rich cargo. Are you trying to tell me that an entire Minoan fleet sank in that bay, and that it survived? No. I don't believe it."

"He saw it," said Keller. As always, he avoided the name, but neither of us wondered who the pronoun "he" referred to. "Two years before the war, when he was on Thera for a few days. To hear him describe it, was an experience one could never forget. The sea bottom for many acres strewn with rotting ships and cargo—anchors, masts, amphorae, even the ropes of the rigging."

The words came pouring out of him. The sheer relief of being able to speak, after years of silence. . . . Or was it more than that? Words are given to us to conceal our thoughts; people sometimes talk about one subject in order to avoid another that is more dangerous. The suspicion flashed through my mind and then was gone, in the fascination of Keller's story.

"It was a summer of bad weather. Storms and winds and earthquakes. He had come, after a season's work in Crete, to pursue a personal theory. He had read the reports of the early excavators—

you know, of course, that Fouque discovered Minoan houses here in the 1870's. Nothing was done to follow up those discoveries, and since Fouque's time the excavations on Crete had opened up an entire new civilization. So *he* came, dreaming, as young men do, of making great discoveries.

"Do you believe in accident? If so, you will say that by pure accident he arrived between two storms, one of which swept the bottom of this bay clear of the sand that had covered the fleet for thousands of years. He had hired one of the fishermen to take him on a trip around the island. The man was reluctant to go because he feared more bad weather, but at last he was persuaded.

"They anchored briefly in this bay, so that *he* might search the base of the cliffs for ruins. Diving, he struck his hand on an anchor that protruded out of the ocean floor. Accident, you say? Cling to that thought. It is not pleasant to think we are the toys of vast forces indifferent to man. . . .

"You were thunderstruck to hear of his discovery. Imagine his sensations, seeing it spread out before his very eyes. But he was trained, he knew these islands and their people. He knew that if the ship's captain learned what he had found, there would be looting, hasty and destructive. He dared not remove any object large enough to be noticed by the crew. He took only one thing—"

"The dagger," I interrupted. "Like the inlaid daggers from Mycenae, Jim. Frederick has it now. How did he get it?"

Keller's mouth tightened. "If he told any other of his find, I was not informed. He told me, because he could not bear that it should be lost, and because he knew I felt as he did about archaeology."

Jim had been frozen throughout the long speech. Now he said, in a croaking voice, "But why didn't he come back? Why didn't he tell someone—other archaeologists, the Greek government—"

"He did come back," Keller said. "Three days later, after the second storm. He came on foot, overland, and swam, recklessly, alone. He found nothing. Another convulsion—accident, my young friends?—had reburied the ships. He had not the opportunity to do more. You must remember that this was before the war, before the development of the self-contained breathing apparatus for diving. His find was deep, deeper than you"—he nodded at me—"have yet gone. Fifty feet, perhaps more. Oh, certainly, divers could work at greater depths, even without the clumsy suits that were the only equipment available then. The sponge divers of the Aegean have been doing it for centuries. But this was an entirely new field. None of the techniques of underwater archaeology had been dreamed of, much less worked out. He was dazzled by the immensity of the problem; and he had also a touch of the hoarding instinct all scholars have. The find was his, his alone, and no one else should see it until he was in a position to handle it as it deserved. Also, I think, he was something of a mystic. It was as if someone had opened the sea to him with one sweep of a giant hand and said, 'Here. It is for you. I have kept it for you for three thousand years.' What had waited so long could wait a little longer. The warclouds were gathering, and the Greek government was not concerned with protecting antiquities. At any moment the waters might be closed to him and his people; to speak out would disclose the secret to those who would exploit it for themselves or neglect it in the more urgent demands of survival. You shake your head; you cannot understand. But I can. Even now, I think I would have acted as he did under those circumstances."

"Oh, I can understand," Jim muttered. "Certainly I can understand his desire to keep it for himself. But it's like a—like a fantastic dream. Even if he wasn't hallucinating, the ships can't be there now."

"I think they are gone," Keller said calmly. "I, too, have searched. When I was younger and stronger, I swam often in the bay. Never did I find a scrap. For ten years now I have done nothing. When Frederick came here, I suspected that he also knew. How he found out I do not know. I never spoke to anyone, not even to Kore."

"How did Kore and Frederick know each other?" I asked, since he seemed to be in an informative mood.

But Keller had finished for the day. "Kore's life is her own to discuss," he said curtly. "She has been loving and faithful to me, and that is all that concerns me. You asked me what I knew; I have spoken."

He swung on his heel in a neat military about-face and walked away.

Jim sat down on the rock, pulling me down with him. He let out a long whistle.

"That hit the jackpot, didn't it? Sandy, why didn't you tell me?"

"I didn't know it was your uncle's discovery. I don't remember exactly what Frederick told me, but he certainly implied that he found the ships himself."

Jim was silent, but his silence was suggestive. I went on, answering the question he hadn't asked.

"Maybe your uncle told him."

"Maybe," Jim said dubiously. "We'll never know, not if we expect Frederick to tell us. I passed the house on the way up here. He was in the courtyard washing pots, as if that were the most important thing on his mind."

"I'm not sure he believes in the ships himself," I said. "His behavior has been so erratic, almost as if he were afraid to pursue the idea for fear it will turn out to be a mirage. Jim, now that you know, what are we going to do about it?"

"Damned if I know. It's too big to take in all at once, and too amorphous. And there are more pressing problems."

"Like what?"

"Like you. I can understand now why you're reluctant to leave Thera. I was pushing you too hard. How about a compromise?"

"Such as?"

"You could move to a hotel in Phira for a few days while we consider the situation. I know you're worried about money, but that's a minor consideration. With what we know now, we can blackmail Frederick if we have to. We need time and freedom from pressure to sort out all the possibilities."

"What about the hotel in the village? Does Angelos still refuse to rent me a room?"

"I wouldn't take it if he offered. Things have gone from bad to worse down there. We haven't gotten any work done for days. The men show up, but they don't do anything; they stand around in groups muttering."

"What is Sir Christopher doing about it?"

"Sir Christopher," said Jim, "is one of the people I want to talk to. I think we need a high-level conference, with everybody being candid for a change."

"Okay," I said. "It's a good idea, Jim. I'll go today if I can find transportation."

The look of relief on Jim's face made me realize how worried he had been.

"I'll get you there," he promised. "I'm glad, Sandy. I was afraid you were going to insist on staying with Kore and her crazy boyfriend."

"I don't ever want to see that place again."

"Why? Has something happened?"

"Yes." I brushed at the knees of my jeans. They were covered with a thin layer of dust. "At first I thought I was just having peculiar dreams. I've had them before—about Theseus and Ariadne and the dancing floor—"

His expression stopped me at that point. "Where did you hear about the dancing floor?" he asked sharply.

"A book I was reading last night."

"Oh." His face cleared. "I thought maybe you had been up the mountain. You shouldn't go by yourself; the terrain is pretty rough."

"Why should I go up there?"

"There's a level spot higher up, with the remnants of stonework," Jim explained. "The local people call it the dancing place. There may actually be a folk memory of some ancient ritual. The dances weren't for entertainment, they had a religious function—"

He broke off with an exclamation, as the rock on which we were sitting shifted sideways. We were facing north, toward the flank of the mountain and the center of the island. We were almost ten miles away from the action, but that wasn't far enough.

A thick column of slate gray went straight up toward the sun. It looked like one of the pillars that held up the sky in the old legends, and when it broke and spread outward, it was as if the vault of heaven were collapsing in a rain of stone and crumbling mortar. Ash began to fall, and then my ears were overwhelmed by a thundering, bellowing roar—the herds of the Earthshaker in stampede. Solid ground became unstable as water. Deafened, and blinded by terror and the spreading dust, I felt the rock on which I sat heave like a living thing, flinging me flat on the ground. I tried to press myself into the dirt, clawing at it with my nails. Even after the sound stopped, I could hear the echoes inside my head.

Hands caught me around the waist and tried to pull me up. I clutched at dusty weeds with both hands, resisting. Another roar, and another shifting of the earth. . . . I couldn't breathe. Dust filled my mouth and nose. I was being buried alive, but the earth wouldn't let me stay buried, it was shaking and heaving, trying to eject me from its womb.

I must have passed out from sheer terror. When I came back to consciousness, Jim was holding me in his arms and yelling in my ear.

"Come on, Sandy, snap out of it. We've got to get down to the village; see if they need help."

He yanked me to my feet. I looked up. The smoke was a dark, menacing cloud, covering half the sky, hiding the sun. Ash was falling over everything. I was coated with it.

"What about them, up there?" I gasped, nodding in the direction of the villa.

"The villa is solidly built and fairly new. Some of those shacks in the village have been on the verge of collapse for years. There may be a tsunami, a tidal wave. Hurry, Sandy."

His face was a grotesque mask of dust and streaked blood and rising bruises. My own must have been as bad. My nose and forehead stung where I had rubbed them against the ground.

"Okay," I said. "Sorry I lost my nerve."

"Don't blame you. I'm supposed to be used to quakes but that was the worst I've ever experienced. Volcanoes aren't in my line either. There may be poisonous gases as well as ash in that cloud. We're in for a rough time."

We staggered down the path. Tumbled rock had obliterated sections of the way, and at one point we had to jump a foot-wide fissure that had not been there before. We had reached the lower slopes before I realized that something was missing. I should have seen the roof of our house from this point. It was no longer there.

"The house," I shouted. "Frederick—"

Jim didn't stop running, he just changed direction. The closer we got, the more appalling the damage appeared. The house was gone; the tumbled heap of plaster and rubble that had taken its place bore no resemblance to a man-made structure.

We found Frederick in the wreckage of what had been the outer wall of the courtyard. He had gotten a few feet along the path when the wall gave way and caught him. The most horrible thing, to me, was the way the ash had already covered his motionless body with a thin gray film.

He had been thrown down with considerable force. One side of his face was scraped raw. Aside from that, the only damage seemed to be a badly bruised and possibly broken arm. He was out cold, but he groaned when I ran my hands up and down to check for broken ribs, and soon he opened his eyes.

"Yell if it hurts," I said, and jabbed my thumb into his side.

"My books," said Frederick. "Are my books buried?"

"They are, and you're lucky you aren't," I said. "How are your legs? Can you walk? There's no point hanging around here; we haven't even any water left, much less medical supplies."

Frederick sat up. He surveyed the situation, his eyes moving from the heap of rubble to the clouded sky, and then back to me, passing over Jim as if he had been invisible.

"I think my arm is broken," he said. "You had better start digging out—"

"Your books? Forget it. We'll get you down to the village—assuming there is any village left. Although why I bother, God knows."

"I have no intention of going to the village," Frederick said.

"I do." Jim stood up. "Better take him to the villa, Sandy. If he'll go."

"He'll go. How about you?"

"I must see if they need any help down there." Jim gnawed at his lip. "Unless you need me—"

"We don't need you," Frederick said, with a sneer that would have done credit to Erich von Stroheim on the Late Show. "Run along and play humanitarian. Perhaps you can extract Chris from under a pile of rock and win his undying gratitude."

Jim gave me an eloquent look and a shrug. I shrugged back.

"As you can see, he's alive and kicking. Don't worry about us. I'll come down later, when I see what's happened at the villa."

"Okay." Jim turned away. I watched him go with an unreasonable sense of abandonment, and then turned back to my father.

"Let's go. Unless you have any objections to seeing Keller again."

"Why should I?" Frederick stood up, pushing my hands away as I tried to steady him. I started to say something nasty, but he looked so awful, all dusty and bloody, with his arm hanging limp, that I bit my lip and remained silent.

We started walking. After a few steps I put my arm around him and he let it remain, which was an admission of something, from Frederick. It took us forever to retrace the route that I had covered in a quarter of an hour earlier that day. The path was almost obliterated, and twice we had to detour around cracks that Frederick was too feeble to jump. The air had darkened, not to the quiet blue of evening, but to a sickly grayish shade that made all objects look corroded and rotten. The ash continued to fall. I was coughing, and Frederick's breath came in strained gasps. He leaned more and more heavily on me.

When the walls of the villa came into sight I could have wept with relief. They seemed to be intact. As we neared the front gate I saw some evidence of damage. Stones littered the path and the gate itself hung askew. An acrid smell of burning reached my nostrils, and with alarm I remembered the charred debris of Knossos. Fire, spreading from lamps and cooking fires, had caused as much damage as the earthquake itself.

In the courtyard many of the earthenware pots, with their green contents, had tumbled and shattered. The smell of smoke grew stronger.

As we approached the front door, Keller came out. He didn't speak, but came quickly to relieve me of Frederick's weight. Frederick was drooping; he didn't seem to realize that he had changed hands. I rubbed my aching shoulders and followed Keller into the house. It felt cool and clean after the outdoors, and I noticed that the windows were tightly shuttered.

"We keep out the ash, if possible," Keller said. "You are unhurt? What has happened in the village?"

His hands were moving over Frederick as he spoke. When he touched the arm, Frederick's eyes opened and he let out a profane remark.

"It is not broken, I think," Keller said calmly, before I could answer his first question. "The servants have gone. You will have to fetch bandages and water. Luckily our reserve tank was not damaged."

"Where is Kore?" I asked.

Keller's eyelids flickered. "She is safe. She rests now. We had a fire in the kitchen. It is extinguished, there is no need to fear. You will find supplies . . ."

He gave me directions. It took me a while to find the things he wanted. Then I held a flashlight while Keller bandaged Frederick's arm. The room was quite dark, but he didn't turn on the lights. Either the wires were down, or he was afraid of risking another fire from shorted electrical circuits.

Except for swearing, Frederick didn't say anything. I wondered about leaving these two old enemies alone together; and then decided cynically that I didn't really care what they did to each other.

"I'm going down to the village," I said.

"You would be better to stay," Keller said. "This house is as safe as any structure could be; I saw to that when it was built."

"You think there will be more quakes?"

"I cannot say. But I am not so concerned about that as about the volcano. The ash is falling thickly."

His voice was quite matter-of-fact; his hands, arranging a sling around Frederick's neck, were steady. Apparently his nerves got out of hand only when his imagination tormented him. In an ordinary physical crisis he was first-rate, and I found his presence a lot more consoling than I did Frederick's.

"I'll risk it," I said. "I may not be able to help, but—"

"Why don't you be honest?" Frederick asked. "It's that boy you're worried about. The whole village could go up in smoke so long as he survives."

"What do you care?" I said. "You didn't even ask me if I was hurt."

"I could see you were not," Frederick said. "Why should I ask?"

I couldn't think of any answer that was rude

enough, so I simply walked out. But when I opened the front door, it was all I could do not to slam it shut and retreat. Day had turned to night, or rather to a dismal twilight. The air stung my eyes and smelled funny. I started to cough.

Then I thought of Jim and the children and old people in the village, and I stepped out into the courtyard. I hadn't gone far, however, before a shape loomed up out of the shadows. I knew it was Jim; I would have known him in the dark of a lightless cave. I greeted him with an exclamation of relief and joy. He didn't reply, just caught my hand and turned me around.

"What—" I began.

"They've gone crazy down there. Come back to the villa."

It was a strange feeling to be walking in and out of the house as if it were a public building. Keller glanced indifferently at us as we ran in, and went on pouring brandy into a glass that he handed to Frederick.

"Ah," said the latter unpleasantly. "The humanitarian has given up."

"There's nothing I can do down there," Jim said. He was still holding my hand, so tightly that it hurt. "I came to warn you. Better not leave the house."

"Why?" Keller asked. "Was there much destruction?"

"Not as bad as it might have been. Some of the

older houses collapsed and the hotel is pretty well demolished. It's not that. It's . . ." Jim ran his fingers through his hair; a gray cloud of dust surrounded his head, halolike, for a moment before settling. "They wouldn't let me help. They were saying some rather ugly things. Some of the kids threw rocks."

"Typical," Frederick said. "When a catastrophe occurs, the primitive mind seeks a scapegoat."

"But they're friends of mine," Jim said. "I don't understand this."

"Sit down," Keller said, motioning toward a chair. "Leave them alone. They will quiet. This has happened before."

Jim shook his head. "I'm going back. I just came here to warn you to stick to the house. You especially, Sandy."

"What makes you think you're any more impervious to rocks than I am?" I demanded. "If you're going, so am I."

"I'm not going to the village. I—I can't find Chris."

"Oh, Jim! The hotel—"

"No, he wasn't there. They told me that much before they. . . . I'm going to the dig. I can circle around, above the village."

I didn't try to argue with him. I knew how he felt about his boss, and indeed the idea that the man might be lying injured in the increasingly foul air disturbed me too. I'd even have gone to look for Frederick under those circumstances.

I followed Jim out into the hall. He turned at the door and took me by the shoulders.

"No, Sandy, you can't come." His voice was very low, almost a whisper. "I want you to keep an eye on things here. There may be trouble. That crowd in the village could turn into a mob. Your father is right. They want a scapegoat."

"No," I said. "It couldn't happen."

"It could. I'll bring Chris here, if I can find him. In any case I won't be gone longer than I can help. Lock the place up tight. And you might ask Keller if he's got any firearms."

With that shocking suggestion he was gone.

I turned slowly back into the house. Earlier that day I had wondered whether anything more could happen to complicate my life. In one sense the cataclysm had simplified the situation. An order of priority had been established. Survive. That was the first problem. Survive an erupting volcano, complete with earthquakes, and a potential mob. After that we could worry about lesser difficulties.

The sight of the two men exasperated me almost beyond endurance. They were sitting and drinking their brandy like two old gents in a club.

"Aren't you going to *do* something?" I demanded of the shadowy figures.

"What is there to do?" Keller asked remotely. "We can only wait. What will come, will come."

"How about Kore?"

"Leave her alone. She is sleeping. I gave her a sedative, she was disturbed."

"Jim said I should ask you if you had a gun in the house," I said, hoping to shake him out of his fatalistic mood.

"As you saw," Keller said indifferently. "They are in that cabinet."

I found the arsenal, with the help of the flashlight. The .22 Kore had used was there. It had several shells in the chamber. There was another rifle, a heavier one, and a couple of handguns, all loaded and ready to go.

Nobody seemed to care what I did, so I went exploring. The house was deserted; no doubt the servants had gone to the village to see if their families were all right. There was a fine drift of ash over every flat surface. Moved by some obscure impulse, I wrote my name: Sandy, on the top of the dining-room table, and then stepped over a pile of broken crystal on my way to the stairs. The house itself had stood, but there were a lot of broken dishes lying around. Pictures had fallen from the walls, too. I started to pick one up and then dropped it again. This was no time to clean house.

The upstairs looked like a hotel in the off season— dark, silent, dusty. I looked into the room I had occupied and saw the book I had been reading lying open on the bedside table. It gave me an eerie feeling to think how much had happened since I left the room only a few hours ago.

I had no idea which room Kore occupied, so I tried one door after another, meeting only darkness and emptiness, until I found a door that wouldn't open. I banged on it.

"It is locked," said Kore's voice, from inside.

"Please unlock it," I said, wondering. "It's only me."

"I know it is you," Kore said. "I cannot unlock. Jürgen has the key."

"He locked you in?" It was a stupid question; she didn't bother answering it. Then, belatedly, I realized that from the first she had spoken in English.

"How did you know it was me?" I asked.

From behind the locked door came an uncanny chuckle.

"I knew."

I had been about to offer to let her out. The lock wasn't very complicated; I could have picked it easily. The queer laugh made me reconsider. Keller might have a darned good reason for locking her up.

"Are you all right?" I asked. "Is there anything I can do?"

"Not now."

"Don't worry," I said. "If . . . anything . . . happens, I'll make sure you get out. You're as safe in there as anywhere."

"I am safe," Kore repeated. Only it didn't sound like a simple repetition of my reassurance; it sounded like a statement of fact.

I retreated. Even the two silent men in the parlor would be better company than that voice.

They were still sitting there when I returned. They reminded me, not of clubmen now, but of those plaster casts archaeologists have made of the victims of the Vesuvius eruption. Hardening ash made a perfect mold of the bodies before they fell into dust; centuries later, scholars poured plaster into the cavities and recreated the dead of Pompeii, men and women, children and dogs, lying as they had died in the last futile struggle for breath.

It was not the most comfortable thing to recollect just then. I poured myself a glass of brandy and drank. Then I went to the window and peered out through a crack in the draperies. I thought the air was a little clearer. It was hard to tell because the sun was setting, up there beyond the clouded skies.

I turned back to my silent companions and lifted my glass.

"*Morituri te salutant*," I said. "That's what the gladiators used to say to the emperor, remember? 'We who are about to die salute you.' I bet you wonder how I know that. Me, the semiliterate.

Well, one of the girls on the hockey team thought that was a cute motto. She used to say it to the coach before—"

"Put that brandy down," Frederick interrupted. "You have no business drinking at your age."

"Ah," I said. "It can talk. Go on, Frederick, lecture me some more. Even your croaking is preferable to silence."

Frederick didn't respond, so I tried again.

"You ought to show a little concern, you know. If I don't live through this adventure, it will be your fault. You got me here."

"You came of your own free will." Frederick's voice sounded livelier.

"You conned me," I said. "Don't you feel a little, teeny bit guilty? Come on, Frederick. Feel guilty."

"Guilty." The word made me jump. I had almost forgotten Keller, silent in the shadows. "We are all guilty. Guilty of mankind."

The reverberant pounding that followed the speech sounded like a symphonic accompaniment. Doom, knocking at the door. Then I got hold of myself.

"It's Jim," I said, with a long breath of relief. "I forgot, I locked the door when he left."

I ran to open it. Jim didn't say hello; he pushed me out of the way and bolted the door again before leading the way into the living room.

"You didn't find Sir Christopher?" I asked.

"No. I looked everywhere. Damn it, can't we have some light in here?"

I gave him the flashlight. It wasn't much help.

"What is the situation?" Frederick asked, blinking as the beam focused on his face.

"The volcano is quiescent, for the moment. The air is clearing a little."

"Good," I said. "Then the village should be calming down."

"No." Jim flicked the light across his body, and I gasped. His shirt was torn and streaked with blood. "When I found no sign of Chris at the dig, I had to go back to the village," he went on. "I had a few words with the priest. He wasn't too coherent, but the gist of the speech was 'Get out and stay out of sight.' "

"The priest," I exclaimed. "But he, of all people—"

"He was trying to help," Jim said. "If I had followed his advice, I wouldn't have gotten these bruises. It was my old landlord, Angelos, who started the fight. He seems to blame us for the damage to his damn hotel. Half a dozen of them jumped me then. Not all the men are crazy; your foreman Nicholas was one of the guys who intervened so I could get away. The women. . . . The women are gone."

"What are you talking about?"

"I didn't see a single female," Jim said. "Not one."

"In their houses, like good Greek ladies," I said. "Tending the wounded, praying. . . ."

"They aren't praying," Jim said. "At least. . . . Where's Kore?"

"Upstairs. Locked in her room."

"You locked her in?"

"No," Keller said. "I did."

"Then you know," Jim said. "You know what she's doing."

The flashlight beam struck Keller full in the face, but he made no move to shield his eyes. The pinpoint pupils, shrinking against the light, gave him a ghostly look.

"I know," he said, barely moving his lips. "There is no harm. She does no harm, it is only a game—"

"Then why did you lock her in? You know it's no game. It's dangerous as hell."

"So Kore's fantasies have found an outlet." Frederick's face was illumined now, as Jim turned the light in response to his voice. "What a fitting occasion. The old gods are angry; they must be propitiated. But Kore's self-appointed role must have been useful all along. By convincing the women of her powers, she controlled the entire village. It always was a woman's cult—"

"You cold-blooded bastard," Jim said. "Perched on your academic pedestal lecturing about cults. . . . You know what your blasted cult involves, don't you? The details are obscure, of course—" His voice was a savage mockery of Frederick's pedantic tone. "But we can be sure that a vegetation cult involved some form of sacrifice. The victim was killed in order that his blood might bring about the resurrection of life in spring. The dying god, Osiris and Attis, Persephone. . . . Kore can choose between several versions of the ritual. Which one does she fancy, Keller? The myth of Persephone, who died and was reborn yearly? It's one of the oldest myths, older than the Greeks, older than ancient Crete, and Sandy makes a perfect patsy, doesn't she? Ariadne, the Most Holy, who was the Cretan equivalent of Persephone. Or is it the Dionysian rite Kore follows? In that case any warm male body will serve the purpose. Is Chris being chased around the hills right now, by a crowd of howling maenads?"

"Absurd," Frederick said. "Hysterical nonsense."

I only wished I could believe it. I knew Jim was right about the cult. What I had not known was the complex and perilous meaning of the role Kore had selected for me. The women of Zoa, filing past my bed that night, in a solemn, ritual viewing of the new "goddess"—Kore's daughter-substitute in a ritual so old that its hoary antiquity weighed down the mind. The priestess was the incarnation of the goddess, and She was the mother, the oldest of all the gods, the Earth herself—dying in winter, born again in spring with the new leaves, the young lambs, the sprouting corn. The women were the food gatherers and the ones who brought forth life. Yes, it was a woman's cult, and the women of Zoa were only following tradition, revering a mother far older than the bright and tender Virgin.

Not all the women were involved, of course, only the more susceptible and superstitious. But there were enough of them, and their influence was great enough to keep Kore and her lover safe all these years. No doubt that was how the game had begun. But now. . . . How far would Kore go to fulfill the demands of her votaries? Was she entirely sane?

Keller's mind was apparently running along the same line. He got up and left the room, almost running. His footsteps pounded up the uncarpeted stairway. He was back very quickly.

"She's gone," he said. "One of the women must have let her out."

Jim started for the door—and ran smack into a chair. As he stood swaying I snatched the flashlight from him and turned it on his face. He closed his eyes and put his hand up, but not quite soon enough.

"Your eyes," I said, horrified. "What happened?"

"The fumes, I suppose," he said fretfully. "Let go, Sandy. I've got to find Chris."

"You can't even see! Are you crazy? What's to prevent them from picking you as their star performer instead of Chris? You fit the part better. You'll blunder right into them."

"Unlikely," said Frederick. "If the performance takes the form I anticipate, it will resemble the bacchic orgies, with some form of circling dance. There will be considerable noise."

He got up from his chair and went to the window. Jim was making feeble attempts to free himself from my grasp. I hung on with both hands.

"The air seems to be clearing," Frederick said. "However, our young hero is in no condition to go out. I see I shall have to assume the role, ill as it suits me."

"You!" I exclaimed.

"Don't misunderstand," said Frederick. "I am immensely curious. The chance of seeing such a survival may never come again. Kore's contributions cannot be denied, but she must have worked with a residuum of folk memory handed down in these islands for millennia. Fascinating."

In that instant, on that last word, my feelings for him died. Oh, I had felt them, much as I wanted to deny them; I had hoped he might have some tenderness buried under his cold, formal manner. I had deluded myself.

"Go ahead," I said. My voice was as flat as my emotions. "Go on, watch the women dancing and cheering and tearing their victim limb from limb.

I hope you will take notes. You may find it a little difficult to write left-handed, but if I know you, you'll manage."

"I will." He put out a hand as Jim surged toward him and shoved him back. "Keep that young fool here. Naturally I will interfere if matters go as far as he suggests, which I don't expect for a moment. The victim will be a goat or a sheep. I shall return in good time."

Jim had fallen into a chair and was struggling to get up. I sat on his lap to hold him down, and tried to calm him.

"Just let me bathe your eyes and fix you up a little. I promise you can go. Later. After you feel better."

As I spoke, Frederick left. I heard the front door close.

Keller helped me work on Jim. We found a lantern that shed more light than the flashlight we had been using. The eyedrops seemed to help.

When Keller had finished, he rolled his shirt sleeves down and buttoned them neatly.

"I too must go," he said. "I must find Kore."

"She's in no danger," Jim muttered. "Sandy is the one I'm worried about."

"Me?" I said, pretending surprise. This was not the time to tell him what I knew about Kore's religious doctrines, especially the ones that concerned me personally. But I underestimated his intelligence.

"Why do you suppose I keep coming back here instead of looking for Chris?" Jim demanded. "I have a pretty good idea what Kore is up to. When I realized that the women were gone from the village, I started putting the rest of it together. Kore's talk about reincarnation and her references to a female deity—whom we naïvely identified as the Virgin Mary—your dreams, the hints the priest threw out. . . . Keller, for God's sake—you ought to know what's going on in that woman's mind, if anyone does. What will she do?"

"She never spoke to me of that," Keller said. "It was her private affair."

"It's not private now," Jim said.

"But I tell you, she will harm no one." Keller was standing just beyond the light; it left his face in shadow, but shone on his hands. They were tight, white-knuckled fists. "You young fools, frantic about imaginary dangers. . . . There is danger walking abroad tonight, but it will not be from my poor Kore. It will be *for* her. And for others."

Jim took the wet cloths off his eyes and sat up.

"I think you had better tell me," he said.

Keller slumped into a chair as if his legs would no longer support him.

"Yes, I must tell you. For thirty years I have kept this burden on my soul. I can bear the weight no longer."

Jim glanced questioningly at me. Was Keller about to go through the same old story again?

"I know about your guilt feelings," Jim said. "But you're mistaken if you think anyone harbors a grudge about that. A murderous grudge, anyway. The idea of revenge—"

"Revenge!" Keller's voice cracked with emotion. "I do not speak of a motive so juvenile! I speak of treachery and fear! How do you think your uncle fell into our hands? It was not by accident, or by our cleverness. He was betrayed, I tell you—given over to us by a man he trusted like a brother, in exchange for immunity. Would such a man hesitate to kill now, in order to keep the secret of his shame?"

Chapter

14

"SO THAT'S IT," JIM SAID. "I WONDERED. . . . WHO ELSE knows this?"

"Myself. Kore." Keller laughed shrilly. "The traitor. Judas, Cain. . . . What I did was bad enough. But he—"

"All right, keep calm," Jim said quickly. "All these years you remained silent. Why?"

"Why should I speak?" Keller's face was shining with sweat. "At the beginning silence was part of the price I paid for his services. It was war. One does many distasteful things to serve one's country. Then, after it was over—to whom should I speak? Was it part of my duty to betray this man, as he had betrayed his comrade in arms? Whom could I serve by doing this?"

Jim's voice cut through the high-pitched monologue.

"And besides, he might have a few secrets to tell about you. I'm sure you did other things, 'in the course of your duty' that might have embarrassed you. No"—as Keller made a wild gesture of protest—"never mind, forget it. Let the past die!"

"It won't die," I said, breaking the silence shock and horror had induced. "Keller said it this afternoon: the labyrinthine prison of time. . . . Jim, why don't you ask the important question? What are you afraid of?"

"A mutual pact of silence," Jim said, gesturing me to be quiet. "And you came here—my God, you came here to protect his find from the man who betrayed him. Was that it?"

Keller nodded eagerly.

"That at least I could do."

He looked hopefully at Jim, as if expecting approbation. The man was mad, all right, but only part of the time. There was a single flaw in his thinking, and even that had its own bizarre consistency.

"I understand," Jim said. "So, this year, when it appeared that the secret was known, you tried to stop the work. The avalanche, that day you saw us on the hill, was no accident. You wanted to put Sandy out of action. She was the diver, the one who was looking for the ships. You planted the amphora, with its booby trap, hoping she would be—"

"No!" Keller's eyes widened. "What do you take me for, that I would harm a young girl? Was I not the one who saved her? She might have died, in the water, if I had not—"

"You didn't plan to kill her," Jim interrupted. "Only to immobilize her. I'll give you that much credit. The mere fact that you were there in time to bring her in is suspicious. How could you have been on the spot unless you expected an accident?"

"Stop it," I said, as Keller began to protest. "All this is beside the point. We sit here talking, while. . . . You don't have to protect me, Jim. I know who the traitor was. It must have been Frederick."

"You're jumping to conclusions," Jim said in a strained voice.

"It was your boss or mine," I said. "Take your pick. Who has the kind of ruthless self-interest for such a filthy action? Why did he volunteer to go out just now? It wasn't altruism, you can be sure. He's never done anything that didn't serve his own interests. What's he doing out there? Who is he after?"

"My God." Jim got to his feet. He pointed at Keller. "You were shot at yesterday afternoon. Was that—"

"*Nein, aber nein.*" Keller's eyes had a queer shine as he looked sideways at Jim. "I am not such a fool. I have taken precautions. A statement, to be opened at my death. He has the strongest reasons to keep me alive."

"You stubborn fool, can't you see the situation has changed?" Jim shouted. "Maybe your precious statement has protected you all these years, but it isn't doing the job now. He's going to kill someone—you, Kore, Sandy—I can't tell, I don't know all the facts!"

"Let them kill each other," Keller said listlessly. "What does it matter?"

"You won't get any more out of him," I said to Jim. "Why are we standing here playing Sherlock Holmes? We've got to stop him."

Before Jim could answer, a ghastly quavering shriek rang along the dark hall.

"It's Kore," I gasped. "Quick, Jim."

The sound aroused Keller from his apathy. He jumped up and ran out of the room, calling Kore's name. Jim went after him, as another, fainter cry shivered the air. Jim yelled at me, something about staying where I was; but I couldn't remain passive while a cry like that one assaulted my ears.

The result would have been the same, whether I remained alone in the room or was alone somewhere else in the house. I made it a little easier for them, that was all. But I didn't expect that particular kind of danger. A howling outraged mob couldn't have broken into the house unheard.

When they surrounded me, I was taken by surprise. I got out one scream, but it was quickly stifled by calloused work-hardened hands—a web of hands and arms, wrapping around me like the tentacles of an octopus, dark bodies pinning my arms to my sides. One of the hands thrust something against my nose. The sharp fumes made me sneeze, but not for long. I pitched forward into blackness, and into the eager, waiting arms of the women of Zoa.

II

I awoke to the worst nightmare I had ever had— the worst, because it wasn't a dream. Yet there was an air of unreality about the scene, and the fact that I was alone made me wonder whether I might not still be dreaming. For a while I wavered back and forth between the two theories.

I had a terrible headache and my stomach felt queasy. I was sitting on the ground; hard pebbles pressed into my posterior. My physical sensations suggested that I must be awake. But when I tried to move, I couldn't, and immobility is one of the signs of nightmare. It took me a while to figure out that I was tied to a tree. My feet were tied too. The ropes were padded; when I pulled against them I felt no pain, only constriction. I tried to squint at the ropes on my ankles, but I couldn't see clearly; my eyes took some time to focus, and the shadow of the tree enveloped me.

The immediate source of light was a fire burning in the middle of a wide-open space. The sky overhead was a ghastly unnatural crimson. Without stars I had no sense of direction, but I knew where I was. I recognized it from an earlier nightmare. Low, uneven ridges of ashy rock surrounded a flat space about an acre in area. The worn, stone-paved surface was the one on which my bare feet had bruised themselves, dancing, the night before. A rehearsal, no doubt, for this evening's performance.

The sickness in my stomach wasn't solely the result of the drug they had used on me. I would almost have welcomed a band of shrieking maenads; the crimson silence, broken only by the far-off rumblings of the tortured earth, was worse than any human threat. My mind was quite clear—too clear. I was remembering a lot of facts I would rather have forgotten.

Score one for Jim. He had been right, and Kore had been training me for the leading role in her lunatic drama. Even the tree—it wasn't much of a tree, all gnarled and straggly, but trees and their man-made derivatives, pillars and columns, were sacred to the goddess in ancient Crete. The Minoans sacrificed bulls and let their blood flow onto the pillars. I looked around the little amphitheater. No bulls. No sacrificial animals visible—except one.

I made myself relax. I had been straining uselessly against the bonds, and all I was doing was tiring myself. Whoever had tied me up had been considerate of my comfort, but she had done a thorough job. My hands were free, but my elbows were pinned by the ropes that held me half erect. I couldn't reach behind me to undo the knots there, and even if I could contort myself into a position where I could touch the ropes on my ankles, untying my feet wouldn't do me much good.

The emptiness was getting on my nerves. Where were they? Howling along the hillside in pursuit of some other prey? The maenads had done that in ancient Greece, and in the still more ancient homelands from which that particularly gory cult had come. The chase culminated in the *diasposmoi,* when the young male victim who represented the god was caught. It was amazing that I remembered the word, but I knew why my mind had produced it—I didn't want to think of the English equivalent. But I couldn't keep it down. Dismemberment. And worse. Ritual cannibalism, to absorb the qualities of the god.

It is surprising how clever one becomes under pressure. I didn't want to remember any of this. I couldn't have remembered it if I had been facing an exam; but now the words stood out in my mind as if I'd just finished reading them. The Orphic rite, the Mysteries of Eleusis, the Sacred Marriage. . . . I wondered if Kore had included that little item in her agenda. Was that what the women were seeking, a mate for the goddess instead of a victim? They couldn't kill him if they wanted him to be of any use in the former role.

A big choking lump rose to my throat. It was no use trying to keep cool and telling myself horrible black jokes. This was no joke. The worst of it was not knowing what was in store for me—and for others. I told myself that surely Kore wouldn't carry the dark rites to their bloody conclusion; a goat or a chicken killed, a wild dance and a lot of wine. . . . But I remembered how easily I had been caught, and I thought of Jim, almost as vulnerable, with his weakened eyesight and bruised body.

A vast network of lightning scored the sky. I cowered against the tree, closing my eyes. When I opened them again, the western sky was a brighter crimson. I knew what the signs meant. Violent electrical storms had accompanied earlier eruptions, and the red glow was the reflection of red-hot lava against the clouds of smoke and ash. In spite of my terror, something in me responded unwillingly to the majestic violence. Kore couldn't have chosen a more fitting setting for her play. Nor could I entirely blame the village women for seizing any means possible of propitiating outraged nature. This was enough to turn anyone's mind.

I pulled my feet up and tried to wriggle around so that I could reach the ropes. I had to do something or I would go crazy thinking. I was still trying to stretch my fingers two inches beyond their proper length when another web of lightning blazed out, followed by a crash that made my ears ache. Thunder, or maybe another eruption; I couldn't tell. The whole world was going insane.

I didn't hear them coming. There was no music, no wild chanting. No organization, either; they sauntered down the slope in small groups, two or three of them together. One group was larger. In the middle, prodded along by the sheer number of them, was Jim.

They had wound ropes around him, but his legs were free. The women pushed him across the floor and sat him down—they weren't rough, I'll say that for them—and then tied his feet. We sat there looking at each other for a while.

"Are you all right?" Jim asked. "They didn't hurt you?"

"Not yet," I said. "How did they catch you?"

"Ambushed me, just outside the villa. As soon as we realized you were missing, we started to look—"

"It was stupid of you to separate," I snapped. "You and Keller together could have fought them off."

Jim accepted the rebuke without comment; he knew it was prompted by frayed nerves.

"Keller didn't go. Your father came back while we were searching the house. He went toward the village to look for you."

"He wouldn't be much help anyway," I said bitterly.

Some of the women were piling up stones on the paving to the right of the fire. The structure was long and low—as long as an outstretched human body.

Jim turned on his side, raising himself on one elbow. He started to speak. I cut him short.

"Look!"

The high priestess had arrived.

The flames were burning high and bright; I could see her clearly. She didn't look very happy. The golden diadem that crowned her black hair was slightly askew, her clothes were rumpled, and I had a feeling that she wouldn't be there except for the escort that hemmed her in. I recognized one of the brawnier women: Helena, the wife of Angelos, the hotelkeeper.

When Kore caught sight of us, she pushed her guard of honor aside and ran toward us. They made no move to stop her. She dropped down on the ground next to me, her ample bosom heaving with haste and agitation.

"They said they would bring you, but I did not think you would be so stupid to be caught," she panted.

"Let's not start out criticizing our behavior,"

Jim growled. "This whole thing is your fault. I'm glad you seem to be coming to your senses, but it's a little late."

"They are mad," Kore moaned, clutching at her hair and knocking the diadem even farther askew. "It was a game, a little game. . . . Oh, yes, I pretended to believe, at times I pretended so well I almost did believe. But something has gone wrong, they are not in my control now. Never would I permit such happenings—"

"No sacrifices?" Jim asked.

Kore shrugged.

"A chicken, a goat. . . ." She must have heard my gasp of released breath; she glanced at me, and grimaced in sympathy. "Ah, the poor children—you did not think . . . ? No, no, there is no danger to you. This is bad, wrong, but it is not what you fear. They wish only to see the Sacred Marriage consummated."

My head turned stiffly, as if on a pivot, toward the low stone structure the women had built. It was long enough for a human body, certainly— and wide enough for two. The women had spread it with an embroidered cloth and were now decorating the structure with branches and wilted wildflowers.

I turned back to stare at Kore. She was still babbling.

". . . then we kill the goats, one for each, and it is over. That is all."

"I'm not going to sit here and watch them slaughter some poor little goats," I said. I didn't dare look at Jim.

"You're crazy," he said, in a strangled voice. "Crazier than she is, worrying about goats, when— If you think I am going over there in front of forty staring women and— No way!"

"You'd rather die?" I inquired sweetly. "That's my line. Only I wouldn't rather die."

"Trust a woman to turn any crisis into a personal insult," Jim said. "That's not the problem, and you damn well know it."

"We could pretend," I said. I was feeling a little giddy now that the danger I had feared seemed to be without foundation.

"Maybe *you* could," Jim said.

"No," I said, watching Helena carefully arranging wilted blossoms across the foot of the stone couch. "I guess I couldn't. Kore, you've got to do something. Talk them out of it."

"There's a knife in my pocket," Jim said urgently. "Cut me loose."

"You make such fuss," Kore said petulantly. "Such a little thing! You are lovers, young and strong. Why can you not—"

"Kore!" I said emphatically.

She wasn't as carefree as she pretended; the firelight reflected from the perspiration that covered her face. With a movement that was half shrug, half shiver, she spread out her flowing

skirts and under their cover began to fumble in
Jim's pocket.

The process seemed to take forever. Apparently
the high priestess was supposed to do some
writhing around; except for a few casual glances,
the women paid no attention to us. Kore cut the
ropes on Jim's feet and was reaching for the ones
that bound his arms when one of the women
called out. She was carrying a load of twigs
toward the fire; now she stopped, pointing
toward the sky. To my incredulous relief I saw a
star.

"Look," I said. "The air is clearing. Maybe. . . ."

"The wind has changed." Jim struggled to a sitting position. "What a piece of luck! That should
blow the clouds away from the island, out to sea."

"Tell them the gods have changed their
minds," I said to Kore. "Isn't that a good omen?
Tell them!"

"I try." Kore got to her feet.

"Damn it, finish this job first," Jim demanded,
squirming.

Kore paid no attention. She was still holding
his knife when she raised her arms and called out
in a high, shrill voice. The women stopped work
to listen. Some of them seemed to be impressed
by her arguments. They hesitated, glancing un-
certainly at one another. But the general opinion
among the hard-core members seemed to be that
the evidence was inconclusive.

Kore sat down again and went back to work on the ropes. "They say no," she reported.

"So I gathered. Hurry up, will you?" Jim's voice sounded strained. "I have a feeling. . . ."

I had it too—the queasy, quavery shaking of the entrails that was becoming only too familiar. The women had hoped to summon the gods and they had succeeded in arousing the greatest of them all.

The ground began to rock gently. Then the sky to the north caught fire. A column of flame shot up amid a roar of erupting gas. In the livid, unearthly glare every blade of grass, every twig stood out as if outlined in fire.

The women broke. I don't know whether it was superstition or natural fear that made them flee; most of them had families, and they knew what might follow. Or perhaps they interpreted the spectacular demonstration as a sign that the gods weren't pleased with the proceedings.

A few of the toughest women lingered. Helena was one of them. A glowing lump of magma struck the ground behind her; she glanced at it and then looked at us. Her expression turned me cold, and in the extremity of the moment it seemed to me that I could read her mind. Maybe the gods were getting impatient because the sacrifice was delayed.

Kore was crawling around on the ground, trying to find the knife, which she had dropped in her terror. Jim was struggling, trying to free himself. Helena was stalking toward us, glaring. Red-hot stones were falling. Then, through the chaos, a voice rose, in a bellow whose volume made it impossible to identify the speaker.

"Police!" Kore gasped. "It is the police!"

"It can't be," Jim gasped back; he was still struggling. "There aren't any— Kore!"

But Kore was gone. I had never seen her move so quickly. The few remaining women had dispersed too. We were alone in the clearing. And the rocks were still falling, red-hot coals of magma from the tormented entrails of the volcano. I was struggling too—a senseless action, but I couldn't help it, it was horrible to be unable to move amid the hail of molten debris. A stone hit the ground six feet away, spattering fragments. One of them stung my leg. I was screaming—I'm not ashamed to admit it—and my eyes were shut tight.

When I opened them again, it was like waking from tormented sleep to the reassurance of reality. The clearing was utterly peaceful. The stars shone down, blurred by lingering dust particles, but serene and steadfast. Then I saw Jim and I knew the nightmare wasn't over.

His final struggle to free himself had succeeded. His wrists were scraped raw, but his hands were unbound; they rested, lax and empty, on the dusty ground. Dust grayed his hair as he lay face down. There was no sign of the rock that had struck him.

There was no rock, because he had not been hit by a rock.

Slowly, shrinkingly, my eyes moved up from the booted feet of the man who stood beside me—up, all the way, till they reached his face, with its magnificent, spreading moustache.

"So it was you," I said.

Sir Christopher stuck the gun in his belt. He had been holding it by the barrel.

"I was the police, yes," he said. "The women were too distraught to realize that the official forces of the island have many other problems on their hands just now."

"That's not what I meant," I said.

"So Keller has broken his silence." Sir Christopher stood musing for a moment. "I thought he might. How unfortunate for you."

"But this is so unnecessary," I groaned. "I thought Frederick was the traitor. If you hadn't given yourself away by knocking Jim out—"

"You aren't thinking," Sir Christopher said reprovingly. "You may have been misled, but you are the only one. You are an undisciplined child; eventually you would accuse your father, and as soon as he learned what really happened thirty years ago, he would have known I had . . ."

It was strange, how he avoided a direct admission. It wasn't caution; who could hear him now, except me? Yet he couldn't bring himself to say the word. He could commit the act and kill to conceal it, but he couldn't say it.

"You mean," I said, "Frederick could prove he was innocent?"

"My dear girl," Sir Christopher said impatiently, "when there are only two suspects, and one knows he is innocent, he knows who must be guilty! Yes; he could have proved that he was on the other side of the peninsula, in the company of a dozen men, during the crucial period. And he is vicious enough to expose me. He is a cold, unfeeling man. I couldn't risk that. Even if I were not imprisoned, my career and my family name would be destroyed."

"Not to mention all those titles you are looking forward to. I suppose it wouldn't do me any good to promise to keep quiet?"

"I'm afraid not." Sir Christopher moved behind me and began tugging at the bonds that held me to the tree.

"This is your fault, you know," he said in a petulant voice. "I tried my best to induce you to leave Thera. Without you, Frederick would have been forced to end his operations and he would never have encountered Keller. It was imperative that I prevented a meeting between them. Keller has become distressingly unstable these last few years, and I feared the sight of Frederick might move him to clear his dirty little conscience.

When I learned that Frederick had made plans to come here, I had to move heaven and earth to arrange my own dig. Then that wretched boy wrote asking to join me. I could hardly refuse without appearing small-minded, could I? I had no reason to expect that he would pose a problem; his name was not the same, and he and Keller were unlikely to meet. Had I realized how much he resembles his uncle, I might have acted differently; but frankly I can't see it myself, I don't know why Keller. . . . Damn these ropes! They seem to be wire wrapped in cloth. Some ritual invention of Kore, no doubt. Her insane cult has been extremely useful to me. But if it had not existed, I would have discovered other means. The ability to make use of the means at hand is a sign of intelligence."

"You were the one who staged the accidents," I said. "The avalanche, the booby trap, even the shot yesterday. . . . That was aimed at me, not at Keller."

"Stop squirming," Sir Christopher snapped. "This is difficult enough without your making it harder."

I started to ask why he was bothering to free me, but I didn't want to give him any ideas that might hasten the inevitable end. It would have been so simple for him to drop one of those handy chunks of magma on my head. Then I realized that he was as anxious as the women must be to conceal any signs of his activities. If I was found dead under these conditions, there would be an investigation, and someone would be held responsible. An investigation was dangerous; some shrewd policeman might stumble on a hint of Sir Christopher's activities. But there would be no need for an investigation if I was found some distance away, unbound, and mashed by a fall or avalanche. Keller would keep quiet in order to protect Kore. Jim might be suspicious, but . . .

I felt as if someone had clamped a giant fist around my ribs. Selfish concern for my own skin had blinded me to Jim's danger. Had he seen the man who knocked him out? If he had not, and if Sir Christopher could be convinced that Jim didn't know of his uncle's betrayal, he might let Jim live. It would double the risk to kill us both.

I thought furiously, so preoccupied that I was only vaguely aware that the wires were loosening. I couldn't blurt out a flat statement of Jim's ignorance, that would be as bad as asserting the opposite.

Then I saw something that made me forget my dilemma. The fire was dying down, so the something was only a shadow, visible for a moment above the low ridge that surrounded the ancient amphitheater. It had looked like the shadow of a man.

I used to pride myself on my ability to react quickly in a crisis. But this was a crisis of monumental proportions, and I had only a few seconds to convince Sir Christopher that Jim was unwitting and to distract his attention from the rescuer—if it was a rescuer, and not just a shadow in my mind. . . . I was further handicapped by my weakness, which was apparent as soon as the ropes fell away from my body. I was stiff as a board and my hands had gone numb. When I tried to stand I toppled over sideways, like a rigid statue of a seated woman.

A man jumped over the ridge and landed, knees bent, on the floor of the amphitheater. He was carrying a rifle, one of Keller's, but he wasn't Keller. He was my father.

"Stand still, Chris," he called, raising the weapon to his shoulder. "Drop the gun."

"You wouldn't dare shoot." Sir Christopher's voice came from the air six feet over my head. "You never were that good a shot, Frederick. Will you risk hitting your daughter?"

"At this range I think I have an excellent chance of missing her," Frederick answered calmly.

I started beating my hands against the ground, trying to get some life into them. Frederick was quite capable of risking a shot; his monumental ego and his indifference to my welfare would overcome any qualms a normal man might feel. When I remembered the battered condition of his right arm I had even less confidence in his aim. I managed to roll over and raise myself on one elbow.

"I'll shoot the girl," Sir Christopher shouted.

"With a bullet that can be shown to come from a gun registered to you?" Frederick gave one of his nasty sneering laughs. "Go ahead."

Sir Christopher fired—but not at me. He shot at Frederick, and hit him. I saw Frederick stagger. He dropped the rifle, but he kept on walking. Sir Christopher shot again. By this time Frederick was so close I saw the blood spurt. My own was at freezing point; it was terrifying to see him come on, apparently undisturbed by the wounds, like some vampire out of a horror show. Sir Christopher was shaken too; his next shot was a clean miss. The fourth one struck the ground as I hit his ankles with my shoulder. He stumbled forward, off balance, and Frederick fell on him.

The pistol was on the ground not far from me. I tried to pick it up, but my hands were still clumsy. The two men were rolling around on the ground. It was the first time I had ever seen a real honest-to-God fight—not a rough and tumble, but a struggle to the death. It made me sick.

I abandoned the gun. I wouldn't have fired it anyway; humanitarian considerations aside, I couldn't risk hitting the wrong man. I started fumbling around for a rock that was big enough to knock Sir Christopher out. Then Jim, whom I had momentarily forgotten, rose up off the ground like Lazarus, and hurled himself into the fight.

He had no trouble separating the combatants; Frederick was flat on the ground, with Sir Christopher kneeling on him and trying to beat his face in. Jim yanked his erstwhile boss to his feet and unleashed the most beautiful right hook I've ever seen. Then I reached Frederick.

The first thing I noticed was his right hand, which lay twisted on his chest in the middle of a spreading bloodstain. The fingers were swollen to twice their normal size. I don't think he could have gotten one of them through the trigger guard, much less squeezed the trigger.

He didn't move or open his eyes, not even when my tears started splashing down on his face.

III

The Red Cross arrived the next day. Whenever I get discouraged with the human race I remember that time, when people from all over the world pitched in to help. The volcano had subsided; I had seen its last defiant outburst in the amphitheater, but there had been a lot of damage and injury. Huge waves had hit some of the coastal villages.

An efficient Swedish nurse made arrangements for Frederick to be taken off by helicopter. The road to Phira was practically demolished, and he couldn't have stood any more rough handling. He had been unconscious since dawn, but he had revived, after we brought him back to the villa, to say a few characteristic words.

"I see no reason . . . to become maudlin," he had wheezed, when I started thanking him.

"You saved our lives," Jim said, because I couldn't talk too plainly. "And deliberately risked your own. Sorry, I've got to say it, whether you like it or not; that was a very brave thing. I saw most of it. I was conscious, but it took me a while to get moving."

Frederick's lip curled. "Waste time," he muttered. "Statement. Chris. Names of men who were with me. . . ."

"It's unnecessary," Jim cut in. "Save your breath, sir. Keller has agreed to testify."

"Good." Frederick's smile was only a shadow of its former self, but it was distinctly malicious. Then he fainted.

In addition to his injured arm, which had not been improved by his activities, he had two bullet wounds, one through the chest and another in his right thigh.

"I can't see how the hell he kept on moving," Jim muttered, as we turned away from the bed. "Come on, Sandy. Lie down for a few hours. Kore will sit with him."

Kore nodded reassuringly at me. She was dressed for the role of angel of mercy in a simple little Dior dress that was probably the plainest outfit she owned; her hair was pulled severely back and she wore almost no makeup. She was wearing her diamonds—there is a limit to the personality change anyone can make—but the golden serpent bracelets were nowhere to be seen. She blinked as she caught my eye, but that was the only sign of embarrassment she showed, then or ever.

She had redeemed herself the previous night; we'd have had a rough time if she hadn't come sneaking back, stung by a belated attack of conscience, to see what had become of us. Or maybe Keller had acted as her conscience. After hearing her story he had set out at once for the amphitheater. They arrived while Jim was tying up Sir Christopher with the handy ropes that had been used on me, and I was trying to give Frederick first aid. Keller had been a pillar of strength; he had constructed a litter out of branches and the embroidered covering of the sacred couch, and after we got Frederick to the house he had worked over him for almost an hour.

He talked as he worked, his account oddly interspersed with curt directions to Kore, who was acting as his nurse. He talked as if he had thirty years' stored-up conversation to unload. We heard it all. His admiration for the young men who were fighting for their countries as he would have fought for his, had their circumstances been reversed; his contempt and disgust when Chris had come to him with his offer.

"It is accepted procedure," he insisted, while his hands moved with quick efficiency over Frederick's body. "Your uncle was the leader, Poseidon himself, it was he whom we wanted; and with two of the three out of action, the underground would be severely crippled. I had no choice. Never did I regret the action. I regretted only the necessity for it. And then to find that Poseidon was one whom I knew and admired. . . ."

In the last few hours of his life, Vincent Durkheim had come to trust the man who was about to kill him. The feeling between them couldn't be called friendship, but in some ways it was more intense than ordinary friendship. Keller's tormented conscience, their mutual interests, and the need of a dying man for comfort and human warmth. . . . I can't explain it or understand it, but I believe it happened. The result was that Durkheim told Keller of his discovery on Thera.

"He died bravely," Keller said. "You cannot comprehend, you young people—it was the last of the popular wars, the war to which we marched with banners flying and patriotic slogans firing our minds. The glamour soon faded; there is no romance in killing or being killed. But there was courage, and he had both kinds—the long, uncomplaining endurance of hardship, and the silent acceptance of his own end. He never knew that one of his friends had betrayed him. I spared him that, at least. His death made an enormous impression on me. I was already questioning some of the orders I had to carry out. . . ."

So Keller came to Thera. And there he remained for years, losing ground slowly but perceptibly in the struggle with his guilt. When he learned of Frederick's presence on the island, he interpreted it as an omen. Sir Christopher had been right to fear an encounter between them, for Keller was almost ready to seek out his old enemy and bare his soul. And Frederick would have acted on the information. He would have been delighted at the chance to bring his rival down in disgrace.

He may have had another motive. I'd like to think so. For it was to Frederick, not to Sir Christopher, that Durkheim left his greatest treasure—the dagger blade he had raised from the ocean floor near Thera, wrapped in a scrap of paper that described its discovery. They had all had their moments of depression and foreboding; in one such moment Durkheim had told Frederick where he had hidden the only thing he hoped would survive him, and after the war Frederick had been able to retrieve it. He expected a will or a letter; the true nature of Durkheim's legacy astounded him so thoroughly that it was years before he could bring himself to investigate it. He didn't know, until he found Keller living at Thera, that Durkheim had also confided in him. Probably Durkheim had not rated Frederick's chances of surviving the war as much higher than his own.

Jim and I pieced most of it together that night, from the things Frederick and Keller said. There was only one thing that still puzzled me, and as we left the room where Frederick lay, I said thoughtfully,

"How did he know Kore? I'll bet you there was something between them—"

Jim laughed and put his arm around me.

"The eternal gossip. The world is blowing up around you and all you can think of are your father's premarital indiscretions."

I stopped at one of the windows and looked out.

"The world has stopped blowing up. How can it look so beautiful, after last night?"

From our vantage point, high on the headland, we could look out over the valley to the rocky coast. There was still volcanic dust in the air; the sunsets around Thera would be spectacular for weeks to come. But the sea lay like silk around the shore, lapping folds of emerald into the narrow inlets, deepening to azure farther out. The squared-off patches of the fields were grayish green, but the crops would survive. It had been a small eruption, nothing to speak of—not to be mentioned in the same breath as that unique cataclysm of the fifteenth century B.C. Probably it would be another twenty thousand years before the baby volcano in the bay had grown big enough to destroy itself again. I wouldn't be around to see that. . . .

"Lie down for a while," Jim said. "You must be bushed."

"No, I'm going down to the village with you."

"How did you know that's what I had in mind?"

"I know you. Let's go down together."

IV

That was five years ago. When I look back on some of the crazy things I did, I can hardly believe I was that young. I'm a settled suburban housewife now—although Jim would deny that. In fact, he says if I ever turn into one, he'll leave me. I went back to school, and I'm still working on my degree—no, not in archaeology. In medicine. The things I saw on the island after the earthquake convinced me that I can't concentrate on anything more abstract than healing broken bodies. There is so much need, especially in the parts of the world where Jim will be working.

Frederick is very contemptuous of my medical studies. I've seen him, off and on, since he recovered. It took him a long time and he's not the man he was. Physically, I mean. His personality hasn't mellowed a bit. He's as mean and cantankerous as ever. But he taught me something valuable: that most people are neither good guys nor bad guys, but unpredictable mixtures of both.

Altogether, the summer on Thera was quite educational; it was also one of those rare cases where justice was served in the end. I got what was coming to me, from Mother and Dad, when I returned—and Jim didn't defend me, he just stood there grinning while they took turns bawling me out. Keller is still on Thera. He won't live much longer, but he'll end his days in relative peace of mind—and with Kore. The relationship between those two has something rather touching about it. As for the relationship between Kore and Frederick. . . . I've got my suspicions, but I don't suppose I'll ever know for sure.

Sir Christopher got what was coming to him, too. He's still in prison. The only person who didn't receive justice has been in his grave for over thirty years. That was the real tragedy, the loss of a young and productive life in the greatest human tragedy, war.

Jim and I have no children. There is time, if we decide we want them, but we'll probably adopt. There's a little girl in a village near Olympia, an orphan, whose old grandmother won't live much longer. . . . And so many others; I'd feel guilty bringing another child into the world when there are so many who are unloved and unwanted already. Wherever she comes from, I'll give her a nice sensible name, like Jan or Penny or Liz. Not a name that carries echoes of a past too distant.

Because that part of it still bothers me. Not much; I don't brood about it, I don't even dream these days. But sometimes, when my hands are busy and my mind is free to wander, I remember those other dreams. Kore's inefficient meddling had its effect, certainly, and now that I understand myself a little better I can see how the old myths suited my particular hang-ups. They are universal, after all—symbols of human fear and guilt and hatred.

But I dreamed before I ever arrived on Thera. I stood in the courtyard of the palace at Knossos and saw the bull games and smelled the acrid stench of blood and dust. Was it only the result of my mixed-up feelings about my father, colored by the particular setting? Or was it something more?

I can explain all of it in rational terms—except for one thing. It's a trivial point, and yet it disturbs me.

The first night I spent at the villa, when I fell into a drugged half-sleep, I heard Kore summoning a spirit from out of the past. I heard her and I understood. I can remember the words she used even now.

Only . . . how did I understand what she was saying? She always spoke English to me; but that night she wasn't speaking to me. She must have reverted to her native tongue in that incantation. And I don't understand Greek.

I know; there are ways of rationalizing that, too, and as I said, it's a trivial thing. And yet . . .

Who are we, really? Combinations of common chemicals that perform mechanical actions for a few years before crumbling back into the original components? Fresh new souls, drawn at random from some celestial cupboard where God keeps an unending supply?

Or the same soul, immortal and eternal, refurbished and reused through endless lives, by that thrifty Housekeeper? In Her wisdom and benevolence She wipes off the memory slates, as part of the cleaning process, because if we could remember all the things we have experienced in earlier lives, we might object to risking it again.

It's a terrifying idea in some ways, but it has certain attractions. It would be nice to think that Vincent Durkheim and all the other young men who died before their time would get another chance. As for me—yes, I would risk it. Aside from all the other things that make life interesting, there would always be Jim.